SCRAPPED

Also by Mollie Cox Bryan

SCRAPBOOK OF SECRETS

SCRAPPED

Mollie Cox Bryan

KENSINGTON PUBLISHING CORP.

http://www.kensingtonbooks.com

KENSINGTON BOOKS are published by

Kensington Publishing Corp.
119 West 40th Street
New York, NY 10018

All Kensington Titles, Imprints, and Distributed Lines are
available at special quantity discounts for bulk purchases for
sales promotions, premiums, fund-raising, and educational
or institutional use. Special book excerpts or customized
printings can also be created to fit specific needs. For details,
write or phone the office of the Kensington special sales
manager: Kensington Publishing Corp., 119 West 40th
Street, New York, NY 10018, attn: Special Sales Department,
Phone: 1-800-221-2647.

Kensington and the K logo Reg. U.S. Pat & TM Off.

ISBN-13: 978-0-7582-6632-3
ISBN-10: 0-7582-6632-4

First Mass Market Printing: January 2013

10 9 8 7 6 5 4 3 2 1

Printed in the United States of America

For my favorite time travelers,
dream surfers, and circle dancers—
Vicki and Richard
Kate
Fran, Kathy, and Dawn

Acknowledgments

Special thanks to Deena Warner for rune research and Dr. Melinda Fergusen for help with medical questions. I'd also like to thank my family and friends, along with my beta readers, Jennifer Feller, India Drummond, and Leeyanne Moore. Much gratitude to the Kensington team: Martin Biro, Adeola Saul, Alexandra Nicolajsen, along with all the sales reps and marketing crew selling those books. You are so appreciated. I'd also like to thank bookstores and the mystery writing community—both have supported me in countless ways. Much gratitude to a group of writing friends who are never too busy to answer questions, lend a shoulder, or extend themselves to me: Marie Bostwick, Mary Burton, Joanna Bourne, Joanna Campbell Slan, Joann Ross, Emilie Richards, Hallie Ephron, Therese Walsh, Alison Hart, Elizabeth Massie, Matthew Warner, and Clare O'Donohue. Heartfelt thanks to Sharon Bowers, agent extraordinaire.

But mostly, I want to express to readers my heartfelt thanks. I'm so glad you love my scrapbookers as much as I do. More to come.

Mollie

Chapter 1

Spending Sunday afternoon watching the police drag a body from a river was not what Annie had planned for the day. She was kicking a soccer ball around in the backyard with her boys when she was called away.

She took a deep breath as she walked through the crowd and over the yellow tape, which roped off the section to the river where the police and paramedics had gathered. Red and orange lights circled and flashed. Ducks swam in the river. A comforting arm slid around a woman standing in the crowd. A group of Mennonites stood from the bench they were sitting on and lowered their heads. What were the Mennonites doing at the park on a Sunday? *Odd.*

Across the river, where the park was more populated, Annie saw children playing on the swings and bars on the playground. Also, a rowdy game of basketball was taking place in another corner of the blacktopped surface. In the grassy area, a Frisbee was being thrown between three friends. Groups of mothers had gathered on the benches, trying not to alert their children or to look too closely at what was happening across the rushing Cumberland Creek River.

A hush came over the crowd on this side of the river

as the nude body of a small red-haired woman emerged from the water in a torn sack, her hair dangling over the side, along with a foot. The body, mostly shrouded by the shredded sack, was placed on the ground. Cameras flashed—again.

Every time Annie viewed a dead person, she silently thanked one of her old journalism professors, who had insisted all his students witness autopsies. "If you're going to get sick, it's better here than in front of a cop. He'll lose all respect for you."

"Hello, Annie," said Jesse, one of the uniformed police officers she had come to know over the past year of reporting about Maggie Rae and her family. Now Annie found herself under contract with a publisher to write a book about the case, which she was just finishing up. But she was still freelancing for the *Washington Herald* from time to time and was called in this morning to check this out. Was this incident another murder in the small town of Cumberland Creek?

"Hi, Jesse. Where's your boss?"

"Behind you," came his voice. Then Detective Bryant walked by her to look over the body more closely. His eyebrows knit, and he leaned in even closer, sliding gloves on his hands. "What the hell is this?"

"Scratches?" Jesse said, looking closer.

Annie was hoping to avoid looking closely at the actual body. Although she'd seen way too many dead bodies during her tenure as a reporter, it never was any easier. And she thought she'd left this behind her when she left Washington. She'd gotten sucked back into reporting during the Maggie Rae case. She was just beginning to get some breathing space—her book sent off to the publisher, nothing much else to report on in Cumberland Creek—and now this. She hoped it was an accident and not a murder.

"No," Detective Bryant said. "Look closer. They are

little markings of some kind. I can't quite make them out. Where's the coroner?"

Annie forced herself to look at the gray-blue arm the detective was holding gingerly in his hand. *Okay, it's just an arm,* she told herself. But she could see the markings.

"It looks like Hebrew," she blurted.

"Really?" Jesse said.

"Look again. That's not Hebrew," Detective Bryant said.

Annie leaned in closer. She had to admit, now that she was looking closer at it, that it didn't look like Hebrew at all.

The detective turned to the coroner as he walked closer to the group. "I want close-up photos of these markings. Photos from all angles."

"Must be a recent drowning," the coroner said. "If that's the cause of death."

"What makes you say that?" Annie asked.

"You can still recognize the body as a person. If it goes too long, it's difficult."

Annie's stomach twisted.

As Detective Bryant dropped the arm, she viewed the face of the victim between the clusters of shoulders of the police as they backed away. Young. Blue eyes staring blankly. Tangled red hair. Her face showed no sign of struggle—like a grimace or a look of anger or regret. The woman looked like a gray-blue rubber doll. Of course, what expression would a dead person have but none?

"Who found her?" Annie asked.

"It was a runner this morning, a Josh Brandt," Detective Bryant answered. "He's home now. I'd appreciate it if you'd give him some time before you zoom in for the kill," he said and grinned, his blue eyes sparkling.

Annie refused to engage with his taunting. She

watched as he brushed away a strand of red hair from the young woman's face. It was the most gentle gesture she'd ever seen him make.

"So what do you think the markings are?" Annie asked the detective.

"I've no idea," he said. "But I'm going to find out. I have a friend that specializes in symbols—if that is what these markings are."

"Will you let me know?"

"Sure. I've got nothing better to do," he said and smirked.

"Any idea who she is?"

"None," he said. "Check back with us tomorrow."

"Thanks," she said and walked away.

It was a beautiful fall day—so much color—golds, reds, crimson, orange, yellow. Fall in Cumberland Creek was as colorful as any painting or photo. It could be an advertisement for the way fall should look, with its mountains, colors, and crisp blue skies.

Annie looked off into the distance at the mountains. Bryant would probably not let her know about those symbols, Annie decided. She would have to research them herself. She was sure of it. She stood on the dirt path and quickly sketched some of the symbols—if that was indeed what they were, and not odd scratches from a struggle with rocks or the limb of a tree. If they were simply scratches, though, the markings were weirdly smooth. Her stomach twisted again. Another murder. They just needed to confirm the cause of death and call it one—but Annie felt that it was. That the body was in a sack made her more certain, and she wondered if the sack had been weighted before the river's rocks and current slashed it to pieces.

She walked along the riverside path toward Cumberland Creek proper, where she lived. She walked right past Vera's dancing school, closed, as were all the town businesses, because today was Sunday. It wouldn't do anybody any good to open on Sunday. There would be no customers. Most of the population in Cumberland Creek spent Sundays in church and at home—except for Annie, Vera, and their friends, who were usually nursing mild hangovers from the Saturday night crop, when they gathered to scrapbook in Sheila's basement.

Annie reached the sidewalk, which veered toward Vera's house. When she'd talked with Vera this morning, she'd said Cookie was coming over and was planning to watch Vera's daughter, Elizabeth, and make her special pumpkin soup, while Vera went to the grocer's. Annie's mouth began to water. The woman could cook.

She could also do some yoga, twisting her body into all sorts of poses as if it were nothing at all. Annie loved Cookie's Friday evening class. She had taken classes when she lived in the D.C. area, but none were like this. Cookie created a safe environment in which you could explore and reach out for new poses—she was not a teacher who pushed you to do anything painful.

Cookie explained to them one evening how she kept a yoga journal as a beginner and how it helped for her to see how much she'd progressed. Now Annie was working on something similar, a combination scrapbook or dream book of sorts—mundane, with ordinary beginning techniques interspersed with writing about a pose or thought. She was using self-portraits. This was a different kind of scrapbooking than what Annie had first learned from the Cumberland Creek crop; it was more like art journaling.

Annie thought about stopping by for a few minutes before heading home, but she should be getting home to Mike and the boys. But it would be nice to see her friends after witnessing the disturbing events at the park. Of course, she'd have to fill them all in.

"Oh God, there you are!" Sheila came around the

corner, nearly knocking Annie over. Her hair needed brushing, her glasses looked crooked, and her T-shirt was a wrinkled mess.

"What's going on?" Annie said, steadying herself. Why was she so tired today?

"Did you hear? They found a dead body in the river," Sheila said, panting.

"Man, this place is amazing," Annie said. "News travels so fast."

"What?" Sheila said.

"I was just there," Annie said.

"Well, for heaven's sake," Sheila said, taking her by the other arm. "Are you heading to Vera's place?"

Annie nodded. Okay, so she wouldn't stay long.

When Vera opened the door, smiling, the smell of pumpkin, cinnamon, and cumin, with its promise of warmth, met Annie, the image of a drowned young woman fresh on her mind.

Chapter 2

"Well, if it isn't the scrapbook queen, looking like hell on a Sunday afternoon," Beatrice said to Sheila as she walked in the kitchen, where they were all gathered.

Sheila waved her off and walked by her. Vera just shook her head. Sheila and Vera were best friends from childhood, and Beatrice loved to pick on Sheila, just for the fun of it.

"Nice to see you, Bea," Annie said.

"At least someone around here has some manners," Beatrice said.

"What are you doing here?" Annie asked.

"I came to see my grandbaby and was just on my way out. The child is sound asleep."

"I went to the store, came back, Mom was here, and Cookie had things under control," Vera said.

Cookie poked her head in from around the corner. "Yes, Elizabeth went straight down after you left. I made soup and tried to get your mother to stay."

"I will now," Beatrice said. "If everybody else is going to eat the vegetarian organic stuff she calls food, I guess it can't be so bad."

Beatrice hated to admit it, but the pumpkin soup did smell heavenly. But she thought all of this vegetarian, back-to-the-earth stuff was nonsense. She suspected that if any of these young, flighty types had to survive from "living from the earth," they wouldn't know the first thing about it. But she couldn't help but like this Cookie—even though she had many of the characteristics Beatrice would have despised in anybody else.

First, she was too damned thin—even thinner than Annie. The woman looked like she needed a big, thick, bloody steak. She was pale and wispy, with long black hair, which she sometimes pulled off her face with a thick, colorful headband. Eastern-looking silver jewelry always dangled from her. Her eyes were almost unnaturally green, and she carefully applied a bit too much eye make-up. While Vera, her own daughter, changed hair color more frequently than anybody she'd ever known, Beatrice preferred the natural look.

Cookie was a yoga teacher and taught classes in Vera's dance studio. Yoga was a good thing, Beatrice knew, but this woman took herself a bit too seriously with all the "*Namastes*" and "Peace be with yous." Who did she think she was? A divine messenger?

Ah, well, she chalked it up to youth. Basically, Cookie was a good sort—very good with Elizabeth, Bea's one and only granddaughter. She sat down at the kitchen table with the other women. God knows what they were chattering about. She wasn't paying a bit of attention. She suddenly thought of going upstairs and waking up Elizabeth just so she could hold her, play with her. Of course, she'd never do that—not in front of Vera, anyway.

"Did you hear me?" Vera was suddenly sitting next to her. "A drowned person washed up in the park today."

"What? In Cumberland Creek?" Beatrice said, clutching her chest. Cumberland Creek, population twelve thousand, going on twenty thousand or so. When Beatrice was a girl, there was a fuss about the population reaching 750. It was two thousand for twenty years or so. She lost count a few years back with all the new housing development on the west side of town. McMansions.

"Yes, in the river at the park," Vera said. "Scary."

"I imagine. Who was it?" she asked Annie, who was sitting down at the table next to Vera.

"I have no idea. Detective Bryant said they might know her name by tomorrow."

"Her?" Beatrice replied.

"It was sort of hard to tell, but there was a lot of long red hair," Annie said, twisting her own wavy black hair behind her ear.

"Hmm. I don't know of many redheads around here. Do you? Of course, sometimes I feel like I don't know half the people here anymore."

"Could be from somewhere else," Annie said, just as bowls of steaming pumpkin soup were being passed around the table.

The scent of the spiced pumpkin reached out and grabbed Beatrice. The scent of pumpkin, spiced with cinnamon and cumin, filled the room. Suddenly she was nearly salivating in anticipation. She reached for a slice of the crusty whole wheat bread—still warm from the oven—and spread butter on it. Goodness, Cookie had gone to a lot of trouble; she had even baked bread.

"Great soup, Cookie," Vera said and sighed. "You didn't have to do this. I wasn't expecting you to bake bread . . . just watch Lizzie while I went out for a bit of exercise and groceries."

"Now, don't worry about it," Cookie said. "Since she went right to sleep, I had some time on my hands. I just wanted to help out. I know how hard it can be. I was raised by a single mom."

Beatrice grimaced at the phrase "single mother," which was not what she wanted for her daughter, who wouldn't let her ex move back in—no matter how much he begged. Thank the universe, Bill had moved out of Beatrice's house and into his own apartment, finally. Beatrice hoped that it would work out—for the baby's sake—but Vera wasn't interested. Beatrice couldn't blame her for that. Also, Vera was seeing a man in New York. They rarely saw each other, and Vera had yet to bring him home to Cumberland Creek. She stole away to New York when she could. Beatrice doubted that it was serious. Bill, however, was seething. Served him right.

So there was another unexplained death in the small, but growing town of Cumberland Creek. Beatrice mused that things had just calmed down from the Maggie Rae case. Just what the town needed: more media attention, more outsiders, as if the new McMansion dwellers on the outskirts of town weren't enough for her and the other locals to manage. Beatrice hated to generalize about folks, but they all thought they were mighty important.

"So, does the death look suspicious?" Beatrice asked.

"I hate to say it," Annie said, dipping her bread into the creamy orange soup. "But it does to me. It looks like she was placed in a sack. I'm not sure she could have put herself in it. And there were these weird markings on her arm."

"Markings?" Vera said. "Like scratches?"

"Sort of," Annie said. "It might not mean anything." She turned back to her soup. "Man, this is good, Cookie."

A smile spread across Cookie's face. "Thanks."

Cookie didn't smile like that often, Beatrice mused. It wasn't that she was gloomy; she always had a look of bemused happiness. But it was in her eyes and the way she spoke.

Beatrice tuned out the chitchatting. Until they knew it was a murder, what was the point in speculating? She didn't want to believe there was another murder in this community. Damn, the soup and bread were just what she needed today. She hadn't realized how hungry she was.

Just then there was a knock at the door. It was Detective Bryant, who walked into the kitchen.

"I heard you were at the park this morning," he said to Sheila. "Did you see anything suspicious?"

He looked happy, like a man with a mission, energetic.

Sheila thought for a moment. "No. It was pretty quiet. But if I remember anything, I'll let you know."

"Oh my God, it smells heavenly in here," he said, stretching his arms, then turning around to see Beatrice. "But look what the devil brought in."

Beatrice swallowed her soup. "Bite me, Bryant."

He chortled.

The detective sure could hold a grudge. But then again, so could Beatrice.

Chapter 3

Vera's back twisted in pain as she placed a sleeping Elizabeth into her crib. After all the years of dancing, who would have thought parenting would be the most physically taxing thing on her body?

"She's down for the time being," she said to her mother, who was sitting next to the fireplace, wrapped in a quilt.

"Go and have a good time," Beatrice said. "This fire is so nice. Think I'll stay right here. Be careful, Vera. It's not safe out there."

"Thanks, Mom."

It had been almost a week since the mysterious body washed up in their park, with nobody claiming it. How sad to think that nobody missed this woman enough to report her absence—or to claim her body.

But still, Beatrice was acting a little more concerned about her safety than usual. Vera wondered if Beatrice would ever be the same. After she returned from her vacation in Paris, a general malaise hung over her, and no matter what Vera said or did, it was clear Beatrice didn't want to talk about this trip, which she and her long-gone husband had dreamed about taking for years. Vera had thought she would return home with countless stories about the city, its food, and its people, but she didn't. Instead, she'd shared a few photos and thoughts, said she was glad she went, but that was it. Vera mused over this as she opened the door to Sheila's basement scrapbooking room.

"How's Lizzie?" Sheila said after Vera sat down at the table and cracked open her satchel of scrapbooking stuff. She was still working on chronicling Elizabeth's first birthday party.

"Rotten, but asleep for now," Vera said, feeling a wave of weariness, reaching into her bag for chocolates. She had found a new chocolate shop in Charlottesville the other day and was smitten with the handmade dark chocolate spiced with chili pepper. Who would have imagined? She sat the box on the table. "Chocolates," she said.

"Have some pumpkin cranberry muffins," DeeAnn said, shoving the plate toward Vera.

"Thanks," Vera said.

"God, these are so good," Annie said, taking another bite of muffin.

"Thanks. We're selling a lot of them at the bakery," DeeAnn said and sliced a picture with her photo cropper. "Business hasn't slowed down a bit for us, thank God." She made the sign of the cross across her ample chest, even though she wasn't Catholic. She was the town baker, and her place was always busy, particularly in the mornings.

"Wish I could say the same thing," Sheila said, pushing her glasses back up on her nose. "Digital scrapbooking is all the rage. I'm losing business with it being so paper based."

"My business is going through a rough patch, too," Vera said. "This darned economy." After a few minutes of silence, Vera brought up the subject of the mysterious body. "You know, I just can't get the dead woman out of my mind," she said. "Any word yet on who she is?"

"Not that I know of," Annie said. "I've called the police a few times. Bryant's supposed to let me know."

"I wouldn't trust that," Sheila said, placing her scissors on the table with a rattle and a clunk.

"Don't worry," Annie said. "I have his number. I'm already researching these symbols carved into her body."

"Symbols?" Cookie asked.

"At first I thought it was Hebrew, but it's not."

"Ooh," DeeAnn said. "That just gave me the chills." Her blue eyes widened, and she leaned on her large baker's arms. "I'm thinking Satanists . . . or witches. . . . Sorry, Cookie."

"Witches don't do that kind of stuff," Cookie said. "We are gentle, earth loving, people loving. I've told you that." She grinned.

"I would assume you are not all the same, though," Annie said. "That there are bad witches, just like there are bad Jews or Christians."

"Well . . ." Cookie shifted around in her chair as it creaked. "You're probably right about that." She turned and asked Sheila, "Now, how do I use this netting?"

Sheila happily showed Cookie the technique. She unrolled the netting from the packaging ball. One side of it was sticky. She placed it on the page at a diagonal and pressed down, then cut it with her scissors, giving it a rough edge, which added to the textured page.

"I honestly still don't know why you call yourself a witch," Vera said.

"Oh, Vera, would you just please leave it alone?" Sheila said. "Good Lord. We are having a crop here, not a trial."

Cookie smiled slightly. "Thanks, Sheila, but I don't mind answering. I call myself a witch because I feel I'm honoring the women who were burned at the stake in the name of witchcraft. I reclaim it. That's all. And if people have a problem with it, they can either educate themselves or not. But I don't dwell on their issues with it."

"Humph," Vera said and laughed. "I guess she told me."

Cookie smiled. "Well, you asked."

"Indeed," Sheila said. "I'd much rather talk about your sex life than Cookie's witchcraft."

"Oh yes, me too," Annie said. "What happened last week? What kind of kinky sex did you have last weekend?"

"Good Lord," Sheila gasped, red-faced, clutching her chest. "The way you just blurt those things out."

Paige, the other steady scrapbook club member, entered the room with a flourish. Paige, DeeAnn, Sheila, and Vera were the original crop. Annie came along last year; then came Cookie.

When Vera thought about how things had changed over the past year, it almost gave her vertigo. She was now the mother of a sixteen-month hellion of a baby, who refused to take naps and didn't want to be weaned. Annie was going to be a published author. Sheila's daughter Donna was now in her senior year of high school—which set Sheila all atwitter from time to time. Paige had announced she was going to take an early retirement from the school system—this year, her twenty-fifth, would be her last. And DeeAnn's bakery was just becoming more and more successful.

Paige's breezy pink silk shirt almost caught on the corner of the ragged table as she waltzed by. "Sorry I'm late." She placed a scrapbook on the table and opened the pages. "I had a flat tire, and it took a while for my husband to get it changed. I mean, Jesus, it's not as if he hasn't changed a tire before. What kind of muffins do you have there?"

"Pumpkin cranberry," Annie answered, holding her page up and eyeballing it. "We were just going to talk about Vera's sex life."

"Oh, really? What did he do to you this time?" Paige asked.

Vera just laughed and waved her hand. They wouldn't believe her if she said that there was absolutely no sex between them the last time she went to the city. They just laughed a lot and talked even more. They had so much to say to one another. She would never tire of hearing Tony's Brooklyn accent as he told her stories about going on tour with this or that dance company. His voice soothed her—it felt like home. And his touch burned her skin with a passion she hadn't known since they were together all those years ago in college, as young dancers. Maybe it was time he visited Cumberland Creek. But how would Bill feel about that? Would he make trouble for them? God knows she couldn't keep his coming a secret. He'd be arriving on a Harley, and if that wasn't enough of an attention getter, he was a beautiful dark man. Not many of those around Cumberland Creek. He'd stick out no matter where they went.

"Yoo-hoo." Paige waved her hand in front of Vera's face. "Where are you? I was asking about the dead body. Did you say she had red hair?"

"Yes," Vera said. "Long red hair. Annie saw her."

"You know, I was just thinking about this the other day. There seems to be a bunch of redheads that live up on the other side of Jenkins Hollow," Paige said, twirling her own wavy blond hair with her slender finger.

Vera looked at Annie, who, at the mention of Jenkins Hollow, coughed on her wine.

"I'm just going to pretend I didn't hear that," Annie finally said.

Chapter 4

Beatrice was thinking about Jenkins Hollow, too. She thought she heard Elizabeth fuss and checked on her, saw she was still asleep, and stood for a moment looking over her granddaughter, whose face shone in the glow of the night-light. What an amazing, beautiful little creature she was—and that shock of red hair, well, if she kept it, the girl was going to be even more unusual. That was one thing Beatrice could claim she had given Elizabeth. Beatrice, of course, was mostly white-haired now.

Beatrice had read how redheads were dying out. The gene pool was getting slimmer and slimmer for them. She knew of a group of families in the Nest, which was a neighborhood in Jenkins Hollow that had always had several generations of redheads. For years she'd ignored the rumors concerning the intermarrying and inbreeding, but her husband had confirmed it one morning, after he delivered a Down syndrome baby that didn't make it.

"It was a mercy to them," he'd told her. "It doesn't feel like that now, of course. But that baby was the product of, well, a brother and sister."

"What?"

"Yes." He'd lowered his eyes. "It's quite a problem up there."

"I've never heard of such a thing," Beatrice said.

"Of course not, Bea. It's all hush-hush," he said and held her hand. "There's plenty in this world you don't know about, and I'd like to keep it that way."

Beatrice smiled at the memory. Here she was, eighty-one years old, and back then she couldn't have imagined some of the things she was exposed to now every day, as a matter of course. Girls running around half naked in public was just part of it; the other was the lack of respect the girls had for themselves. It was almost as if sex was the only thing they cared about. And as if they thought they had invented sex. She looked at her grandbaby and felt that same sense of protection that Ed must've felt for her. And yet she knew it was futile. Elizabeth would start out seeing much more in her life than what Beatrice never could have imagined all those years ago.

She supposed the redhead must have come from the hollow, and believed the police would find out what happened—eventually. She hoped it was an accidental drowning. She ran her hand through her mostly white hair. Thinking about it all—the possibility of a murder here, in Cumberland Creek—sent spasms of fear through her.

Back to Jenkins Mountain. Beatrice used to hike on the ridge that looked over Jenkins Hollow and out over the river. On one side of the river was a group of Old Order Mennonites—those that still dressed in plain clothes and eschewed "modern" conveniences, like electricity and cars. There were plenty of other kinds of Mennonites around, though, like some of her neighbors, who dressed normally and embraced technology but still held true to some of the basic tenets of the religion. Beatrice didn't know exactly what the schisms between the Old Order Mennonites and the other sects were based on. All she knew was that most of the Old Orders kept to themselves. They always had. Although they were neighborly, they were never overly so.

On the other side of the river and around a small hill was the Nest—the neighborhood that was a melting pot for castoffs, inbreeds, and other troubled sorts. Most of them were impoverished and still didn't have running water. Ironic since the river life force that fed the valley started deep in the caves on Jenkins Mountain.

Beatrice sighed. She hated that so many of them were exactly what the rest of the world envisioned when they thought about Appalachia—that they were all inbreeds, that they lacked education and were impoverished. Damn.

She had traveled all over the world and still thought the Cumberland Creek Mountains and the Blue Ridge Mountains were the most beautiful places on the planet. That included Jenkins Hollow. From the ridge, you could look down on the settlement, with its beautiful white clapboard church at the center and the steep mountains folding into one another in the background.

As you looked farther and farther into the distance, the mountains grew smaller and smaller, but they sort of looked as if they were fanning out from one another. In the fall of the year, you couldn't ask for a prettier place to visit. It was unique because it was so hard to get to that the tourists left it alone. Hell, many of them probably didn't even know it existed. There were no tourist shops, fences, or paved paths.

So many legends existed about the place. It was a remote place when she was a child that everybody had a scary story about. Ghosts. Aliens. Wild, marauding Native Americans or mountain men. Several of the ghost tales were about jilted lovers taking their own lives. Then there was the story that claimed a curse was

placed on Mary Jenkins, one of the settlers of the
region, because she took up with a Native American
chief and bore his children, provoking the suicide of a
young Native American maiden, Star, who had been
promised to him. She cursed them before she leapt to
her death. None of the story was probably true, mused
Beatrice. Still, it was interesting to ruminate on it in
terms of some of the landmarks on Jenkins Mountain.
Lover's Ridge. Suicide Plunge. Star's Tears, which were
boulders shaped like tears.

Beatrice leaned her head back in the rocker. A streetlight shone on the wall just where a puffy little lamb was
jumping across it. She pondered life and the random-
ness of it. Ghosts. Lambs. Churches. Precious sleeping
babies. Mountains. Rivers. And dead redheads washing
ashore.

She felt the drifting sensation of sleep and then
jerked back awake. Was she falling? She grabbed the
chair to steady herself and blinked. Oh, it was just a
dream. Just a dream.

Chapter 5

Annie pulled her lasagna out of the oven while she listened to the football game in the living room. She took in the scent of oregano, garlic, and tomatoes. All her boys, including her husband, were planted in front of the television, watching football, even Sam, who was just four. She slid the pan back in. She'd give it another twenty minutes.

She sat back down at the kitchen table, where she thumbed through a huge book of ancient symbols. None of them seemed to match her carelessly drawn symbols from the drowned body. Was DeeAnn onto something? Was it a satanic ritual of sorts? Annie wanted to dismiss that, but she'd learned a long time ago not to rule anything out at the beginning of a story.

"You getting anywhere?" Mike asked as he walked into the room, tossed his beer bottle into the recycling bin, and opened the fridge for another.

"Not really," she said and sighed. "These symbols look so strange. They must have a connection to the death."

"Humph, maybe not. You know some of these young people are into carving themselves up. Cutting themselves. I don't get it," Mike said, then opened his bottle. The burp hissed into the air.

"I don't think she could cut herself on the upper arm like that. She seemed to be very young," Annie said. "Though it's getting harder and harder for me to tell how old someone is, let alone someone dead in a river for God knows how long."

"I hear ya," he said and kissed her head, then left the room.

Just then the doorbell rang. It was Cookie, who was dropping off some new die cuts for Annie. Sheila's new Cricut machine made die cuts, which the women were enjoying placing in their latest scrapbooks. Sheila just chose the design, plugged the cartridge in, and slid the paper or cardboard in, and out came a sheet of easily punched-out designs—hearts, spirals, and even *Namaste* symbols.

Annie was always working on at least one of her boys' books, so she had plenty of cutout soccer balls and birthday cakes. But the croppers had spotted a *Namaste* symbol in one of the cartridges, and they all had asked for one, since Cookie had gotten them so into yoga and they were all working on a yoga scrapbook-journal project.

Annie heard the front door open, and her sons greeting Cookie with squeals, hugs, and kisses before she waltzed into the kitchen.

"Mmm. What are you making? It smells so good," she said, arms full of paper bags.

"Lasagna. Why don't you stay for dinner?"

"That sounds like an offer I can't refuse," Cookie said, placing her bags on the table. She fished around in one. "Here's your *Namaste*. Isn't it beautiful? I love the crimson you chose. It will look great on that beige page of yours." She ran her thin, pale fingers over the rounded edges. "Look at that," she said. "What a clean line."

"It's nice," Annie said, not quite as enthusiastically. She was still distracted by the symbols. She loved the ancient Egyptian symbols. "Look at this," she said, pointing to the page. "These symbols are so beautiful."

"Oh yes, the scarab," Cookie said, leaning over the table, her long black hair falling over her shoulders. "I have a necklace that has that symbol on it."

"You do?"

"It means 'spontaneous creation,' or some such thing. Good luck and all that," Cookie said and laughed. Annie loved the way she laughed, with no holds barred. "But what are you doing?"

Just then dark, curly-haired Ben came running into the kitchen. "Can I get some water?"

"Help yourself, baby," Annie said. "You know where the cups are."

He stood on the stool and rattled around in the cupboard until he found the perfect cup.

"I'm sorry. Where were we?" Annie said.

"What are you doing with this book?" Cookie said, leaning over it, her black hair falling on its white pages.

"I am trying to find a match for the symbols that were"—Annie lowered her voice—"carved into the drowned body."

"Oh, can I see?" Cookie asked, her eyebrows lifting as she straightened herself.

"Sure," Annie said, and slid the paper with her sketchings over to Cookie, whose green eyes lifted further.

"Runes," she said.

"What?"

"It looks to me like what you have here are rune symbols. You won't find anything about them in this book of Eastern religious symbols. Runes are Germanic. I should say, originally Germanic. Then they traveled up through Britain and into Scandinavia, and each of those cultures gave them their own little twist."

"How do you know this stuff?" Annie said and smiled.

"Some pagans are still using them for divination. I

don't know that much about them. Just what they are. I've seen them in shops and so on, but they never called out to me."

"Oh," Annie said, with one eye watching Ben get water from the refrigerator spout. "Where can I find out more?"

"Now, see, that's going to be tricky," Cookie said, sitting down at the table. "There's a lot of stuff out there—even on the Internet. But what's good information . . . I don't know what to tell you. It pains me to say this, but a lot of pagans are just making stuff up—even the stuff that's not supposed to be made up. Like claiming they know the true meaning of the runes . . . I mean, I think there are people who do. I can check around for you."

"That would be great. I'll look around, too," Annie said.

Annie found Cookie intriguing. She never talked much about her past. When she was asked about it, she would say it wasn't important. "I live in the present moment." But she always knew the most obscure facts—like what a blue moon really was, or what herb to plant during what phase of the moon. And then there was the time she talked about quantum physics, which captured Beatrice's heart—a woman who had studied physics, then quantum physics, her whole life.

But there was this other, commonsense, earth mama, good cook, and great friend part of Cookie, which was most endearing. In the year she'd lived in Cumberland Creek, she had immersed herself in several networks of people and had plenty of friends—especially the scrapbook club, the group of women who cropped every Saturday night come hell or high water. It had taken Annie a whole year of living in Cumberland Creek to find any kind of friendship. Cookie was just different, attracting people wherever she went. She oozed warmth.

"When will supper be ready?" Mike yelled over the football game.

"In a few minutes," Annie yelled back. She looked at Cookie and frowned.

"What can I do to help?" Cookie said.

Chapter 6

Bill would be here any minute, Lizzie was fussing,
and Vera was still in her nightgown, though it was nearly
supper time.

"Land sakes, let me take her. She probably needs a
change. Now, go get dressed," Beatrice said as she
walked in the door.

The three of them had vowed to get together for
Sunday dinner when they were all in town. They thought
it would be a good thing for Lizzie, a consistent tradition for her, this child who was often schlepped between
households and people. Coming together every Sunday
was a touchstone for all of them—the primary care-
givers and this miracle of a growing, healthy child.

Vera could hear her mother changing Lizzie as she
rifled through what clean clothes she had. Good God.
What had become of her? She was such a mess,
couldn't keep track of anything. She finally found a
shirt that wasn't too wrinkled and a pair of jeans that
had been washed—what?—a few weeks ago?

She'd been lured into playing with her daughter all
day, and the time had just slipped right by. Elizabeth
often pulled Vera into her play world, and there she
would stay forever, if she could. She knew what Beatrice

said was true—she doted too much on Elizabeth. But she was going to have only one go-around at this parenting thing and didn't want to miss a thing. And today she felt the passage of time sharply, the appreciation of life. Today's paper reported that the drowning was not an accident. The murder of the unknown young woman reminded her of Maggie Rae's death and the loss of her young life—a loss Vera still mourned—even as she held her own baby girl. New life.

She heard Bill enter the house and greetings being exchanged. Elizabeth was thrilled with seeing her father, which made Vera's heart sink. Lord, she wished she could have forgiven that man and they could be the happy family all children wanted and deserved.

"Heard about the murder?" Bill said later, while seated at the table. "Pass me the potatoes, please."

"Yes, I did. I was a bit shaken up. You can imagine," Vera told him.

"She was a redhead," Beatrice said, spreading butter on a roll.

"You are the only redhead I know in Cumberland Creek. You and Lizzie, that is. Must be from out of town," Bill said.

"Thanks. I'm glad you remember my red hair, Bill, but there's some redheads in Jenkins Hollow," Beatrice said.

"Da-da-da," Lizzie said and giggled.

"Yes, that's your dad," Vera said, exchanging a look of pride with Bill, who was spooning mashed potatoes into Lizzie's mouth.

"Mmm, good," he said, exchanging silly grins with his daughter.

I could love him again, Vera thought. She felt her heart open from time to time, and then he'd anger her and she would go back to thinking, *Never again.* The last time she was almost ready to forgive him, she had heard about him dating a young lawyer from Charlottesville. *Of course young,* she thought and grimaced.

"Are you okay?" Beatrice said.

"Huh? Oh yeah, I'm fine," Vera replied.

"You're awfully quiet, and you had that faraway look in your eyes."

"Mama, I'm thinking about there being a murder in Cumberland Creek. For some reason, I keep thinking of the body and the poor young woman who nobody has even claimed."

"And then people keep bringing it up," Beatrice shot at Bill.

"For God's sake, I just asked," he said, turning back to Vera. "I wonder if she was from up there. The river flows from there. If she drowned on the mountain, it would make sense if she ended up at the park."

Vera shrugged.

"This is tasty ham. Did you use my recipe?" Beatrice asked.

Vera nodded. "Except I baked it just a wee bit longer." She watched Bill lift Lizzie from the chair and sit her on his lap. But she was ready to go and wouldn't sit still. She took off across the kitchen like a lightning bug.

"Such energy," he said, grinning. "Hey, what do you know about this Cookie person?"

Beatrice groaned.

"Why? She seems like a nice person. She's great with Lizzie," Vera answered.

"We don't really know much about her, do we? She's new to town, and suddenly a dead body shows up."

Beatrice sat up a little straighter.

"She's been here almost a year, Bill. She waited all that time to kill someone? Really?"

"I don't know her. She just seems kind of weird."

"I agree," said Beatrice. "She is weird. But she's

likable, I tell you. A good heart. Always helping where she can. But the rest of that stuff . . . I dunno."

"What stuff?" he asked, moving across the floor to catch Lizzie.

"She calls herself a witch," Vera said, then bit into a thick slice of ham.

He snorted. "Really? What does she do? Twitch her nose? Wave a magic wand? Does she know Harry Potter?"

"It's not like that," Vera said, moving dishes around, piling them on top of one another as she sat at the table.

"They say it's an actual religion," Beatrice said. "I've looked into it, and it is. Quite interesting, really."

"I bet," he said. "New Age mumbo jumbo."

"Well, yes . . . and no," Beatrice said. "I'm still thinking it over."

"Well," he said, grabbing Lizzie from the floor, swooping her over his shoulder to giggles and squirms, "while you're thinking about that, think about what a witch would be doing someplace like Cumberland Creek. I mean, we're about thirty years behind the rest of the country. Why would she want to be here?"

"I can tell you one thing," Vera said. "I don't know what I would have done without her this past year. And she can call herself a witch or an ogre. I really don't care. I like her, and believe me, Bill, she didn't kill anybody. Hell, she doesn't even eat meat, because she loves animals. She's so tenderhearted. So give it a rest."

Chapter 7

Beatrice couldn't believe her ears. Monday mornings came and went, but to hear a chain saw at 7:00 a.m.? That just beat all. She tried to get up out of her bed quickly. Well, as quickly as she could. Her body was stiff each morning—and it was getting worse. When she finally untangled herself from the blankets and swung her legs to the floor, it sounded like the sawing had stopped. What on earth? Who would be cutting anything at this time of day?

She sat in her bed and listened. Nothing.

Should she get up and get the day started or lie back down? *Humph.* Maybe she was dreaming. Her stomach growled, and she reached for her shawl, remembering the muffins in her bread box. She'd pop them in the microwave and smear them with butter. That would make a fine breakfast. Pumpkin cranberry muffins. And if they weren't enough to fill her, she was sure about the blueberry muffins in the freezer.

She padded down the stairs and noticed the soft sunlight shining directly on the portrait of her husband, dead now twenty-some years. Until she had gone to Paris, he had been with her—as a ghost—off and on all those years. Oh, some folks thought she was a crazy old coot, and maybe she was, but he was a great comfort to her. Knowing he was still around, even if as a ghost, took the edge off her sometime loneliness, though for the most part she didn't mind being alone.

Life sure was funny. She had thought she had it all figured out. *Keep busy. Keep your mind occupied. But the next thing you know, you're boffing some Frenchman you barely even know.* God, what was she thinking?

And of course she hadn't heard from Jon since she came back to Cumberland Creek last month—and her late husband's ghost also appeared to be giving her the cold shoulder. Men would never change. Neither would women. *A handsome Frenchman tells you you're pretty, and even at the age of eighty-one, you buy it. He whispers lovely words into your old ears, and you melt. How ridiculous.*

Up until then, she had never so much as looked at any man but her husband—and had never even wanted to. She didn't know what came over her in Paris. She'd felt too young and free there, and Jon was ten years younger than her, which didn't seem to bother him at all.

After they met at the museum and went for their first coffee together, they were inseparable. A month of silliness. But still, she thought, grinning, the experience was sweet. She shoveled a muffin into her mouth. *Mmm. Good.*

She had never acted so foolishly in her life. A giggle erupted. Even if he didn't call her, who would have imagined that at her age, she could still manage to attract such a young, handsome man?

Of course, Ed, her dead husband, was upset with her. She knew it. Felt him leaving her, finally, as she kissed Jon, opened her heart to him. That broke her heart, and she missed him—but maybe it was time she moved on.

Cookie had said he'd be back. She was the only person Beatrice confided in. Her daughter had never

believed in the existence of ghosts and thought Ed was
a figment of Beatrice's imagination. Annie was open to
the idea, but she was so analytical sometimes, it even
scared Beatrice, herself a trained scientist. And she had
a feeling that Annie would rush to tell Vera about the
affair. She certainly didn't want Vera to know. She'd
never let it rest.

That was exactly what Beatrice was trying to do.
Make peace with it. She didn't need Vera poking her
nose into everything.

"Maybe Ed is just giving you some time," Cookie
had suggested.

"Or maybe he's moved on."

"He should have moved on years ago, yes?"

Beatrice's stomach had tightened. She knew she was
part of what held him here. She'd nodded, trying to fight
back the tears.

"Oh, Beatrice, we are never too old for a broken
heart, are we? But don't ever be sorry about, um, er,
Jon. You are human. There's enough room in that heart
of yours to love again. My goodness, you've been a
widow for twenty-five years."

Cookie knew all the right things to say—strange brew
of a person that she was. Wouldn't eat meat of any kind,
sometimes wore way too much eye make-up, and other
times she ran around town without an ounce of make-up
on her pale face. Beatrice had caught her dancing around
the nursery with Elizabeth, humming and grinning at the
child. *She can't be that bad. Witch and all.*

Chapter 8

At first Annie thought the phone ringing was her alarm. She hit the clock, and the irritating sound wouldn't stop. Finally, in her haze she reached for the phone.

"Hello," she said. Her husband sat up reluctantly in bed, startled.

"I know you have two boys sound asleep," the voice said.

Pulses of fear shot through her. "Who is this?"

"Detective Bryant. You need to get down to the landfill, if you have someone to stay with those boys."

"Why would I want to do that?" Why was Bryant always bringing up her sons?

"What the hell?" her husband said.

"There's been another murder. Thought you'd appreciate knowing. That's all," the detective said.

She sighed, mentally going through child-care options. "Um, er, I'll be right there. Thanks."

She had just filed her story about the first murder. The identity of the young woman had been revealed as Sarah Carpenter. The scrapbookers were right. She was from Jenkins Hollow. Annie had yet to piece together the story of who she was, and was hoping she could do it via the phone and the Internet. Jenkins Hollow was her least favorite place on the planet.

"I have to go. Another murder."

"It's three in the morning. I don't want you out," Mike said.

"Oh, for God's sake, Mike, I am not a child. I've been in worse situations—"

"Who was it on the phone? Bryant?"

"Yes," she said and yawned.

"This time of day? Who the hell does he think he is?" he grumbled.

"He's a cop. I'm a reporter," she said, getting a little miffed at his tone. "I used to get calls like this before we moved here. You know."

"Okay, okay," he said, sinking back into his pillow. "But I don't like it."

Annie decided to ignore that remark—for now.

"Call Beatrice in the morning. She'll be happy to stay with the boys," Annie said, lifting herself from the sea of warm blankets. It was early autumn—and a warm one at that—but it was chilly at three in the morning.

She threw on a black pair of jeans, noted that they were a little tight, and went searching for a sweater to throw on over her T-shirt. She found the bathroom and tended to her teeth, brushed her unruly black hair, pulled it back, and smeared lipstick on. That would have to do. Where were her sneakers? Ah yes, she'd left them in the living room. She used to know where all of her shoes were, used to have plenty of designer flats to choose from, all lined up in neat rows in her closet. Now she could barely keep track of her old, worn-out sneakers.

She grabbed her bag and tiptoed out of the house.

Annie had never trusted the safety of landfills. All that trash had to be releasing toxins into the air. She didn't allow her boys up there to play for that very reason. Even though a lot of parents brought their children there to play because of the huge open spaces, she couldn't see it.

As she pulled up to the parking lot, a group of red lights flashed on the far edge of the lot, near a huge recycling bin, where most of the flurry was erupting. She parked and grabbed her camera, press credentials, and recorder out of her bag. First, she saw Jesse, wiping his face with a bandanna. Then Detective Bryant's contorted face, looking at Jesse, placing his arm around him. A gesture of unbelievable gentility from such a brute of a man. Then he saw Annie and placed his hand up, as if to say, "Stop."

"What's wrong?" she called.

"Don't go any closer, ma'am," she heard a female voice say.

"Bryant called me and got me out of bed. I was invited here."

The officer looked confused. "Called you? We've been here for several hours. I don't know anybody who gets cell phone service here. The tower over there interferes too much, along with the mountains."

"I didn't call her," the detective yelled, shaking his head. "You need to get her out of here."

"What?" Annie attempted to move forward.

"Ma'am, there's a potentially hazardous chemical here. You need to go home."

"Was there another murder? I need to know for the paper," she said as the officer nearly pushed her back toward her car.

"Yes, ma'am, but you don't want to see what's over there. It's gruesome."

Annie noted the officer's tone. She was serious. Annie wasn't certain that she wanted to push on this.

"Any details you can give me?"

"Details?"

"Anything about the body? Who is it?"

"I can't tell you anything right now. They are not letting me get close enough to it. They've called in the CDC."

"The CDC?"

"Centers for Disease Control."

"I know what it stands for," Annie said. "But why?"

"Evidently, there's a potentially dangerous substance surrounding the body. Like I said."

Annie looked at the group of people standing around the body. No wonder they were still. It was dark, the only illumination coming from flashing red lights and a few flashlights cutting light into the dark. But Annie could still see the worry in Detective Bryant's face. *Wait.* Did he say he hadn't called her?

She tried to remember the voice on the phone. It had sounded enough like him. But at 3:00 a.m., who knew what anybody sounded like? One thing was clear: someone wanted to make sure she was here. And she was going to stay put. She leaned on her car and folded her arms, shivered slightly in the brisk air, watching the clouds of breath in the soft peach light.

Did she want to see what the officers were getting sick over? No. Did she want to breathe in a potentially hazardous chemical? No. She'd stay right where she was and wait.

It wasn't long until a white van came along the slanted road to the parking lot and people dressed in white suits and masks came tumbling out. That gave her heart a start. *Nothing like the CDC to make your heart race.* Why would they be so interested in this particular case? It didn't make sense—unless this situation was already on their radar. She watched as the group approached the crime scene and one person fell back, pulling off his mask just as vomit spewed from him, which made Annie's stomach wrench.

A few minutes later Detective Bryant and several police left the area and walked toward their car.

"All clear," he said. "It's not anthrax."

"Anthrax? God, is that what you thought it was?" Annie said.

He nodded. "You look like hell," he said and smiled.

"You're no Prince Charming, either," Annie said and smiled back. "I guess I need to check out the crime scene."

"I don't think you should," he said, his blue eyes heavy but still sparkling as the sun began to rise over the mountains. "It's . . . ghastly."

"Ghastly?"

"A dismemberment."

"What?"

"The worst thing I've ever seen," he said, looking away from her, his voice cracking.

Good God, he was human, after all.

She swallowed. "Any similarities with Sarah?"

He nodded. "Red hair. Young woman," he said, taking a handkerchief from his pocket, wiping his sweaty forehead. "Those same symbols carved . . ."

"Serial killer?"

He nodded. "Hard to say, but it could be. But let's not set off a panic in the community. Okay?"

Annie nodded and turned toward her car door.

"Annie?" he said, getting between her and the door. "I, ah, want you to be careful."

"Of course," she said, not knowing whether to be touched or pissed because of his patronizing tone. "I can take care of myself, Bryant."

"If you're getting phone calls from someone in the middle of the night who claims to be me, and you believe them, I have to wonder if you can."

Chapter 9

"Sarah Carpenter," Vera said over her omelet. "What do you know about that family?"

"Not much," Beatrice said. "What's the paper say?"

Vera shook the paper out, folded it over, and placed it beside her cheese-coated plate.

"Eighteen-year-old Sarah Carpenter—"

"Eighteen? Lawd, have mercy."

"Eighteen-year-old Sarah Carpenter," Vera said, starting again, "was found in Cumberland Creek, in the middle of Cumberland Creek Park. The daughter of Rachel and Paul Carpenter, Sarah was a homeschool graduate and a member of the local Divinity Homeschooling Cooperative, where she played piano and taught preschool. According to local officials, the cause of death is inconclusive, though an accidental drowning has been ruled out. 'The investigation is under way, and we'll endeavor to keep the public informed as it progresses,' said Detective Bryant, Cumberland Creek Police Department. 'We have nothing else to report right now.'"

"What a lying bastard," Beatrice said. "What about those markings? Maybe somebody knows something about them. What an ass. What's the point in keeping that a secret?"

"I think everybody knows by this point, but maybe he wanted to keep it out of the paper for some reason. I'm surprised that Annie didn't report it. She never lets him stop her."

"Speaking of Annie, her husband called and wants me to sit with the kids this morning. You mind if I take Lizzie over there?"

"Not at all. Where's Annie?"

"She was called out on a story in the middle of the night. Mike didn't seem to know much. Believe me, I grilled him."

"Humph," Vera said. "I bet you did."

Vera scooped up their plates and placed them in the sink, turned around, and looked at Lizzie. "Done?"

"Done," she said, nodding emphatically, and raised her arms for her mother to lift her out of the high chair.

Beatrice reached for the paper and glanced over the article. "Hmm. It says where the funeral is on Wednesday."

"Where?" Vera asked, smoothing back Lizzie's hair. The child gave a little squeal. "Lizzie doesn't like people messing with her hair."

"Neither do I," Beatrice said and chortled. "Just like her gram."

"Don't wish that on her, Mama."

"Now, would it be so bad to have another bright, beautiful woman in this family?"

Vera couldn't help herself and laughed. Her mother was one of the most intelligent women in Cumberland Creek. Of course, that didn't say much. But at one time, she was also one of the smartest women in the world—some breakthrough with her physics research. Vera didn't understand a thing about it. Nor did she understand the other part—the quantum physics. Beatrice fell in love with it later in her career and received international recognition for her work. Vera sighed. She, the daughter of a physicist and a physician, had struggled all the way through school with math, then science, especially chemistry. Which reminded her. Her mother had stopped talking so much about him.

"You haven't mentioned Daddy in a long time," Vera said.

Beatrice's back was to her. She was at the sink, rinsing off the dishes. But it looked like she stiffened. Well, Vera might not be a physicist, but she was a dancer, had studied movement her whole life, and could read anybody's body—even a person like Beatrice, who was astute at keeping the personal to herself.

"What is it, Mama?"

Beatrice loaded up the dishwasher, grabbed a black-and-white checked towel from the drawer. "Vera, your father is gone. When I was in Paris, well, he finally left me," she said, her voice cracking ever so slightly. Jaw firm.

Vera searched her mother's lined face, bright blue eyes, slightly pursed lips for an answer. She had never believed that her father was haunting her mother. There were no such things as ghosts. But she knew Beatrice believed it with all of her heart. Nobody had questioned Beatrice Matthews too thoroughly about it. After all, she was a brilliant, formidable woman. Still walking to get her groceries, still reading good books, helping to take care of a small child. And her mind was as good as— if not better than—it was when she was thirty. So, Vera had always conceded, if her mother wanted to believe her father was hanging around, what was the harm? But now this, this had her concerned. It was not like her mother.

"Just like that?" Vera said. "He left?"

"Yes, Vera. Just like that. Now, give me the baby, and don't get your panties in a cinch over it. I need to get over to Annie's place. "

Vera put Elizabeth in the stroller, which she kept in

the foyer, with a diaper bag ready to go. "Okay, Mama," she said. "Whatever you say."

"Well, now," Beatrice said. "Forty-one years old and you're finally learning to listen to me. Ain't that remarkable!"

Vera kissed Lizzie, then Beatrice, and watched her mother walk down the sidewalk with Lizzie in the stroller. She glanced around. The sidewalks were empty; she was pleased to note there were no suspicious characters hanging around. She suddenly wondered what the hell happened to her mom in Paris—and she planned to get to the bottom of it.

Chapter 10

Beatrice had it all under control. Annie's boys were off to school, Mike was off to work, and Elizabeth was napping in her portable crib in Annie's living room. She rinsed off the last of the Chamovitzes' breakfast dishes and was thinking about going home as soon as Elizabeth awakened when Annie walked in the door.

"The boys in school?" Annie said immediately to Beatrice when she saw her standing at the sink.

"Well, how do to you, too," Beatrice said.

"Oh, I'm sorry, Bea," Annie said and dropped her bag on the table. "I'm a bit off this morning."

When Annie dropped the bag, Beatrice saw her tremble.

"Here now," Beatrice said, pulling out a chair and gently guiding Annie to it. "You look like you've seen a ghost."

Annie looked directly into her eyes and smirked.

"Okay, okay, the irony's not lost on me. Me and my ghosts," Beatrice said.

"Oh God, my neck feels like a tightrope. Maybe I'm getting a headache."

"Coffee?" Beatrice said, noticing the circles around Annie's dark eyes.

"I was not thinking."

"I know. You look like hell."

"Thanks, Bea," she said, taking the full hot cup from Beatrice's hands. "I've been up since about three."

"What on earth is going on?"

"Another murder," Annie said hoarsely.

Beatrice clutched her chest and sat down. "Who?" she finally said, fingering her disheveled sweater.

"I don't know yet."

"What do you know?"

"I know . . . some incredibly sick and scary stuff."

Just then a baby's cry interrupted them.

Beatrice rushed to her granddaughter, pulled her from the crib, and sat down on the rocking chair. "Hey, Lizzie. Granny's here."

Beatrice felt her only grandchild's weight on her, and she loved the warmth of it. The tenderness and reverence. Maybe it was true that being a grandparent was better than being a parent. She appreciated each step of Elizabeth's life—in a way that she couldn't have done as a young mom herself. When you were in the thick of it, it just wasn't easy. Still, there were moments she would never forget with Vera, and sometimes she wished she could go back and freeze those moments. Sometimes she looked at Elizabeth and remembered those days with a startling freshness.

Poor Annie. Now that both boys were in school all day, she had a whole new set of worries. The local Weekly Religious Education program was just one of those worries that Annie had expressed to Beatrice. It was "Bible" education given by the local church—really they were proselytizing. If it were an "education," she'd have no problem with it. But her two Jewish boys had no reason to attend Bible studies at the church. It was just beginning, Beatrice feared.

Annie sipped her coffee and watched Beatrice rock Elizabeth on the well-worn glider rocker.

"So?" Beatrice finally said. "Are you going to make me wait and read it in the paper?"

"Another young woman. Arms were cut off. There was a white powder all over the place. The CDC came. Thought it was anthrax, but it wasn't. It was just a very fine specialty flour."

"Jesus. You did have quite a morning." Beatrice took a deep breath. Was this really happening in her sleepy little town?

"A couple more things, Bea."

"Yes?" Did she want to hear more?

"She had those same markings. And she was a red-head."

"You don't say," Beatrice said, eyes widening. "Are we talking serial killer, then?"

"It looks like it. And there's another interesting piece to it," Annie said, getting up to fix herself a bowl of cereal.

"God, what else could there be?" Beatrice looked at her with her eyebrows lifted.

"It seems to be getting personal."

"What do you mean, personal? Personal for who?"

"For me. The phone call I received in the middle of the night? It wasn't from the detective. It was from someone else, someone who wanted to make sure I was there."

"You told the police that, didn't you?"

"Bryant knows. They are going to put a device on my phone," she said, opening the refrigerator, grabbing the milk. "It was a compromise. He wanted to post guards at my house. I don't need Cumberland Creek's finest hanging around my house. I want some time to unravel this before my life gets completely turned upside down."

"That's foolish," Beatrice said. "C'mon."

Annie had just started to speak when the doorbell rang.

"Yoo-hoo," came Cookie's voice as she entered. She looked from Beatrice to Annie. "What's going on? I feel like I've walked into a hornet's nest."

Chapter 11

Annie was working on Ben's soccer book. She was thrilled that Sheila had finally gotten in the soccer ball embellishments she'd ordered a couple of weeks ago. She placed the ball on the corner of the photo. Her oldest son with that grin on his face, holding a ball. She loved it. This was one way her boys were fitting in—with their athleticism.

Annie took a long sip of her beer and thought about this group of women who were her friends. Sheila, with her morning runs and scrapbooking business, everything in her home and life so precise, except for her own grooming; DeeAnn, with the hands and heart of a baker, always finding a reason to laugh; Paige, with her tie-dyed hippie clothes and decidedly un-hippie lifestyle; and Vera, always a little too made up, a butterfly stronger than stone. Cookie, the outsider that everybody adored, was caught up in some shimmery paper across the table.

"Oh, isn't that beautiful!" DeeAnn exclaimed over a scrapbook page that Cookie was working on.

Annie glanced away from her boy's photo on the page to Cookie's white slender fingers holding the paper. It was just like DeeAnn to get excited over a shiny thing.

"It's for my book of shadows," Cookie explained.

"Your what?" Annie said.

"A book of shadows is a witch's journal. I keep track of things and write about rituals and moon phases. My observations. Stuff like that," she said. "My other one is getting kind of used and full. I thought I might start a new one, using some scrapbook techniques."

"I love that glitter paper," DeeAnn said, holding out some nachos with her homemade salsa. "Have you tried this?"

"Now, be careful. I don't want salsa spilling. Take it over to the snack table, please," Sheila said.

DeeAnn rolled her eyes but did what she was told. Food and precious photos didn't mix well.

Annie went back to her soccer book, sipping her beer. Beer and scrapbooking had become synonymous with her Saturday nights. If her old friends in D.C. could see her now.

"I wonder what Vera is doing right now," Sheila said and giggled.

"One thing she's not doing is this," DeeAnn said.

"Oh, it's a good thing we have Vera and her sex life to talk about," Paige said, fussing over the Cricut personal cutting machine. "None of the rest of us old married ladies get much sex."

That's what you think, Annie thought.

"That's because our husbands are *too tired* from work. What does that Tony guy do with himself, anyway?" DeeAnn said, scooping up more salsa. Her large hands dwarfed the salsa jar.

"God only knows," Sheila said. "He's teaching dance somewhere, I suppose. Chelsea Dance?"

Again, it became very quiet. The spurts of quiet were probably what Annie liked the most about their gatherings. They could be quiet among themselves, and it wasn't a problem. DeeAnn was working on a scrap cookbook; Paige was working on her niece's wedding scrapbook; Sheila was scrapbooking her daughter Donna's senior year of high school.

But tonight an air of fear seemed to permeate. The news that a second body had turned up had sent the town—especially the women—into a state of fear and shock. The victims were both young women from Jenkins Hollow, a place that seemed to be legendary for outcasts.

"I just can't believe it," Sheila suddenly said. "Another murder."

"Did they ever find out who the second woman was?" DeeAnn asked Annie.

"Yes, Rebecca Collins," Annie said, pushing back the images that came to her from her morning at the landfill a few days ago. "We're going to her funeral."

"Did you say that Bea went to Sarah's funeral?" Sheila said, pushing her glasses back on her nose.

Paige piped up. "Bea's not going to miss a funeral."

The women laughed. It was true Beatrice Matthews didn't miss a funeral within fifty miles of Cumberland Creek proper.

Paige was one of the few croppers who still had deep ties to Jenkins Hollow. But she was recently ostracized by her church because her son was gay and she'd just reconciled with him. She stood up for him one Sunday during the preacher's antigay rant, and that was the end of her church relationship. It was the church she was raised in, the one her family had always gone to, and it held many memories of weddings, baptisms, funerals. Paige was devastated, but also angry.

"Of course, my mother wouldn't miss one, either," Paige said.

Annie nodded affirmatively. "Both of us went and wished we didn't. It was sad and bizarre."

"What do you mean?" Sheila said in a hushed tone.

"Very few people were there. I mean, there were five of us. Bea, me, Detective Bryant, and her parents. There was no wake, no friends. Nothing."

It was the second Christian funeral Annie had attended since she moved to Cumberland Creek. The two funerals were a year apart from one another. This one was so different from Maggie Rae's, which was attended by everybody in town, and then some. The wake was huge, with tables and tables of food. Sarah's memorial service was sparse, and it left Annie feeling weirdly frightened. Was Sarah that isolated that she had no friends? Or was there a statement being made? If so, what was it? Or were people afraid to show up for some reason?

Annie was met with silence from the scrapbookers.

"That makes sense," Paige finally said, her blue eyes lit. "It makes sense in some weird kind of way. Those people are very superstitious, very backward."

"Do you mean they think her bad luck would rub off?" Cookie asked with one eyebrow lifted.

"I don't know, really. Who knows?" Paige said, waving her hand. "But there'd have to be a reason for it, and I'm betting it has to do with one of their strange beliefs."

"I keep hearing about their strange beliefs," Annie said. "But I have no idea what you're talking about. Is there a certain religion? What is it?"

"Who really knows?" Sheila said. "No outsiders know all about them. Some Old Orders don't even believe in funerals. Maybe people didn't even realize she was gone at the time they buried her. They bury their dead quickly, sometimes before the service. One thing I can say for sure is that some of them may call themselves Old Order Mennonites, but they are not Mennonite."

"Oh, heavens no," DeeAnn said. "That's some odd brew of weirdness going on up there. They keep real close to themselves. I've heard of cousins marrying. I've heard of animal sacrifice. And even drugs and rituals."

DeeAnn, hailing from Minnesota, had married a local man and had settled in Cumberland Creek with him. She was a culinary school graduate and owned and operated her own bakery, yet Annie had always thought she was a bit sheltered.

"Sounds a little far-fetched to me," Cookie said.

"Humph. This coming from a witch named Cookie," Paige said good-naturedly and rolled her eyes.

"They call me Cookie for one simple reason, Paige," Cookie said. "If you bite me, I taste really, really sweet."

Laughter ensued.

"Let's turn up the music. Gosh, I love that new Usher song," Sheila said.

Annie emptied her glass of beer, smiled at Sheila dancing between the chair and the shelves that held every color of paper you could imagine. Tomorrow she would be slaving over her next article for the paper, trying to keep Ben and Sam occupied, fixing some kind of supper, and trying to keep some semblance of sanity. But tonight she'd finish this book, eat some chips and salsa, and drink another one of those dark chocolate stouts. Yes, indeed.

Chapter 12

Vera loved the train. But as it moved away from the city this time, she felt it in her guts. Leaving Tony was getting harder and harder. They had both said this relationship was just for fun. Both of them divorced. She with a baby. He with a new teaching job. And besides all this, he was in New York and she was in Cumberland Creek.

She felt an intense pang for him move through her body—like a wave of heightened awareness. She ached; her guts twisted; her heart sank. And then she caught herself. Wasn't this the stuff of cheap romance novels? She was almost forty-two years old and couldn't continue this emotional roller-coaster ride with him. For how many years could it go on? Where could it lead? She could never leave Cumberland Creek to be with him—because of Elizabeth. She couldn't take the child away from Bill and Beatrice. Meanwhile, he was so Brooklyn. It wouldn't be fair to ask him to leave behind his city—this place that pulsed with energy and life—for her sleepy little town.

Perhaps it wasn't so sleepy anymore. Two murders within a month of one another. Both young women with red hair. Unique markings called runes were carved into their bodies.

"You don't hear about that stuff in New York," Tony had told her over bagels that morning. "It's so safe here now."

"Yes. I feel safer here now than I used to," she said, looking around his tiny studio apartment. His years of dance had not left Tony well off—quite the contrary. He had to give up the touring because his knees finally gave way. But he was able to teach and commanded a decent salary, most of which he was saving for a knee replacement.

But she loved the simplicity of his place and his life. A wall with a desk that held his computer, next to that a keyboard and stereo, then what counted as his kitchen—just a wall with a sink, stove, fridge, and a few cupboards. She smiled at the thought of the first time she baked him an apple pie there. It was a challenge. But, oh, he loved it. Raved about it between fork-fed bites from her own hand.

Of course, along the opposite wall was mostly just his huge bed, where his touch made her feel more alive than she had in years.

Someone gave a laugh on the train—it had the same quality as Tony's. He laughed again. It was so similar that she had to turn around and look. Of course, it wasn't him. But when the laugh came again, Vera realized she was crying. That laugh. She could picture Tony's smiling mouth, open, framed in deep dimples, with that sound rolling out of it. How could he fill her with such pleasure and such bittersweet longing at the same time?

Every time she left him, she was grateful for the transition time on the train or plane. The train was nicer for this very reason. She felt as if it was transporting her between two worlds. Two lives that she struggled to keep separate. Tony wanted to come to Cumberland Creek, and that thought made her uneasy.

"Are you ashamed of me?" he'd asked her just last night, his deep brown eyes softly looking at her through long black eyelashes. "What?"

She'd wanted to cry. "This time together has been like a dream I don't want to wake up from. I don't want to share you."

He'd kissed her with such passion at that moment that it almost took her breath away. The next thing she knew, they had gotten so carried away that they knocked all his plants down that were perched along the headboard of his bed.

Vera smiled. She'd keep that to herself—along with all the decidedly kinky things that went on this weekend. He was leading her to explore a side of herself that had been stuffed inside for far too long. In a way, she felt foolish. Here she was, a slightly overweight new mother, feeling like a lithe teenager. She lost all sense of herself in his arms. What they had seemed to go beyond the physical trappings of their bodies, though the trappings were what brought them such joy.

She opened up her laptop and clicked on the local news, hoping there had been no more murders in her little town. She scrolled down and breathed a huge sigh of relief at the lack of news—there was only Annie's recap of the events about Sarah's death.

Jenkins Mountain—one of the biggest mountains in the Shenandoah Valley—houses several communities. One of the communities is a tight-knit Old Order Mennonite enclave, which is where Sarah Carpenter was raised.

"The Mennonite faith encompasses many branches," says the Reverend Paul Thomas. "Some dress simply. Some dress in modern clothing. But

we are all Mennonites, and we are all Christians seeking a simple, peaceful way of life."

At first glance, one might think peace might be found surrounded by the pristine mountains and farm fields of the region. Long days are spent working the land or canning the garden's crops or picnicking with your church. This place is far from the temptations of neighboring cities, like Charlottesville, Waynesboro, or even small town Cumberland Creek—which is where Sarah's body washed up approximately ten hours after she drowned.

"We know it wasn't an accident. There are marks that indicate that she was held underwater until she died," says Detective Adam Bryant of the Cumberland Creek police.

Sarah's murder, the second murder in the area in two years, is shrouded in mystery. Part of that mystery is her life on the mountain. Given that the community is in mourning and enforces strict mourning precepts, many of her family and friends are not available for questioning.

But as a typical young Mennonite farm woman, she probably began each morning with prayer, then farm or kitchen chores. Sarah had three brothers and two sisters. Given her age, she may have begun each day in the kitchen, helping prepare food for the family.

One thing we know about Sarah is that she played the piano and gave lessons to the local children as a way to earn money—which she no doubt gave to her parents.

Her social life would have consisted of visiting with neighbors and friends who were also Mennonite. She would have attended church functions, since the Jenkins Mountain community does not have a bar, a grocer, or even a restaurant.

Just then Vera's cell phone blared Beethoven's Fifth. She brought it to her ear.

"I miss you," Tony whispered into the phone.

She smiled and reached into her bag for a chocolate. "I miss you, too."

Chapter 13

Nothing like a good funeral, even if it was a couple of hours away in Jenkins Hollow.

Beatrice dressed in her Sunday best, a dark blue suit, and placed a strand of pearls around her neck. Real pearls, mind you, and it was getting to the point where funerals were the only occasions she could wear them.

Not that she liked to see grieving. But what Beatrice did like was to see a community come together in fellowship and offer condolences. A keen observer of humanity—or at least that was what she thought about herself—Beatrice loved to see the spectacle of clothes and food at many of the local funerals. Southerners always brought out the best for such events.

She'd missed Maggie Rae's funeral as she had just had surgery to remove a knife from her neck. Vera was supposed to report back to her, but her observations were weak.

"What did Violet wear? The same black dress she always wears? She's been wearing it for thirty years. I swear."

"Well," Vera had said. "Hmm. I can't remember what Violet was wearing. It seems to me it was dark. Yes. Maybe it was black. Oh, Mama, who cares?"

Beatrice was not so vacuous that she cared only about what people wore. But she made note of certain individuals' clothing and what it said about them. For example, Violet's husband was one of the wealthiest men in the town, yet she didn't appear to ever buy anything new. Her funeral dress was a black shirtwaist dress, her spring and summer "wedding" dress was a light blue silk, and her fall and winter, a red wool. The same dresses for thirty years. Or at least that was how it appeared.

So Beatrice wondered if Violet chose not to buy anything new or if her husband refused to buy anything for her. And what was that all about?

And then there was Mathilda Rogers, who always brought a "little" something to wakes. Damn little. Once she brought a plate of a dozen chocolate chip cookies to a wake. A dozen? Why did she bother? Why bring anything at all if she was going to be so stingy about it?

She mentioned it once to Vera, who said that maybe there was a financial problem.

"Humph. I don't think so. She plays bingo like it's going out of style, and I've seen her spending money at the hair salon," Beatrice had said.

"Really, Mother, don't you have anything better to do?"

"Don't you ever notice anything about people? How do you function in the world?" Beatrice had said. Why couldn't Vera be more like Annie, who noticed even more than Beatrice?

Vera had waved her off, as she often did, as if she were exasperated with her old fool of a mother. *Damn her.*

A car beep sounded at the front of Beatrice's house. She stood at the door with her purse slung around her arm. Ready to go.

She mumbled as she crawled into the backseat of the car, next to Annie, who was looking elegant in black,

with chunky gold earrings and a lovely gray angora
scarf around her neck.

"Hey," Annie said.

"Hey back. How are you?"

Annie shrugged. "Fine, I guess."

"I'm fine, too, Bea," Sheila said, grinning, from the
front passenger seat of the car.

"Who asked you, scrapbook queen?" Beatrice said,
turning away from her. Her relationship with Sheila was
one of consistent, but good-natured banter. Her mother,
Gerty, was Beatrice's best friend—she died several
years ago from breast cancer. "Listen, Annie, do you
think we can get some clues today?"

Annie started to talk, but Vera interrupted.

"Mama! This is a funeral. Behave yourself."

"I've been going to funerals since you were a glimmer in your daddy's eye. Don't tell me how to behave at
a funeral. I just thought it might be a good place to
observe the family, see if anybody suspicious shows
up," Beatrice said.

Vera stopped the car at a red light. "Well, don't go
around questioning people."

"I am on a story," Annie said. "But I certainly would
be very careful about who I spoke to and what I asked."

"Oh, Annie, I'm not worried about you," Vera
replied. "It's Mama. Sometimes I never know what's
going to come out of her mouth—or who she is going
to try to shoot."

Sheila laughed. Annie smiled.

Beatrice folded her arms and leaned them on her
purse, where, they all knew, she kept her gun. She looked
at Annie and shrugged.

Chapter 14

Even though it was the opposite of the Cumberland Creek Episcopal brick building—which sprawled over half a city block with its cavernous hallways—the white-clapboard, one-room Jenkins Creek Baptist Church still reminded Annie of the day she went to Maggie Rae's funeral. Witnessing Maggie Rae's family, most especially her children, dealing with her death was gut wrenching.

As the four women approached the church, a cold wind swept up and Annie pulled her scarf tighter around her neck. The sound of the creek chilled her. *Damn*. She had to find the bathroom.

"Bathroom," she whispered just as they entered the church.

Vera pointed her outside, in the direction of an out-house.

"You are kidding."

Vera shook her head.

Annie shrugged. She had used worse places. She padded over to the outhouse, opened the door, and was pleasantly surprised to find a clean experience.

When she was done, she made her way back to the church, just as a hush was coming over the funeral congregation. She glanced around for her companions. There they were in the middle, of course.

Annie found her way to the pew, feeling as if everybody was watching her, and sat down as delicately as possible. Nothing like making a grand entrance.

The minister, a much younger man than what Annie had expected, approached the pulpit and began to pray. She tuned him out. She was here to check out the crowd—except she couldn't shake the feeling that someone was watching her. She glanced around and saw what must have been Rebecca's family, finally seated at the front of the room. While everybody's heads were bowed, Annie took the opportunity to turn around quietly—and there he was, Zeb McClain, Tina Sue's husband, who was not praying, but was instead looking directly at her. Zeb had been implicated in Maggie Rae's case, but the Jenkins Hollow community had provided sound alibis for him.

He was dressed in Old Order Mennonite clothing, hiding his well-sculpted physique, for which Annie was grateful. She'd already seen too much of the man. His steely blue eyes, square jawline, and full lips were all a part of the man that visited her in her nightmares.

Her stomach twisted. She turned her face quickly, feeling the hot creep of embarrassment mixed with anger. *Damn.* Of course, he would be here. This church was on the outskirts of Jenkins Mountain proper. But even though he stood there, dressed in plain, dark Mennonite clothing, he was not praying. He was watching her!

He wasn't the only one watching her.

Detective Bryant sat two rows in front of her. His head wasn't bowed, either. He turned and caught her eye. Nodded. She pursed her lips. Beatrice elbowed her. She didn't miss a thing.

The piano started to play "Amazing Grace," and a large woman stood and began to sing.

"Amazing grace, how sweet the sound . . ."

Annie didn't know the song as part of her culture, but she still found it incredibly beautiful and moving. The sunlight was beaming in through the window, and it lit a corner of the piano and the singer. Twisty, bare branches visible through the window reached across the blue sky.

"To save a wretch like me . . ."

Wretch. Now that was an interesting word. She sighed and supposed that most of those gathered here today would agree that she fit the bill. *Wretch.* Annie smiled to herself. She turned to see if Zeb was still looking at her and was startled to see that his icy blues were refusing to leave her. She gave him her harshest stare. Who did he think he was? Beatrice elbowed her again. She turned back around and lifted her eyebrow.

"What?" she mouthed.

Beatrice motioned to her purse, opened it, and gave her a glimpse of her gun.

Annie waved her off. Beatrice and that gun were going to get into trouble one day. She hoped it wasn't today. But then again, that gun could come in handy if the big brute of a man suddenly came at her. Annie decided to stick close to Beatrice.

Zeb, sitting at the edge of his pew, was one of many people in that section of the congregation who were dressed in the plain clothes of Old Order Mennonites. Annie flashed back to Maggie's Rae's funeral. Zeb was sitting in front with the rest of the family. But Annie distinctly remembered another group of Mennonites standing in the back. Seeing people dressed like it was 1900 always left an impression on her. She didn't see such things while she was growing up in Bethesda, Maryland. The first time she remembered seeing anything like it was in Amish Lancaster, Pennsylvania. She realized some people equated their garb with a peaceful, simple life, but it unsettled Annie. She was aware of the "romantic" notions the public held about Mennonites and their "peaceful," simple lives. Maybe she was too cynical and world weary, but she would not be surprised to learn of more stories like the one she'd just read about Mary Schultz. She was a young Mennonite woman who recently murdered her father with an axe, claiming he'd abused her. Now her lawyers were claiming she was mentally unstable. And who wouldn't be after years of abuse? Annie knew that was one hell of a story—a story the woman was not telling and one the courts were also keeping under wraps.

Annie glanced around the church and noted how different it was than the Episcopal church in town. No statues of Jesus on the cross, no stained-glass windows, and no carpeting. It was austere and simple. Annie felt okay about being in this space, whereas the bigger town church made her uncomfortable.

She shifted around in her seat; Bryant looked back at her. God, that man annoyed her. He could certainly be more helpful. Annie felt another set of eyes on her; she looked across the aisle at a young woman, who smiled shyly. She was blonde and pale, with a large mole on the side of her face, and looked to be about eighteen or nineteen. She wore the white prayer cap of all the young Mennonite women. She must have known Rebecca and maybe even Sarah. Annie made a mental note to try to talk to her during the wake.

A wailing sob came from the front of the room— Rebecca's mother—and her husband placed his arms around her. They looked in the direction of the simple wooden casket, which was closed, of course. Their daughter had been hacked to pieces, covered in flour, with rune symbols carved into her. How would they ever get over this?

Chapter 15

Vera knew that it was expected that she attend funerals—even as a child, she went along with her mother. Beatrice had always said it did no good to shield children from death. It was a part of life. But Vera did not think she would want Elizabeth anywhere near this place.

She heard a baby cry and turned to watch the mother scuttle off during the service. Maybe she had nobody to keep the baby. Her eyes met the other woman's, and she made a connection with a sympathetic smile. Mothers knew what it was like to have a crying baby at a church service or concert. She was still amazed at how becoming a mother had opened her heart. Other mothers. Other children. Babies. She only wished that she could have more children—her heart was so full.

She brushed some lint off her black wool slacks. Her mother had rolled her eyes at her when she saw she was not wearing a dress. But Vera didn't care. It was cold, and these days pants were every bit as appropriate as a skirt. She stood with the rest of the crowd as the family exited the room to go to the basement, where the food was already laid out, awaiting the bereaved family and other mourners.

Vera could not help but wonder if the murderer was in the crowd. She looked over those gathered. There was John DeGrassi, from the only Italian family she knew, a simple, hardworking shopkeeper. He owned the only general store in Jenkins Hollow. His eyes were heavy with grief, she decided. He was not a killer.

Then there was Shelly Martin, dressed in a dark floral dress, whose daughter, Christy, had recently gone off to school to study physical education. She was one of Vera's best dancers but had decided against a career in the field. Smart cookie. Shelly had always had a bit of a dark side. She dyed her hair platinum blond and sported several tattoos. But could she kill someone?

Detective Bryant glanced toward Annie. He was watching her. Annie received much male attention everywhere she went. She was beautiful in a unique way—dark skin, high cheekbones, large brown eyes, thin, tall. Damn, she could have been a model. But she was too smart for that—you could see the brightness in her eyes.

Sheila's arm bumped into Annie as she pushed her glasses back up onto her nose. Sheila had actually put some more make-up on this morning than her usual smear of lipstick. And she looked great in that navy blue suit. Sheila had the body of a twenty-five-year-old. Vera sighed. It was all those years of running, which Vera hated. How could anybody get excited about it?

"It's not exciting," Sheila had told her one day. "It's that monotony that is a blessing. One foot in front of the other. That's all I need to think about at that moment."

The four women walked down the stairs together quietly—not much could be spoken, just felt. A young woman heinously killed. Her family was at a loss. You could see it in their eyes. All of them looked hollow.

A stab of fear shot through Vera. What if something

like this were to happen to Elizabeth? How could she manage to survive? To go on living?

The service was over, and the crowd meandered to the basement of the church. Long card tables were jammed full of the usual wake food—pies, pasta salads, cakes, shrimp, a meat tray with ham and roast beef, several cheese platters, several types of chicken (barbecued, fried, baked), corn pudding, and turkey.

The wake was usually Bill's favorite part of a funeral, but he was keeping Elizabeth and so he wasn't here. The last funeral they had attended as a couple, they were still married, happily, or so she'd thought.

"Oh, look at that red velvet cake," Beatrice said quietly as they moved into the food line.

"I can't believe all this food," Annie said, looking as if she were shell-shocked.

"Oh, this is nothing," Vera said. "You should have seen the food at Maggie Rae's funeral."

"It's part of our tradition," Beatrice said.

Once all their plates were piled high, they were able to find seats together at one of the tables.

"How's the scrapbook queens?" a male voice said behind Vera. She recognized it.

"Detective Bryant," Sheila said. "We are fine. And you?"

"Just keeping an eye on things," he said, looking at Annie. "How about you?"

Annie nodded after taking a bite of red potato salad.

"Don't worry. I have her covered," Beatrice said.

He laughed, his blue eyes lighting up and his dimples deepening. "Now, that worries me, more than anything."

"You don't look bad once you're cleaned up a bit, Detective," Beatrice said.

"Mama! For heaven's sake," Vera said.

He waved them off and then walked away. He was dressed in the same blue suit he'd worn for all the other recent funerals—it was probably custom-made. He was so broad at the shoulders and narrow at the hips, Vera imagined he couldn't buy directly off the rack. His sandy hair was combed nicely for a change, she noted.

Vera bit into a perfectly seasoned piece of barbecued chicken. Now, these mountain folks knew how to barbecue a bird. Annie shoved a piece of shoofly pie, chock-full of molasses and brown sugar, into her mouth and chewed.

She grimaced. "Ahh," she said. "What is this? It looked good . . . but—"

The next thing Vera knew, Annie was running outside for fresh air.

"Shoofly," Beatrice said, smacking her lips after another bite of red velvet cake. "Someone should have warned her." Sometimes it took a while for outsiders to develop a taste for this toothsome molasses and brown sugar pie. Not only was it sweet enough that it could make your teeth ache, but it also had a surprisingly spicy bite. Some folks just couldn't handle it.

Chapter 16

Beatrice was looking at the Eiffel Tower, marveling at its height, the smooth yet geometric lines of it. She suddenly realized she was lying on the ground, in between beds of flowers on soft green grass, and beyond the lit tower was the Paris night sky.

Ed was present, his hand resting in hers, and as they looked at each other, his face beamed. He had always wanted to take her to Paris. Here they were, a dream come true.

But wait. She turned to see where the music was coming from and turned back, and he was gone. A sinking, sickening feeling came over her. Where was her husband? Her best friend? How could he leave her?

Beatrice awoke with words from *Leaves of Grass* turning over in her mind. What a dream. She reached up to her cheek and wiped a salty tear from her face.

"Stupid old woman," she said out loud, then heard a weird noise downstairs. What was that? Something outside, or was it in her front room?

She reached in the drawer for her trusty pistol, felt its cool steel. She slowly unraveled herself from the blankets, sat up, and placed her bare feet on the floor. Her bedroom door was already open—she had started leaving it open because more and more she was concerned about intruders, with all the recent unexplained incidents. She wanted immediate access to whoever was fool enough to enter her home uninvited. Not just her, but her and her gun, which freaked Vera out to no end. That made Beatrice grin even as she heard another scuffling noise. This time she was sure that it wasn't in her head and that it was at her front door.

She glanced at her digital clock: 5:30 a.m. What fool of a thief would be out and about at that time?

She walked gingerly down the hallway and saw streams of soft morning light coming through her stained-glass window. She began to descend the steps. So quiet. One step creaked—it always did. *Confound it!* Her heart skipped a beat as she wondered if the person at her front porch could hear it. She stood quietly for a moment and then began to move again. She swore she could feel the blood rush through her body. If only her joints did not ache so much this morning, she'd have already shot the guy.

The phone interrupted her last step to the first floor. *Blast!* Who would be calling at this hour? She let it ring. Let the goddamned answering machine pick up.

"Ms. Matthews? It's Detective Bryant," the voice said. "I don't want to frighten you, but I am on your front porch and can hear you rattling around inside. So maybe you just better put that pistol down and open the door."

What? What was he doing here? He knew her too well, knew all about that pistol. She had just taken another gun safety class, and he happened to be the teacher, supplementing from his day job as a detective.

She peeked out the peephole, and he waved.

She unlocked the door. "What's going on, Bryant?" she said as she flung it open.

"I'm sorry to disturb you—"

"Get on with it," she said, waving her hand around.

"There's been some vandalism."

"Why are you involving me?"

He stepped back and pointed to her house. "C'mon out here, Ms. Matthews."

She realized what a fool thing it was to have come downstairs without her robe and slippers as she stood in the cold October morning, looking at the strange rune symbol painted on her pink house.

"What on earth?" She put her hands on her hips and looked at him.

"Doesn't make much sense, does it? Until you realize the idiot was probably after Annie and her family."

"What do you mean? How do you know that? Why Annie?"

"Your house number is six-ten. Hers is six-oh-one. It took me a while to think of that. But that has to be it," he said, with a look of crushing concern.

Beatrice shivered. "C'mon in out of the cold, Bryant. Let me get you some coffee."

Chapter 17

Every time Mike and the boys left the house on Mondays, Annie felt an onslaught of freedom and relief, tinged with a little guilt. Should she feel this happy because she had the whole house and the whole day to herself? She didn't know what mess to tackle first, while her work called to her.

She straightened up the kitchen, always first, putting the dishes in the dishwasher, putting away all the cereal boxes and the milk and so on. She called Hannah Bowman, the young woman from the wake, who wasn't at the bakery where she worked, so she left a message. Then she allowed herself to be drawn to the computer.

She looked up "runes." A site all about runes—Runepedia—came up on her screen. Annie read over the first part and saw that Cookie was right. Germanic written languages used runic alphabets before adopting the Latin alphabet. As she read on, she was surprised to see that there were Scandinavian variants, known as "futharks," the Anglo-Saxon term for which was "futhorcs." She read on and learned that there was an actual study of runic alphabets called runology, which formed a specialized branch of Germanic linguistics.

Germanic linguistics? Cookie didn't mention that.

Annie wondered if she could find an expert in Germanic linguistics who knew about runes. That way they could approach the symbols with some semblance of academic rigor and not rely on these New Agers, whom even Cookie greeted with suspicion.

As Annie read further, she saw that the earliest runic inscriptions dated from around AD 150. Runes were first replaced by Latin letters when a culture that used runes underwent Christianization by around AD 700. But people never really gave up using runes—they continued to use them for "special purposes" in Northern Europe. Then the term "special purposes" popped out at her several times. *What special purposes?* She read more. The three best-known runic alphabets were Elder Futhark (around 150 to 800 AD), Anglo-Saxon Futhorc (400 to 1100 AD), and Younger Futhark (800 to 1100 AD). Younger Futhark was further divided into the long-branch runes.

Those further divisions were going to have to wait. Annie's eyes were beginning to glaze over. Better get more coffee and a shower, and then maybe she could start making sense of this.

Just then the doorbell rang. She walked to the door, still in her threadbare sweatpants that she called pajamas and a long Redskins T-shirt. She looked through the peephole. *Detective Bryant and Beatrice. Oh, boy. The two of them together?* They were like oil and water. *This ought to be good.*

She opened the door. "What's going on?"

"Can we come in?" the detective asked.

She glanced around at her messy home. Toys on the couch. Clothes thrown over chairs. Papers from the school on the coffee table and kitchen table. She shrugged. "I guess." She grabbed the papers off the kitchen table and placed them on the counter. "Sit down. Can I get you some coffee?"

"No," Beatrice said. "I'm fine."

"Me too," Detective Bryant said.

"I need another cup," Annie said, turning her back on them, then pouring the coffee. She paused to listen to the noise of it and breathed in the scent of it. Then she turned around and sat at the table.

"I told him that you need some guards," said Beatrice.

"I'm not surprised," Annie responded.

"I'm going to ask you again. Why won't you let us at least have a car outside?" he asked.

"I just haven't had the chance to think. I was on deadline. The place was full of commotion. You know that," Annie said.

"That is in the past. Today is today, and I think you're going to need someone watching over your home at least," he replied.

"I think we are overreaching here. Must be a logical explanation for that phone call," Annie insisted. "Maybe someone else from the police called. You know, one hand doesn't often know what the other is doing around here. You have a lot of new guys on the force. And I'm beginning to think the phone call was, um, just imaginary."

"Pretending it didn't happen won't make it so," Beatrice said.

"Bea, I'm not a child. Don't talk to me like that."

"Then stop acting like one," she snapped back. "It's gotten more serious than you know. More personal."

"What?"

"Early this morning one of the officers who was driving around town spotted a weird symbol painted on Beatrice's house," the detective said.

Annie's stomach tightened. "Why Bea?"

"We figured that it was meant for you. They got the address confused," Bryant said. He explained the similarity of the addresses.

Annie felt the breath leave her and tried to get some air.

"So, between the phone call and now this, I'm afraid that we are going to have to place you under watch . . . whether you want us to or not."

Annie shot a look at Beatrice. Exactly what she didn't need while she was working on this story—the Cumberland Creek police force under her feet.

"You know, other symbols, like the swastika, are painted in barns in Jenkins Hollow. You told me that it was just some kids being stupid, that it was nothing to worry about," she said.

"Between you and me and Bea, I can tell you that there is something to worry about. I can't tell you why. But you need to know this could be very dangerous for you and your family," he said.

"These people are anti-Semitic?" Annie said weakly.

"Oh yes," he said loudly. "But that's only part of what they are."

"Lord," Beatrice said. "What's wrong with people?"

"That is not your problem," Bryant said. "We have everything under control."

"Like hell you do," Beatrice said. "There's been two murders in this town recently. You have nothing under control. Nothing."

"Did it ever occur to you that there might be even more murders if we didn't have some control here?" he retorted.

Annie felt a chill travel up her spine, even as she held the hot coffee in her hands.

"Last time you two got your heads together, you almost got killed," he said to Beatrice. "Now, personally, I don't like either one of you. But I don't want to see you dead." He crossed his arms over his stomach.

"Mighty kind of you," Beatrice said, while Annie was trying to keep breakfast down.

Chapter 18

Vera was on her way to pick up Elizabeth from Bill's place when she saw the strange symbol painted in black on her mother's pink Victorian house. Double take. She slammed on the brakes and pulled alongside the house, leaving the car running as she ran up to the patio, where Cookie was knocking on the door.

"I can't get any answer," Cookie said, her green eyes filled with worry. "The door is locked."

Vera reached under the doormat and found the extra key—even though she had told her mother that this was an unwise place for it. She opened the door, and the two of them searched the house.

"She's not here," Vera said. "Where would she be?"

"We had plans to go to the craft show in Charlottesville today," Cookie said. "She must have forgotten."

"Maybe she's at Annie's," Vera suggested, picking up the phone.

Sometimes it hurt Vera that her mother and Annie had gotten so close. She knew she'd never be as smart as either one of them, but damn, Beatrice was her mother. That ought to count for something.

"Hello, Annie?"

"Yes."

"Is my mother there?"

"Yes."

"What's she doing there?"

"She's fine," Annie said. "We're just having coffee and discussing the day's events."

"The day's events? It's only eight in the morning," Vera said.

"Yes. Why don't you come on over?"

"Will do," Vera said and hung up.

The next thing Vera knew, Cookie was getting in the passenger side of the car. It wasn't as if either one of them needed to ride the two blocks to Annie's place. It was just that the car was convenient.

"Oh, bother," Vera said, remembering that she needed to pick up Elizabeth.

"Give me your phone. I'll call and tell him to meet us at Annie's," Cookie said when Vera explained her predicament.

"How weird to see a rune symbol on your mother's house," Cookie said after talking to Bill.

"Is that what that is? I don't even want to know. All kinds of weirdness going on here these days. I just hope Mama's okay."

"I'm sure she's fine if she's with Annie."

When they opened the door to Annie's bungalow, the two were sitting at the computer and looked up like nothing was wrong.

"Goodness, Mama, you gave us a start!"

"Oh," Beatrice said to Cookie. "I forgot about the craft fair."

"I guess I can forgive that after seeing that huge thing painted on your house this morning," Cookie said.

"What happened, and are you okay?" Vera said, rushing up to her mother and hugging her.

"Oh, for heaven's sake. Can't you see I'm fine? Stop

fussing over me. I'm looking for a painter to come and paint over that damned monstrosity and the whole house while he's at it," Beatrice said.

Annie smiled weakly at Vera. Annie looked beautiful in her grungy clothes, without a stitch of make-up on. The always made-up Vera marveled silently at that.

"Oh, well, good. You need to get that taken care of ASAP," Vera said. "Mama," she added, holding up a brown paper bag, "I brought you some of the poppy seed rolls you like so much."

"Oh," Beatrice said, her eyes lighting up. "Let's have some."

Annie sliced a roll as each of them claimed their spot around the tiny table. A high chair still sat in the corner, even though Annie's boys hadn't used it in years. Her fridge was covered with drawings and memos. Cereal boxes had been haphazardly placed on top of the fridge.

"Oh my God, this is good," said Cookie, taking another bite. "This is just the way they make it in Eastern Europe."

"You've been there?" Annie said.

"Ah, um, yeah, I was, as a child," she said, obviously a little uncomfortable talking about herself, as usual. "Where did you get this, Vera?"

"From a little neighborhood bakery in Brooklyn. I try to pick Mom up a roll or two when they have it," Vera answered.

"I never had it before Vera brought it home. I'm quite taken with it," Beatrice said. "I've only had poppy seeds in lemon poppy seed rolls. I understand you can make all kinds of things with it."

"We ate poppy seed cake every year for the holidays," Cookie said, grinning and suddenly looking like she was seven years old.

"Cake? Really?" Beatrice said.

Each of the women sat in silence for a few minutes, enjoying her poppy seed roll and coffee.

"So, Mom, what are you doing at Annie's? Why didn't you call the cops?" Vera finally asked.

Chapter 13

Chapter 19

Walking to the grocery store, Beatrice always thought about the time she was stabbed there and didn't know it until she got home and Vera pointed out that she had a knife sticking out the back of her neck. It was so odd to not feel that. According to the doctors, no nerve endings existed where the blade was plunged into her—right through her coat and scarf. It was a cold morning, like this morning, except then it was spring, and now it was fall. Beatrice preferred the cool spring to the cool fall. Perhaps it was because of what came after—summer and winter. God, she loved her seasons. She reached up and touched her scar, as had become her habit. Also, she paid more attention to who the people were around her. Today maybe more so than other days.

She walked in the store and turned the corner to head for the produce. She loved looking at the tables and tables of fruit from all over the world. Loved the smell that came off of it. When she was a child, she had never heard of a pomegranate. Now she could buy one at the local grocer.

"Good morning, Ms. Matthews," the produce manager said to her as he fussed over the bananas.

"Morning," she said. What was he so friendly about?

She'd known the Stickles family for years, and *friendly* wasn't the term she'd use to describe any of them. Especially Fred, this young man's father, who once hit a neighbor's dog with his car and never turned around to see if it was okay. This boy appeared to be on the cusp of having serious mental problems.

"What's going on over at your house? I saw some graffiti," he said.

Beatrice shrugged. So that was it. He wanted the scoop.

"Yeah, when I drove by, cops and stuff were everywhere," he said.

"Yep," she said and kept walking. She reached for the roll of plastic bags and unrolled it. The damned plastic always gave her fits. She tore off a bag, opened it, and shoved her bananas inside. She was thinking about getting a pomegranate.

"So, what happened?" he persisted.

"I'm not sure," she said. "Some young fools probably."

She dumped her bananas in her cart and decided to make a run for it. She didn't want to talk with this kid about the symbol on her house. She didn't like the way he had inserted himself into her life. Why, he hardly knew her. But then again, it was probably the talk of the town by now, with the way the grapevine worked so eloquently in Cumberland Creek. The problem was half the time it was full of half-truths and innuendos.

"So, are you a Nazi or a witch or what?" he asked as she walked away.

"Excuse me?" she said, turning around.

"I asked if you were a Nazi . . . ," he mumbled.

"Absurd. Why don't you . . . I don't know . . . go and read a book, young man?" Beatrice said, turning away from him.

"That symbol—"

"Phillip," said Eric, the general store manager, coming

to the rescue. "Finish up there. They need you in the deli."

Eric looked at Beatrice and shrugged. "Sorry," he said.

She waved him off, as if to say, "Whatever." She moved through the aisles, checking out the specials and new products.

As she was leaving, she noted that the Stickles boy was in the office, which was in the corner and raised, so she couldn't see much of it. But the top part had a window in it, so she could see he was in the office with his hat on his head. Was he getting ready to leave? *Hmm.* She hoped she didn't run into him again. The stupidity and crassness of some people were hard to take. The older she got, the worse it was. She found it hard to keep her thoughts to herself. But if people were going to offer their uneducated opinions, it was her philosophy that they got what was coming to them. Yes, indeed.

As she walked down the few blocks to her house, she waved to the schoolchildren getting ready to cross the street. Too soon, Elizabeth would be in school. Her heart sank.

Two bags of groceries in her arms, one in each now, she made her way to her house and stood at the gate. When she set the bags down to dig out her house key, she heard someone on the pavement behind her. She turned and saw the Stickles boy walking by her house. She placed her hands on her hips. Had he been following her the whole time?

He turned and looked at her, his eyes glaring. His middle finger lifting with attitude.

Beatrice laughed. Maybe she should be offended? But she found it hysterical that he actually thought that she cared what he thought about her. *Humph.*

Chapter 20

Finally, Annie found an expert in symbols, which was more difficult than she had thought since she lived so close to the University of Virginia. The language department transferred her to the classics department; the classics department transferred her to the anthropology department. She wanted to scream.

Eureka, she found a professor in German linguistics.

"Thanks for the fax," the professor said.

"Certainly. I'm looking for information about those runes," she told him. "If that is, indeed, what they are. I have a friend who says they are, but she doesn't seem certain."

"Oh yes. They definitely look like runes. These neo-pagans have attached themselves and their beliefs onto them. In some cases, they are making things up. In very rare cases, they know what they are doing . . . well, as much as they can know."

Cookie had made a similar statement.

"What would you think if you saw one of these rune symbols painted on a house?"

The professor was silent for a moment. "I'd think it was some crazy teenagers being ridiculous, which is sort of dangerous enough. Or I'd think that someone who kind of knows the rune system was warning the person who owns the house." He paused. "With this one particular symbol, maybe . . . troublemaker? Or trouble ahead? Depending on the interpretation."

"Anything there about red hair?" Annie asked.

He laughed. "No, I don't think so. I can have a friend look at them. A friend who is an expert in runes. I know enough about them, but they are really not my specialty. Why do you ask?"

"Two young women have been murdered in our community. They both had red hair. I wonder if that's of some significance. You know, there's all these strange sorts of beliefs about redheads."

"If you're dealing with these New Agers, I wouldn't think red hair would mean a thing. But other groups . . ."

"What other groups?"

"I think I remember reading that the Nazis wanted to stop redheads from breeding. Then there are several biblical characters often portrayed with red hair. Though, who knows what they really looked like."

"Which characters?"

"Judas for one. Mary Magdalene for another . . . maybe even Adam."

"Whoa," Annie said.

"Whoa, indeed," the professor said. "I really need to get going. But I'll have my friend contact you."

"Thanks," Annie said before hanging up the phone.

Mary Magdalene. Judas. Adam. An interesting group of characters. But how did they relate to her story and the murders, if at all?

She wasn't sure Adam related at all. But Mary Magdalene and Judas? Lust. Betrayal. She sat back in her chair. Interesting. But both of these young women were innocents. Or at least that was what everybody thought.

Chapter 21

Vera hung up the phone and tapped her nails on her desk as she watched her students getting ready for their ballet class. Slipping off their jeans or sweatpants, putting on their shoes, and stretching out. This was a small class of twelve-year-olds hoping to get into pointe shoes soon.

It was hard to get off the phone with Sheila, especially when she was so excited. One of her scrapbook designs was selected as a semifinalist in a national competition. The woman was so thrilled, she could barely put her sentences together.

Vera was happy Sheila was finally getting some recognition for her design work. After all, she was an art major in college, on a scholarship; then she married and had babies. Now maybe Sheila was finally coming into her own. What Sheila didn't know was that Cookie had taken some of her designed pages and had sent them off to other competitions, as well.

"I'm so impressed with her work," Cookie had said. "Don't tell her I'm doing this. Remember what she went through just to get one design sent off on her own."

"What we went through, too," Vera said, laughing. "If

I had to answer one more time which design I like best, I'm not sure, but I think I may have screamed."

"I hear you," Cookie said. "But it's so important to her."

"Ms. Matthews?" A voice that snapped Vera back to the present.

"Yes?" She turned to see Chelsea, one of her students.

"I'm supposed to tell you Valerie is sick today."

"Oh, thanks," Vera said, getting up from behind her desk. One of her ankles clicked. More parents were in the waiting room today. It was like that when Maggie Rae was killed, too. Parents who would ordinarily just drop their children off at their activities became more vigilant for a while.

"Okay, girls, to the bar," she said. She picked up the remote control and turned on the music. "Let's start with pliés, of course, two demi, one grande, eight times, and turn and do the other side."

All of them were lined up in a neat little row, all with black leotards, pink tights and shoes, hair pulled back into a bun. Six of them. They were at a point in their development as dancers where it could go either way. Usually out of six twelve-year-old girls, three might come back next year, and the following year perhaps two. One might try to pursue a career.

"Knees over the toes, ladies," she said, watching Melissa's coltish legs give a little wobble. Melissa's bright red hair made her stand out among the other dancers. She was the only redhead in the middle school and in the dancing school. She had forgotten about her earlier. Vera wondered if Melissa could be in danger. Was the killer after all redheads? Just teenaged redheads? Or was there some other connection between the two victims and the red hair didn't matter at all?

"Girls, we are looking a bit tired this afternoon. Let's

do it all again. This time, pretend we are not tired, eh? Can we see that energy?"

While the girls were getting ready for floor work, stretching and working on their splits, Vera always joined them on the floor. She liked to stay in shape and tried to do stretches and splits with each class. She also used the time to chitchat with the students. Sometimes it was about junk food or football games or boys.

"So what's on everybody's minds today?"

"We are worried about that killer on the loose. My mom won't let me go anywhere with my friends," Chelsea said.

The others chimed in. It seemed that it was a general rule with the parents around town.

"And then there was that symbol painted on the pink house," Melissa said. "Kind of freaky."

"I agree," Vera said, wondering how many of the girls knew that her mom lived in the house.

"My mama says it's witchcraft. She says that there's a real witch in Cumberland Creek," Melissa said.

Stunned, Vera stood up, brushed off her sweatpants. "Well, now, Kelly and Melissa, you've got a lot to learn. Both in ballet class and in life, sorry to say. So let's get busy."

When Beatrice finally arrived at her house, a paint crew was scrambling around, and she hadn't even had a chance to call a contractor.

"Detective Bryant called us," one of the painters told her.

"Good," she said and smiled. Then she saw the godawful pink they were putting on her house. "Wait! That's not the right color."

"He said pink."

"Everybody says pink, but it's really dusty pink. Look at the difference." She pointed to a patch of paint.

"I'm sorry, ma'am, but I don't see a difference."

"Baloney! Look at the difference," she said. "Take those sunglasses off."

"Oh," he said, taking the glasses off and squinting from the sun. "Yeah, but it's a slight difference."

"Stop painting right now, and go get the right shade, please," she told him. She looked at one of the young men who was painting. He looked like he was about twelve, but she wouldn't swear to it. She couldn't judge ages anymore. "Stop right there, young man!"

After she sent the painters on their way, Beatrice checked her e-mail. And there it was, an e-mail from Jon. She was so angry that she'd not heard from him that she thought about deleting it—but curiosity got the best of her. She clicked and it opened:

My dearest Beatrice,
I hope this e-mail finds you well, love. I have finally figured out how to use e-mail. I had to ask my grandson. My son, he would ask too many questions.

Humph, she thought. *About time.*

After we parted, I had a slight accident. It is nothing, really, but a twisted ankle, which made it a bit hard to get around. Can you imagine me sitting most of the day? It was terribly depressing. Darling, I am terrible at expressing myself on this machine. Would it not be best for us to be together? You must move to Paris and grow old with me.

Beatrice smiled. That would be the day.

It is terrible to feel like such a young man in an old man's body. But at least I can still please you.

Lawd. Red-faced old woman.

As I hope to again.
With all my love,
Jon

Beatrice sat back and mulled the e-mail over. She would wait a few days before she got back to him. After all, he had waited more than a month to e-mail her.

She leaned back and checked the local newspaper—such as it was. She read over an article about the second woman who was murdered, Rebecca Collins. She remembered Rebecca as a child, at Bible school camp one year. They used to live in town and then moved out to the country. Where was that? It had to be Jenkins Hollow.

So it must be a serial killer who has it in for redheads. She twirled her one remaining strand of red hair around her finger. But often, as in her study of quantum physics, these things went beyond the purely physical. What did the two women have in common, other than the red hair? Maybe, just maybe, the red hair was a pure coincidence. Well, they lived in Jenkins Hollow. The Collinses were not Mennonite; they were Baptist. She knew that from her church days—and from attending Rebecca's funeral. They were both eighteen. They both had ended up dead—one drowned, as the paper had reported, and the other dismembered. They both had those runes markings on them.

Did they know one another? If so, how well? That was the question. Of course, she couldn't go butting her nose in up in Jenkins Hollow, but she had a cousin, Rose, who lived up on the mountain that looked out over it. Perhaps it was time for a visit.

Chapter 22

All the arrangements were made. Annie hated the
drive to the prison, with its twisty mountain roads.
Queasy barely touched it. She'd visited several times for
research for the book, which was now at the publisher's
office, thank God. If she had to look at it one more time,
she would scream. She had worked on it. Rewritten it,
checked her facts, rewritten it again. She was so finished with that book.

But she felt compelled to visit this Mary Schultz, the
young Mennonite woman who recently murdered her
father with an axe, claiming he'd abused her. It was fascinating to ponder, but what Annie wanted was inside
information about the communities at Jenkins Mountain. Not only did she want to avoid the place, but it was
also a closed-off community. Nobody would talk to her.

By now, Annie knew the prison drill—she wore a
T-shirt and sweatpants, nothing with buttons, which, if
they fell off of her, could be saved and used as a
weapon. Annie handed her bag to the prison guard, who
searched through it. She looked at Annie and smiled a
weary smile.

"How are you today?" she asked politely.

"Fine," Annie said. "How about you?"

"Uh, well, another day, another dollar."

"I hear you."

The guard kept the bag. "Go ahead."

When Annie walked into the room, she was shocked at how fragile and small Mary was. This woman killed her father? How could that be? She was expecting a big farm girl—not this petite person in front of her.

The papers didn't give much information. Everything had happened quickly, and for months it was all handled within the Mennonite community. No press access until the young woman was brought to the local authorities by her church pastor, who claimed that she was insane and could not be cared for by her family or the community. In fact, she was a threat to them.

"Good morning, Ms. Schultz," Annie said.

Mary looked up and nodded, barely meeting her eyes. Pale. Plain. Brown hair cut short, uneven, as if she'd taken a pair of old scissors haphazardly to her hair.

"I'm Annie. How are you doing?" she said, sitting across the table from her.

A pause. "I'm still alive, and that's something, I suppose."

Annie smiled. "Indeed," she said. "I hear you've had a rough time of it."

Mary smiled weakly at her and almost met her eyes. "I'm not going to talk to you about my case," she said. She spoke succinctly, her voice soft and quiet. "My lawyer doesn't think it would be a good idea for the appeal. And I agree with her. I don't want any sensationalism."

"I understand. But if you ever change your mind, I'd love to write your story. But right now, I'm working on another project," Annie told her. "I'm writing articles about the murders. You heard about them, of course."

"Yeah," she said, running her fingers along the edge of the table.

"Do you know those families?"

"Yes."

"What do you know about them?"

"What do you want to know?"

"Let's start with the Carpenters. They were Old Order Mennonites, right?"

"What's that got to do with anything?"

"I'm not sure," Annie said. "I'm just asking."

"Well, yes. They are one of the few families left in the hollow who are actually real and Old Order. They go to my church . . . or my old church, I should say."

"What do you mean by 'real'?"

She shrugged. "They've never been involved with any of the others. . . ."

"I'm not sure I follow."

"A good bit of mixing is going on. It's very rare these days that the generations stay what they call pure in their faith," she said.

Pure in their faith? What the hell was that supposed to mean?

"You know," Mary said and smiled, "just like all young people . . . a Mennonite might fall in love with a Baptist. . . . It's complicated when it's Old Order . . . you know. . . . Depending on the family . . . there could be a shunning. That's bad . . . really bad. . . ."

Annie thought of the young woman's funeral she'd attended. Nobody went except her parents.

"Was that Carpenter girl being shunned?" Annie said out loud, but mostly to herself.

"I don't know. I've had a few problems of my own, and I'm not exactly a favorite in that community right now," she said. "But I could ask around."

"I'd appreciate it," Annie said. "Look, Mary, there's no real reason for you to help me. I appreciate anything you can give me, though. Someone is out there murdering young women. I'm supposed to write about these women, write about this case. I've got a job to do. I know you're having a rough time. I can see that."

"I killed my father," she said point-blank. "I belong here. This is justice, right? Even though the man abused me for years, my killing him was the worst of the crimes."

"I read that you went to the church and asked for help."

"I did. And I wrote to other churches. Nobody would help. All I kept hearing is that I needed to forgive my father," she said. Suddenly tears were sliding down her cheeks. "This is better. Being here. It's better than being out there. My family? My church? They've turned their back on me. I've not exactly been shunned, but I have nobody. And all I've ever done is everything they wanted me to. Except . . ."

Annie willed away tears and swallowed hard. "I think you did the right thing in defending yourself," she finally said. "No matter what the justice system says . . . or your family or church."

Mary looked at her with a glimmer of something. Was it hope?

A knock on the door. That was it. "Time's up, Ms. Chamovitz."

"Okay, thanks," Annie said. "I'll be back. Once you get settled in, think about things. Maybe you'll have information for me."

Mary nodded.

Annie took a deep breath. She hated this place. She'd visited this place too many times over the past year. It was dingy and sterile, just as you would expect a prison to be, but it seemed that the women's side of the prison was worse. It left her with a feeling of profound sorrow. But this was better than going up to Jenkins Hollow and snooping around herself. It had to be.

Chapter 23

"Invisible ink? That is too much!" said DeeAnn at the weekly crop. "It could be fun."

"But, of course, someone would have to know it was there to put the solution on it to read it," Annie said.

"Well, sure. But you could leave it as a part of a time capsule for your children, for example. Send them on a treasure hunt for it. It might make getting a sweet note from Mom a little more fun," Sheila said.

"But I love that vanishing-ink pen. That makes a lot of sense to me," Annie said. "I love the fact that I can draw lines on my pages with it. Journal along those lines, and in a few days the lines vanish. How cool is that?"

"Very. So many new products, so little time," Vera said.

"And money," DeeAnn said. "Good thing we share."

"Speaking of sharing, I heard that you went to the prison again," Vera said to Annie, then reached out for an angel food cupcake.

"Yes. I saw Mary Schultz," Annie said.

"What did you find out? Anything?"

"She won't talk to me about her case. I totally get that. But I did find out that the Carpenters are an Old

Order Mennonite family. I'm wondering if there was a shunning of that young woman."

Paige spoke up. "Shunning? That would have to be because of a serious issue. We don't do them . . . my church, that is."

"But you're not Old Order. I'd not even know you were a Mennonite by looking at you," Cookie said.

"I wouldn't know you're a witch by looking at you," Paige said and laughed. "But yes, there's a big difference between us and the Old Orders. But we respect them a great deal, you know. A shunning is serious business. When a young person is shunned, it's usually because of romance. You know, they've gone against their parents' wishes. They've married someone outside the religion. And that's it. No turning back."

"It seems kind of unchristian," DeeAnn said. "But that's just little ole me talking. It just seems like being a Christian would give them a bit more forgiveness. . . ."

"That's all very New Testament," Annie said and drank from her beer glass.

"Yep," Paige said. "And we are all about the Old Testament."

"It's so harsh," DeeAnn said.

"Not any harsher than the fire and brimstone," Vera said.

"That's not harsh," Paige said, lifting her voice. "C'mon."

Vera could hear the history teacher in Paige's voice, who didn't come out very often at the crops, but her dance students claimed Paige was one of the toughest teachers at the school.

An awkward silence filled the room.

Cookie cleared her throat, looked up at them through her long strands of black hair, which had fallen in her face. "It's all Christianity, right? Just different takes on the same philosophy."

"So, if there was a shunning . . . Let's say Sarah was involved with someone, and Rebecca was her friend and may have known something. But a shunning is not murder. Why kill them?" Annie said.

"I had an aunt one time who said she'd rather be killed than shunned. It's a very painful experience," DeeAnn said.

"Maybe the reason they were killed had nothing to do with the shunning," Sheila said.

"Could've been some crazy man who hates redheads," Cookie said. "Could be that simple."

"Yes, but what about the rune symbols carved into them? I mean, to me the killer is leaving a message on them," Annie said as she doodled the runes on a page of scratch paper.

"I'd be more interested in hearing about Vera's weekend in New York than about all this religious stuff. What's gotten into people? All we talk about are murders and religion," Sheila said and bit into a chip.

"Yes, I think it's time you told us what happened last weekend," Annie said and smiled.

"A lady never tells," Vera said, smiling back at Annie, feeling her face getting warm.

"Well, now, doesn't that beat all?" Sheila said, cutting a photograph.

Vera sat with her page, pictures, and pens, smoothed her hands over the thick paper. The sex between her and Tony sizzled—even when they were younger. He was the only man she'd slept with besides her ex-husband.

Tony reached inside of her soul somehow and touched a wild part of her—so wild that it scared her sometimes. It was like a wild beast escaping out of a cage. And lately her sexual thoughts dwelled on Tony, but occasionally, on other men, as well.

It was the oddest thing to be forty-one, almost forty-two, and suddenly discover a rampant, evolving sexuality that had been so repressed for years, she hadn't even known it existed within herself. It was certainly not a topic for discussion at a scrapbook crop.

Did DeeAnn just say she had gotten a gun? Vera thought.

"Yes. I went and learned how to use my gun. It's in my purse. I have a permit for it. I'm not listening to any of your liberal nonsense, Annie. I'm almost as liberal as you are—but not with a goddamned killer on the loose in Cumberland Creek."

"I'm just saying that it seems a little drastic. Yes, there've been two murders, but they seem related. You don't have red hair, you don't live in the hollow, and you aren't eighteen. It seems to me the last thing we need in Cumberland Creek is another woman carrying a gun in her bag," Annie said. "How many times has Bea almost shot someone by mistake?"

Sheila's stifled giggle escaped, sending them all into fits of laughter.

Chapter 24

Beatrice loved Sunday mornings so much better since she had stopped going to church twelve years ago. Church was always more of a social and community event for her because she was never a believer in the traditional sense. Oh, she believed in God, all right, and knew God as well as anybody could. But she had a different view of Him and certainly a different view from what the local Baptist church claimed. Some folks thought that meant she was an atheist, and she'd even heard the whispers at Dolly's old beauty shop. She was that weird non-believing quantum physicist. But if only they knew that the mystery of the universe was always its beauty, and the more she studied it, the closer to God or Spirit she felt.

Sundays in Cumberland Creek were glorious days because most people were in church. Between the hours of nine and eleven, one could walk the whole of the town without seeing anybody, which suited Beatrice, who was not a woman for small talk and gossip. So as she stood on her porch, waiting for Vera, she took in the quiet of her growing town.

Trouble was, with the growth came more problems than just annoyances, like lines at the grocery store and post office. Why, before all of this recent nonsense, Cumberland Creek had little crime in its history, with no murders in thirty or so years.

She wrapped her scarf around her neck and ears and relished the rustling sounds of the crumbly fallen leaves blowing in the breeze. She couldn't believe that Friday would be Halloween already. She couldn't wait to see Lizzie dressed up like a pea pod. How cute was that going to be? Just a year ago, she never would have imagined enjoying Halloween as much as she did now. For that matter, enjoying life as much as she did now. So much of that had to do with her granddaughter. Unfortunately, she barely remembered Halloween with Vera. She recalled an angel costume—or, wait, was that a ghost? *Bah.* Who knew? It was too long ago.

Beatrice loved having Vera in her life. But she didn't have many specific memories of Vera's childhood. The memories, some of them were just one big—albeit happy—blur. She remembered more about her work and her husband than she did about Vera. She took very few pictures. It wasn't like today—everybody had a camera, and mothers, especially the scrapbooking ones, always took these little digital cameras everywhere. They didn't want to miss a move and not be able to chronicle it.

Last year Beatrice handed Vera all the scrapbooks she had kept of her daughter for years, even with how busy she was as a young mother. She surprised herself that she had so many of them. These scrapbooks were mundane compared to what people did these days. They consisted of pictures snapped of Vera during special occasions, like birthdays and graduations. And then the dance recitals had taken over. Even so, Beatrice had managed to put something together, even during her busy career years, albeit without stickers, fancy cutouts, and glitter.

Vera's car pulled up to the curb, drawing Beatrice

back to the present. "Are you ready?" she yelled at Beatrice.

Beatrice just shook her head. "What do you think? I'm standing here for my health?"

Vera waved her mother's attitude off and reached over to open the door.

"Where's Elizabeth?" Beatrice said, looking into the empty backseat.

"She's with her dad. She's got a little fever. Teething, I think."

"Aunt Rose will be disappointed."

"Well, if it matters that much to her, she could come down off that mountain," Vera said, looking into her side mirror and pulling back onto the quiet road.

Beatrice chortled. "I've been telling her that for fifty years."

"I've never understood it."

"Me neither," Beatrice said. "But it makes her happy to stay. It's her domain, and it seems to work out for her. Where are you going?" she asked, because Vera was going in the wrong direction.

"Annie's coming along. I thought it would be good for her to meet Aunt Rose. I asked Sheila to come, but something's up with her oldest daughter, Donna," Vera said as she pulled over to the curb and tooted her horn.

Annie's door flung open, she turned to kiss her husband, and they were off.

"So this woman has never ventured off the mountain?" Annie said later, after she was situated in the car, as they turned off the main road.

"That's right," Beatrice said. "And she has an in with all the mountain folk—even the nesters and Mennonites. She's an herbalist. Knows her stuff. They call her before they call a doctor. That used to drive Ed crazy."

"Oh, I remember . . . ," Vera said in a faraway voice.

Beatrice loved this old road. She knew every twist

and turn, every bump and dip. She loved the way fields on either side gave way to heavy woods, with high tree branches swaying over the road.

"You know who else knows a lot about herbs? Cookie," Annie said. "She also knows about runes."

"Runes?" Beatrice said.

"Yes. Cookie figured out that's what those symbols are that were carved into the bodies and painted on your house."

"You don't say," Beatrice said, digging in a cloth bag. "Scone? I just made them this morning. I call them my good-for-travel cinnamon scones."

Annie reached her hand in the bag and pulled one out for Vera, who reached for it and then suddenly swerved as a loud *thud, thud* came from the rattling car.

"Damn," Vera said, pulling over. "Must be a flat tire. Anybody know how to change one?"

Annie shrugged, still eating her scone.

"Surely we can figure it out," Beatrice said. "But what a pain in the ass. Can't you call someone?"

"Mother," Vera said, opening her door. "Who would I call out here?"

"Does the cell even work?" Annie pulled out her phone. Dead.

"Lord, how did civilization manage without the cell phone?" Beatrice said, getting out of the car. "Let's see. That is a very flat tire." She bent down and touched it. "What is that?" She reached her finger and felt along the rubber. There was not just one, but three huge nails puncturing the tire. "Nails."

"Do you have a spare?" Annie said.

"I've no idea," Vera said. "Bill's always dealt with these things. Where would it be?"

"Probably in the trunk," Annie replied.

Beatrice harrumphed. "Yeah, probably. Thank God

you didn't bring Elizabeth. This will probably take some time."

Annie and Vera slipped out of the car to a cool day and took in sweeping views of mountains and farms in the distance. Annie rolled up her sleeves.

"I'm sure we can figure this out," she said, lifting the trunk.

After messing with the jack and getting nowhere, Annie tried to place it again. "It looks like it should go right there," she muttered as she crouched down beside the tire, smelling the rubber, the grease, and the gravel from the road. It would help if she felt better. She felt so weak these days. Maybe she just needed more sleep.

"Oh, here comes a car," Beatrice said.

"Maybe they'll stop," Vera said.

"That's Cookie!" Annie exclaimed.

Annie stood up, and sure enough, it was Cookie in a rental car—a yellow Volkswagen Bug. She waved and pulled along the slim berm that dropped off into a ditch along the hillside.

"Look at you ladies. I wish I had my camera," she said, grinning, with her hands on her hips, after getting out of the car. She was wearing old blue jeans and a thick gray wool sweater. The color brought out the gray in her green eyes and was set off by huge dangling silver earrings.

"Would you just be quiet and help if you can?" Annie said, smiling, brushing her hands together.

"Shoot, I can change a flat," Cookie said. "But he can probably do a better job than me. Upper body strength and all that," she added and pointed at the Bug. A large man was trying to get out of the small car. "Found him walking along the road. I offered to give him a lift."

He was dressed in what the locals called "plain clothes"—black Mennonite garb—and tipped his hat to the women. "How do?"

Annie noticed the three earrings in his right ear. He was no Mennonite.

Beatrice took over. "Fine to meet you, Mr., ah . . ."

"Name's Luther Vandergrift," he said, sizing up the women with a few brief looks.

"Can you help us out?" Beatrice said.

"No problem," he said, taking off his hat and crouching next to the car.

In no time the old tire was off, looking like a pitiful, huge fake snake with nails sticking out of it. Huge nails.

"What are you doing way out here?" Vera asked Cookie while Annie tried to help Luther by sliding the new tire onto the rim.

"It's my annual retreat. I told you about it. I do it every year, a few days before Halloween. That's why I couldn't come with you to Aunt Rose's today."

"This is a retreat? I thought you were going to a spa or something," Vera answered.

Cookie smiled. "No. I take my tent, some food, water, notebooks. And it's just me and the sky."

"It's too damned cold to be camping out up here this time of year," Beatrice said.

"I do okay. I've got a great sleeping bag."

"What about the bears?" Vera said.

"I'm okay with the bears," Cookie said, moving her head around so her dangling earring caught the light. "If they are okay with me."

"You're certifiable," Beatrice said.

"So they tell me."

"Thanks," Luther said to Annie while she helped hold the spare tire in place.

She smiled back and nodded, half listening to the other conversation, trying not to stare at his earrings. It wasn't as if she hadn't seen men with earrings—there were plenty of them back in D.C., where she used to live and work. You just didn't see many of them around

Cumberland Creek. If you did, it was usually a teenager. Certainly not any of the Old Order Mennonites.

Annie wasn't certain, but she thought one of his earrings was a cross. She couldn't make out what the other two were. His beautiful blond hair looked like spun gold, falling in waves around his ears and down onto his neck. It made seeing the earrings' details difficult.

He gave the tire one last wrenching and grunted. "There." He stood up, and Annie saw very clearly that one of his earrings was the same rune symbol that was painted on Beatrice's house. Her heart began to pound in her chest, and she felt the rush of blood through her body as she tried to take a breath. The feeling just tipped her right over the edge. She'd been just feeling lousy. Now this.

"Are you okay?" he said and grabbed her, steadied her as her knees wobbled.

"Annie?" Vera said.

The women swarmed around her, and she realized this was not what she wanted. She needed space and air and room to move, but they were all around her, fanning her as she lay on the ground now. His face between the women's concerned faces, all looking down at her.

"Maybe she got a whiff of fumes," someone said.

"I'm fine," Annie said. "Really. I just need some air." She struggled to get up, and the man reached for her. His blue eyes met her deep brown eyes, and they locked, softened momentarily, but his touch made her pulse race. She felt fear and anger ripple in waves through her arms and shoulders as he placed his arms around her and led her to the car.

This was not like her. She had looked into the face of murderers and rapists, dogfighters, crooked cops, and she had dealt with them all. She was slightly embarrassed. And ill. Was she coming down with something?

Cookie was on the other side of her. "Take some deep belly breaths, dear. You're going to be fine."

Cookie looked her in the eye, and momentarily Annie thought, *She knows. Cookie knows about the earring, and she's trying to calm me down.*

For God's sake, she was on a mountain—not too far from Jenkins Hollow, thinking her yoga teacher and friend was sending her psychic thoughts and Luther was transmitting evil through his fingers. He didn't even know her. As long as Annie could get air and space and she could think her way around this, she'd be fine. *Get it together, girl.*

As she sat in the car and took a deep breath, she looked closely at Luther's face and smiled faintly. She took a deep drink from one of the water bottles that they had brought. Her thoughts were still jumbled, but she wanted to remember his face. As she recalled some of the research she'd done on runes, she thought that this was too much of a coincidence and that she could be looking at the face of a murderer, the man who strangled one young woman and placed her body in the raging Cumberland Creek River, the man who chopped the arms off of another young woman and left her body in pieces in a huge recycling bin. And she certainly couldn't allow Cookie to drive off with him in her car. But a persistent pain jabbed in her gut.

She leaned her head back onto the car seat and took a deep breath. *Think. Think. Think.*

"I've never known a Mennonite man to wear earrings. Who are your people, son?" Beatrice said, loud enough for everybody to hear.

Leave it to Bea. Annie lifted her head and watched as the young man put his hat back on.

"I'm new in the area, ma'am. You don't know my people. And I am not a Mennonite."

Chapter 25

Vera's sweaty hands felt the cool steering wheel sliding beneath them. What a day. She glanced in her rearview mirror to see if Cookie was still behind them. She had insisted on following them to the nearest tire shop. Then they would have to turn around and head back to Cumberland Creek. "That doughnut of a tire is not going to take you up these mountain roads. It's closer to the nearest shop than it is to go back," she'd said.

And she'd left the man to walk the rest of his journey along the dusty mountain roads—which was fine with Vera and the rest of the women in the car, all of them thinking how incongruous that he was dressed like an Old Order Mennonite and yet was wearing earrings. But Annie was the only one who had seen the rune earring.

Damn. Annie, of all people. She'd been seriously spooked by the whole hollow. And who could blame her, really? It didn't take long for any of them to make the leap from the rune in his ear to the possibility of him being the killer of those two young women—as irrational as it was. Now that Annie knew more about runes, his weird earring was hard for them to shake. So, Vera wouldn't be seeing her aunt Rose today. Her mom was in the backseat on the cell phone, now explaining the tire situation. At least they were back in cell phone range.

"After we get the tire on, I'm heading over to the police station," Vera told them. "I think we need to tell Detective Bryant about that man." She looked at Annie for some response, but she was staring out the window, deep in thought and pale. "Did you hear me, Annie?"

"Yes, yes, I heard you," she said and went back to staring.

"Well, that's that. We'll have to go up next Sunday," Beatrice said, clicking her cell phone shut.

"Busy weekend with Halloween coming up," Vera told her. "But I guess we could squeeze a trip in on Sunday."

"If we are not sacrifices to the gods of Halloween," Beatrice said, grinning.

Cookie had invited them to a Halloween ritual. She called it *samhain* and pronounced it "sow-hane." After trick-or-treating and once Elizabeth was asleep, the women were going to gather in Vera's living room for a real "witch" ritual.

"It's my favorite ritual. It's our new year and the time we remember our loved ones who've died. I want each of you to bring a photo or an object that belonged to someone you loved that has died. It will be wonderful to share this with you," Cookie had said.

"Sounds silly to me," DeeAnn had remarked. "But if there's a feast after, I'm in!"

The vegetarian potluck feast had hooked Vera, too. Besides, what was the difference between this ritual and any number of rituals she'd participated in at the local Baptist church? She trusted Cookie wouldn't be conjuring evil spirits or sacrificing chickens. But she wasn't sure what to expect.

She pulled into the Jiffy Lube.

"Finally," Beatrice said. "Could you drive any slower?"

Vera ignored her. Driving with the doughnut of a wheel was not easy—no matter what her mother thought. Besides that, Vera was a little shaken. A flat tire was one thing, but that Luther guy was an oddball. Oh, sure, he helped them out and was nice about it. Dressed in the simple clothes of an Old Order Mennonite man and not being Mennonite? What was going on in that hollow?

The women made themselves at home with the free coffee in the waiting area while the car was in the shop. Vera took a sip and loved the way the coffee's warmth traveled down to her stomach. It seemed to be getting colder, instead of warmer, throughout the day. The skies were tinged with murky gray. Was it going to rain? Snow?

Annie sat down next to Cookie and pulled out her notebook. Cookie elbowed her as she turned to speak to Beatrice, who was sitting on the other side of her. All of Annie's things went flying. All the women bent to help her pick them up.

"What's that?" Cookie gasped, picking up a loose page from the floor.

"Let's see." Annie looked it over. "Ah, those are the symbols that were carved into the bodies of those young women. The runes. I think this is the one that was painted on Bea's house."

Cookie's face whitened. "I don't know why I didn't see it before."

"What is it?" Beatrice said.

"It was the same symbol on both of the women?" Cookie asked.

"Yes. On their arms and backs. I thought you said you didn't know much about them," Annie said, still gathering her papers.

"I don't know many of them," Cookie said. "But I think I know those symbols."

"Well, for God's sake, Cookie. If you know something, spit it out," Vera said.

"What I know about runes is the simple divination patterns. That in itself is kind of controversial. I'm sorry I didn't see the combination before. Anyway, some scholars think it was more of a language than a divination tool," Cookie said. "But this looks like the Three Lifetimes Spread, which is what a rune reader would use to portray character."

"And?" Vera said.

Cookie placed the paper on the floor. "You see, it's five symbols." She pointed to each of them and counted. "The center rune is your present character, the top rune is your future lives, the bottom rune is your past lives—"

"Lives?" Annie said. "Reincarnation?"

Cookie nodded. "The left rune is your future in this life, and the right rune is your birth or childhood." She paused, running her long, skinny fingers across the page. "If a rune is reversed, it has the opposite meaning from the upright rune. We have a reversed rune here at the bottom. Nauthiz reversed, which would mean 'bringer of pain, suffering.' Here's another reversed one. Um, I think it's called Fehu, which would mean something like 'mindless joyousness that should be avoided at all costs.'"

"That's the one they painted on your house, isn't it?" Vera said, squinting her eyes.

Beatrice nodded. "What about this one? I like this one," she said, pointing at the center of the page.

"That is called Uruz, which means 'strong woman,' 'wild ox,' 'darkness,'" Cookie replied.

"How could it mean all three of those things?" Vera said.

"They weren't meant to be read in English or even taken literally, Vera. Stay with me here," Cookie said and paused. "This rune is Wunjo reversed. That means 'a crisis, difficult passage, or an absence of joy.' The top rune is Isa, or ice, 'something that impedes or a kind of spiritual winter.'"

"What does it all mean?" Annie said.

"It's obvious," Beatrice said. "It means a strong, stubborn woman who needs to be tamed. You came about from much darkness and tragedy, and you offer joys of the flesh that only cause trouble. You have left pain in your path wherever you've been, and ahead of you is only coldness and loneliness."

"Beatrice, you are a woman of many talents," Cookie said and smiled.

"Humph," Beatrice said. "It's not brain surgery, my dear."

Chapter 26

Beatrice hated the police station almost as badly as she hated the hospital. Yet she'd spent more time in both of them the past few years that she ever had in her previous seventy-nine years. But the group decided they would go together to tell Detective Bryant what they had learned. She didn't care for the man but had softened to him with the latest incident of the rune being painted on her house because of his concern for Annie. She completely agreed with him that Annie needed to be more careful. She breathed a huge sigh of relief when Annie allowed him to alert school officials to watch her boys carefully, and to instruct the local patrol to go by her place several times a night. It wouldn't be intrusive at all.

She unwound her red scarf. Damn, it was hot in here—one of the many reasons she hated the place. Also, it needed a good cleaning. Couldn't they get somebody to come in and clean the place up? It wasn't just the piles of papers and pens all over the place, the half-opened drawers, and the clothes flung over chairs. It was also the real dirt on the floors and the windows.

You could hardly see out. Then you never knew what drunk or other lowlife the officers would have trudging along in front of them on their way to the cells. It just made Beatrice uncomfortable. She couldn't wait to leave.

Detective Bryant came into the room. "Ladies, what can I do for you?" He looked directly at Annie.

"We think we have some leads for you," she said to him.

What was wrong with her? Beatrice looked at her, and she seemed pale, certainly not herself.

"Why don't you all come into my office?" he said. "Follow me."

Finally, a soft chair, Beatrice thought when they entered his office, and plopped herself into it.

Annie and Vera told the detective about the suspicious young man, and he asked what he looked like. Beatrice whipped out her cell phone.

"I've got a picture of him right here," she said.

"Mama, why didn't you say?"

"I just did," Beatrice said, handing the phone to the detective.

"Ms. Matthews," he said, looking at the picture, "I'm going to need to keep this phone until I can get this photo downloaded into our system. Just in case."

"Damn. When do I get it back?"

"Maybe tomorrow," he said, just when his cell phone rang. "Excuse me."

"I guess I'll have to use my landline. I was just thinking about getting rid of it," Beatrice said.

"Okay." Detective Bryant put his cell phone down on the desk and sat down in his chair. "Do you have something else for me? You said something about the rune symbols . . . if that's what they even are."

"Yes, we know what they mean," Annie said and told him.

"Who told you that?" he asked when she was finished.

"Cookie Crandall," Annie answered.

"How does she know about runes?"

Annie shrugged. "She said she didn't know much about them, but she knew what these meant."

"Interesting," he said, leaning back in his chair. "I'll give her a call."

"She's on her way to a retreat," Beatrice said. "Up on the mountain."

"Alone?"

"Yes," Beatrice replied. "We tried to talk her out of it."

"I see. She's not afraid, knowing a killer is on the loose?"

Nobody replied.

"Sometimes that woman doesn't have the sense God gave a goose," Beatrice said to break the silence.

"That's not exactly what I was thinking, but I hear you, Ms. Matthews."

"Maybe we should try to find her," Vera said.

Annie spoke up. "Why are you all so worried? If anybody can take care of herself, it's Cookie. C'mon. She hikes and camps by herself all the time."

"Yeah, well, she also picked up a guy she doesn't know and gave him a lift," the detective said, with an edge to his voice. "You know some very smart women can be stupid when it comes to placing themselves in danger." He smirked as he looked at Vera, Beatrice, and Annie.

"We aren't here for a lecture, Detective," Annie finally said. "We thought we could help out the investigation."

"And get more information for your story?"

"Now that you mention it, of course," Annie said, sitting up even straighter.

Beatrice beamed. Annie could handle that detective. She looked over at Vera, who was playing with a loose string on her knit purse. Where was her daughter's head these days?

Later, the blue light of the computer washed over Annie's fingers as she tapped the keyboard. Done. She'd like to let it sit a day and then proofread it, but she didn't have the time. It was almost midnight, and her eyes hurt from the strain and her lower back ached. She probably needed an ergonomic chair. Who could afford it? She was making so little as a freelancer for the paper, it was barely worth working. Still, she liked to keep her fingers in it.

Tomorrow she'd finish the final touches on the boys' Halloween costumes—somehow. She wasn't a seamstress. It was good that they chose costumes that needed very little sewing. Ben wanted to be the Mad Hatter from *Alice in Wonderland,* and Sam a cowboy.

She slid her glasses off her face, placed them on her desk, and thought about the day's events. Evidently, the person who killed both young women knew them, thought they were evil, and considered them troublemakers. But why? That would seem to be a key piece of the puzzle. Maybe Rose could have answered it. Maybe not. Maybe she would next week. But Annie wasn't sure she could wait.

She climbed in next to Mike, who was softly snoring, and snuggled next to him under the blankets. Thoughts of bills that needed paying, lunches that needed to be packed, money that needed to be sent to the school for pictures . . . Oh, and there was the soccer game on Saturday. . . .

The alarm went off sooner than she wanted. When Annie lifted her head from the pillow, she felt a rush of dizziness and nausea. She'd felt the same way yesterday. She lay back down and closed her eyes. Maybe it would go away.

Mike came into the room "Honey, do you know where my red tie is?"

"No," she managed to groan.

"Annie?" He came over to her and leaned on the bed. "What's wrong?"

"I don't know. I feel sick. Just give me a few moments."

She pulled the covers closer and closed her eyes. She woke back up in a quiet house and looked at the clock. Eleven thirty. Feeling a little like Alice in Wonderland, she sat up slowly. No dizziness or nausea. But she had to pee badly, and oh God, she was so hungry. When was the last time she ate?

When she entered the kitchen, she wanted to cry. It was a complete mess. Mike had left the dirty pan that he had used to fry eggs on the stove, not even bothering to place it in the sink to soak. Bits and pieces of cereal were all over the counters and the floor. The boys' cereal bowls were still on the kitchen table. Dishes were piled in the sink—and the dishwasher was not more than a foot away. *Oh well,* she thought and shrugged. At least she'd gotten some sleep before she had to deal with the mess.

Thank God enough coffee was left in the pot for her to pop a cup in the microwave and heat it up.

She took her hot cup to her desk and flipped the on switch for the computer. She was going to look up this Luther character. She couldn't remember exactly if she had been dreaming about him, but he was definitely on her mind this morning. Had she gotten his last name? *That's right.* It was Vandergrift. She keyed in his name and clicked on the first link. She read over the obituary of his mother, a linguist who had specialized in ancient Nordic languages. *What?*

The phone rang. *Damn.*

"Hello," she said.

"Hey, Annie. It's Steve. How's it going?"

"Fine, Steve. What's up?"

"We loved those articles on the murders and wondered if we could get a little more."

"What more is there to say?"

"The publisher would like a background piece on the area where they lived, Jenkins Mountain."

"Seriously?" Annie said when her cell phone began to buzz. "Can you hold on? My other phone is ringing. I need to get it."

She picked it up.

"Mrs. Chamovitz?"

"Yes."

"This is Ralph Miller, assistant principal at the elementary school."

"Is everything okay?"

"Well, yes," he said, hesitating. "It is now. But Ben's been in a fight, and we'd like you to come to the school to pick him up. I think he just needs some cooling down time."

"What? What happened?" Annie's heart raced. *Ben? In a fight?*

"We'll discuss it when you get here."

"I'll be there right away."

Damn. Her editor would have to wait. And so would Luther. Wouldn't you just know it? Days went by and Annie rarely heard from her editor—or had any interesting research leads. And this was the first time she'd been called to the school. There had to be a mistake. Her son? In a fight?

"I'm sorry, Steve," she said into the other phone. "I have to go to the school. Can we talk about this later?"

"Sure," he said. "But not too much later."

He hung up. Her heart sank. She knew what he was thinking. *School? I need a story, and she has to go to school?*

Oh, the world was unkind to mothers.

Annie hadn't even taken the time to run a brush through her hair. And as she sat in the office waiting room at the school, she realized she had a little ketchup stain on her black jeans. *Damn.* Maybe nobody would notice if she just kept her bag over it. To top it all off, she was starting to get cramps.

"Mrs. Chamovitz, you can go in now," said the perky blond secretary.

Annie stood and felt dizzy, again. She steadied herself on the chair and walked into Ralph Miller's office. He stood and smiled, reaching his hand across the desk.

"Nice to see you, Mrs. Chamovitz. Please sit down."

"Thanks," she said. He looked like a kind old man, with nice little creases around his eyes and mouth. Impeccably groomed gray hair. Not good looking, kind of plain, but in a pleasant way.

"Ben hit a young man this morning," he said.

"Did he hurt him?"

"Yes. He has quite a shiner."

"Oh, dear," she said. "I don't understand. He's never had a problem before. What happened? Do you know?"

"As far as I know, it had to do with, um . . . ," he said, looking away briefly, then back at her. "Your religion."

Annie's heart nearly stopped. Her cramps were getting worse with each breath. Now she felt sweat beads forming on her face and head.

She was speechless.

"Today was the first day of our Weekly Religious Education program. All the other children were being bused to the church. Of course, you opted for Ben to stay behind. Questions came from his classmates."

Her boy. Her sweet Ben. She imagined him all alone, surrounded by taunting children. She wanted to cry. "And?" she managed to say. Was her heart even beating? Was she even still breathing? "Where was the teacher?"

"The teacher was there, of course," he said. "That's why we know exactly what happened. One boy provoked Ben and started taunting him."

"What? How?"

"That's not the issue. The issue is that Ben attacked him, punched him in the eye."

Annie tried not to laugh, but a bubble of embarrassed pride welled up in her chest. Her son had defended his faith.

"Mr. Miller, we do not condone violence in our house, and I've always told my kids that if they get into trouble at school, they will be in trouble at home. We will deal with Ben. But you have to tell me what the boy said."

He looked down as embarrassment washed over his face, and then looked quickly away.

The cramps in Annie's gut were getting so horrible that she was not sure she would be able to stand up when the time came. She sat back in her chair, took a deep breath, and tried to remain as calm as she could.

"Where does a child get such an ignorant attitude, Mr. Miller?"

How horrible was it? The principal couldn't even meet her eyes, let alone tell her what the child had said. Even though she was not naive about such ignorance, Annie had never been confronted with this before.

"You find many attitudes in this school, Mrs. Chamovitz. But, unfortunately, we can't tolerate an outburst like this and need to send a clear message to all parties. We have to ask that you take Ben home for the rest of the day. Violence will not be tolerated in our school."

"What about ignorance?"

"Excuse me?"

"I mean, what will happen to the other boy?"

"I can't discuss the other child with you. Privacy matters."

"Okay, then," she said, swallowing, then taking a deep breath. Just then an image of Cookie came to her mind. She was so different in her beliefs and views, yet she handled all the potential sticky issues with such grace and such matter-of-factness. She found herself pretending to be Cookie. "Let's discuss the ignorance of the whole WRE program."

His mouth flung open.

"Seriously, we need to come to terms about this. My children are Jewish, they attend your school, which is a public school, and it seems their civil rights are at issue," she said as a pain ripped through her gut and she fell to her knees.

"Mrs. Chamovitz?"

Chapter 27

Vera was at her desk, going over the billing statements for the first of November, to be sent out next week. Every month she wished she could hire an accountant, but things were tighter than ever. Enrollment was way down, and she was afraid she'd have to raise tuition, which she hated to do. Dance was for everybody, not just the middle class. But at the same time, she couldn't continue like this with the way the economy was tanking. And the latest talk was of a new dance school opening in town. Who knew what that would mean?

Her eyes rested on a picture of Tony that was framed and next to her computer. She'd see him again in two weeks—and this time he sent her the train ticket. She knew he couldn't afford to do that a lot. But this was special—the whole weekend was on him. He had a surprise for her.

Back to the statements. The business. She thought about giving it up sometimes, but then she thought about the girls she knew for whom dance meant everything. The Dasher girls, for example. They had lost their mom in a tragedy, yet somehow they managed to keep dancing, and she could see how they poured themselves into it.

Suddenly, she remembered the strawberry blond hair of the youngest Dasher girl, who was in her Saturday morning "baby" class. Not exactly red, but still. She drifted to the river in her mind. She imagined a strand of red hair floating there, twisting around a tree branch, and she shivered. There had been no trips to the park since the body had washed up there. She couldn't bring herself to do it.

Both of the victims were from Jenkins Hollow. Both had red hair. Both had these rune symbols, which basically meant they were thought to be evil, marked women. How many more could there be? If it was a serial killer, how many others could fit this pattern?

Just then the phone rang, and she nearly jumped off her chair.

"Hello. Cumberland Creek Dance."

"Vera Matthews please."

"Speaking."

"This is Jennifer Blake at the elementary school. There's been an emergency with Annie Chamovitz, and she has you listed as an emergency contact for her children. Can you pick her boys up at the school?"

"An emergency? Is she okay? Where is she?" Vera leaped to her feet.

"She was rushed to the emergency room about an hour ago."

"I'll be right there."

After she called Beatrice, who had Lizzie for the day, she hightailed it to the school, where both Chamovitz boys were sitting in the front office with their backpacks.

She smiled. "How about some ice cream, boys?"

Ben smiled.

Sam's brows knit. "Where's my mom?"

"She got sick and was taken to the hospital. The doctors are taking good care of her," Vera told them.

* * *

Later, with a house full of children and women, who had gathered at Vera's place when they heard the news, Vera received a call from Mike, Annie's husband.

"She's all right. She's, ah, out of surgery, and as soon as she's up, we'll be coming home."

"Surgery?"

The adults in the room quieted.

"Yes," he said and sighed. "She had an ectopic pregnancy. We are lucky we found it so early." His voice was strained. "I need to call her parents, and . . . I'll pick up the boys in about an hour."

"I can keep them, Mike. It's not a problem," she said.

"I feel like I want my boys at home with us right now," he said and sighed. "There was trouble at the school today, and I need to talk to them."

"Okay. Good-bye," she said and hung up the phone, thinking she was so glad she had made that huge batch of chili. That, along with Sheila's corn bread, should help them out tonight.

"She's fine," she told the group of women who were gathered around her. Sheila, her longtime friend, DeeAnn, Paige, and her mom—the women she'd always had in her life. She couldn't imagine life without them. Now she couldn't imagine life without Annie, as well. Or Cookie, for that matter.

"Ectopic pregnancy," she said in a low voice, partially because she didn't want the children to overhear, partially out of respect for Annie's baby, who was gone, whom Annie didn't even know she was carrying.

"That is so dangerous," Sheila said. "She's lucky to be okay."

"Indeed," Paige said.

"Let's pack up a box of food," Beatrice said, rubbing her hands together. "We need to feed this family."

* * *

"I popped him," Ben was telling Sam loudly.

"Who did you pop?" Vera asked, only half listening as she poured the chili into a Tupperware bowl.

"Edward Carpenter," he said. "A boy at my school."

"Why would you do that, Ben?"

"He called me a devil Jew boy and told me I was going to hell with the rest of the Jews, and so I popped him."

With that, Beatrice dropped her tin foil–wrapped rolls into the box with a thud. Her eyes met Vera's, but she didn't say a word.

Chapter 28

Two days later Annie was feeling a bit stronger and Beatrice had taken up residence on her couch. Beatrice finished the boys' costumes, made an overflowing pot of chicken soup, baked bread and pies.

"That coconut pie is simply the best I've ever had," Mike said before he left the house that morning.

"Thanks. It's an old recipe of my mom's," Beatrice told him. Funny, when she was a younger woman, she didn't care to bake. Now she loved it and always had a freezer full of her baked goods.

Annie, always a thin woman, looked devastatingly thin to Beatrice. She moved like a ghost through her little house, checking e-mails, looking over books full of ancient symbols and runes, reading romance novels that DeeAnn and Sheila brought her.

Beatrice thought she'd be okay. She just needed to rest and eat to get her strength back—and Beatrice was going to see that she did so. Annie's mother could not make it to help take care of the situation.

Annie had lost a lot of blood—so much that the doctors had considered a transfusion, but she was otherwise so healthy that they thought she could manage without one. Transfusions could be risky.

She plopped herself down on the other end of the couch. "I've been thinking, Bea," she said. "I should have seen this coming. I knew I wasn't feeling like myself. Why didn't I pay attention?"

Beatrice smiled. "Stupidity, I guess."

Annie laughed. "Okay. Hey, thanks for finishing the boys' costumes. I was worried about that."

"No problem," Beatrice said.

Halloween was two days away. Beatrice looked out the window at the graying, cloudy sky. The wind was picking up, and leaves and branches were blowing around. Another storm?

Annie picked up a tablet. "Hannah Bowman."

"What?"

"Hannah Bowman," Annie said. "She is the young woman I met at the funeral. Same age as Sarah and Rebecca. She's so hard to reach."

"The Bowmans that live up in Jenkins Hollow are Old Order. She may not have a phone. They're good people. I've known them a long time," Beatrice said.

The doorbell rang. That would be Paige, bringing pizza for lunch.

"Well, hello," she said, walking in the door and hugging Annie.

"Now, this will help fatten you up. I also brought some treats from the bakery. Vegan chocolate cupcakes."

"Mmm," Annie said.

"Vegan? Since when does DeeAnn make vegan anything?" Beatrice asked.

Paige shrugged. "She's just experimenting."

Annie plunged a cupcake into her mouth. "Mmm."

"Let me try," Beatrice said and took a dainty bite of one of the cupcakes—but, damn, she needed another bite, a bigger one. She nodded. "Good."

"It's getting a bit cold out," Paige said, digging in a plastic sack and pulling out paper plates. "The temperature must have dropped ten degrees since this morning."

"Glad the boys went to school dressed warmly," Annie said.

"Have you heard anything about the case?" Paige asked.

Annie shook her head.

"You'd think they'd have caught him by now," Beatrice said. "Land sakes, we just about handed Bryant the murderer on a silver platter. I'm sure it was the guy who helped us change our tire. Or at least he knows about it. "

"You're sure it's him?" Paige said, passing around the plates.

"He's a bit strange, Bea, but it doesn't mean he killed those women," Annie said.

"One thing is for sure. That man was bizarre, very different, not local, and he also was some kind of weirdo, with that damned rune in his ear."

"Doesn't mean he killed those girls, though," Paige said, opening the box of pizza. "I heard they brought him in for questioning and let him go. Not enough evidence."

"What? Why did they bring him in? Just because of what we said? That doesn't make sense. Damn, I need to call Bryant. Maybe he'll tell me why they brought him in," Annie said, placing her pizza slice on a plate, licking her finger where some of the sauce had spilled.

From everything that Beatrice could gather while pretending to watch television, Paige was correct. The young man was questioned and had rock-solid alibis. Rumors were sometimes true. But there was something else. Beatrice strained her ears to hear. *FBI? Halloween? Runes? Cults*? What the hell was happening?

Annie hung up the phone. "They couldn't hold him. His name is Luther Vandergrift. We knew that. He is new to the area. We knew that. He doesn't drive, doesn't have a regular job. He lives on some farm up around the hollow." She took another bite of pizza.

"Now, let me think," Beatrice said. "There aren't too many working farms up there. It never was a good place to farm. It's very rocky."

"It's a new farm," Annie said.

"What are they growing?"

Annie shrugged.

No, Annie wasn't herself. The old Annie was sharper than a tack and would have asked what they were growing—even if it didn't matter. She was always curious. But maybe the pain medicine was muddling her mind.

"The police are on high alert, and a few undercover FBI members will be hanging around Cumberland Creek. Isn't that strange?" she said.

"Why the alert? The FBI?" Beatrice said.

"Halloween," Annie said after she swallowed her pizza. "They are expecting trouble. You know, copycats, pranksters, and stuff. Halloween is the night all the troublemakers come out."

"I've heard that a lot of parents are keeping their kids home this year because of the killings," Paige said.

"I can understand that," Annie said. "But the rest of it? I don't know."

Beatrice didn't know how to feel, either. "It seems like a bunch of superstitious mumbo jumbo to me. Halloween, indeed."

Chapter 29

All the children were in bed—quite an achievement for all concerned—and the Cumberland Creek Scrapbook Club members, plus Beatrice, were gathered at Vera's house. Vera's house was the best spot because it was large enough for all of them. Elizabeth, once asleep, would sleep through a train wreck. Of course, she'd be up bright and early, but Vera was used to being tired now and considered it a normal state of being.

She looked at Cookie, who was unusually lovely tonight. Her hair was up off her neck, and she wore a jeweled band around her black hair. Rhinestones? Whatever they were, they sparkled against her dark hair and brought out the light in her green eyes, as well. Her earrings matched her blue dress. She was actually wearing a little mascara and eyeliner.

Cookie wore a long blue velvet dress, which cascaded to mid-calf and flowed around her as she walked. The dress had a low V-neck, which showed off her breasts. A bit too much for Beatrice, Vera knew, as she caught her mother looking at them and then at her. Beatrice rolled her eyes. But Vera thought Cookie's breasts looked beautiful, so she tried not to pay attention to Beatrice's antics.

The women—Sheila, DeeAnn, Paige, and Annie, along with Vera and her mother—gathered in a circle around Cookie, who stood next to a decorated table. Pictures of deceased people adorned the table, along with a huge seashell, a statue of Mary, candles, a wooden bowl of water, flowers, and silk scarves. Each piece of this altar alone was not unusually pretty, but gathered on the altar, the pieces had a simple beauty, and it touched Vera. Her throat tightened. What was wrong with her?

"I like to keep things simple," Cookie said. "Some of my cohorts go way out. You won't see fancy things or become overwhelmed with the ritual, I promise. But women have been meeting like this for generations, gathering around the fire or the altar. Some of the things here represent some deep connections we have and will always be so. Maybe some of you are already feeling a pull that you don't quite understand."

Vera's eyes met Cookie's.

"I want you to know that's okay. You are safe here. If anybody feels uncomfortable at any time, please let me know."

Vera loved the sound of Cookie's voice—it was quiet, yet strong, never wavered.

"Why don't we get on with it? I'd like to eat sometime before midnight," Beatrice said.

The group giggled nervously.

"Okay, first I'll call quarters, and we will remember our loved ones by sharing our memories," Cookie told them. "It's important to honor our ancestors tonight. Magically, it's the night the veil between our worlds is the thinnest."

"Hail to the North," she said with her arms out, palms up, facing Vera's fireplace. "Place of patience, endurance, stability, and earth." She dipped her hand into a bowl of dirt and let it fall back into the bowl. "Hail to the East," she said, picking up a feather and placing it in the bowl. "Place of wisdom, intellect, perception, and inspiration. Air," she added with a flourishing of the feather.

Vera caught her Beatrice's eye, seeing that her brows were knit. She saw Sheila's face clearly, as well, and she seemed enraptured by the theatricality. Beatrice was not.

The fire in the fireplace popped, and some of the women jumped a little.

Cookie struck a match and lit the black candles that were on the table. "Hail to the South, place of passion, strength, energy, and willpower. Place of fire."

Just then a knock sounded at the door.

"Bother," Vera said. "Let's ignore it. Go on, Cookie."

Cookie picked up the water bowl, and the knock at the door became louder and more forceful.

"Vera Matthews," a male voice said. "It's the police. Open up please."

"Oh, for God's sake," DeeAnn muttered.

"I better let them in," Vera said, feeling torn out of a nice, almost meditative mood. "This better be important."

She opened the door to a sweaty, excited Detective Bryant.

"Where is your daughter?" he asked.

"What?"

"Elizabeth. Where is she?"

"Upstairs, sound asleep," she replied, baffled.

"Can you please check?"

"Certainly," Vera said, her heart and mind suddenly brought to full attention, away from the dreamy place she'd been enjoying. Pulse racing, she ran up the stairs. What was going on? Why were they concerned about Elizabeth?

She opened the door and looked in her daughter's

crib. The light of the moon was shining on her face. She twitched her nose and then was still once more.

Vera shut the door behind her and rushed downstairs.

"What on earth is going on?" Beatrice was saying.

"Cookie Crandall, you are under arrest," the detective told her. "You have the right to remain silent. . . ."

Vera got to the bottom of the stairs just in time to see the kindest woman she'd ever known handcuffed.

"Now, you see here," she said. "I don't know what's going on. But Elizabeth is upstairs, sound asleep. Now, let go of Cookie."

"No, ma'am. She's under arrest for suspicion of murder," he said.

Cookie's mouth dropped, and she looked pleadingly at her friends. "I never—"

"Don't say anything," Beatrice cautioned, shushing her. "We'll call Bill, and he'll have you home in no time," she said and turned around to look Bryant in the eye. "And for the record, this woman couldn't hurt a fly."

He completely ignored Beatrice as he handed Cookie off to a uniformed police officer. She turned and looked at the women one more time before she left. Were those tears? She dropped her head and went with the officer. She looked defeated—as if all the air and beauty that were in her a few moments ago had evaporated.

Chapter 30

"What murder are you arresting her for?" Annie said after the uniformed officer took Cookie away, trying to keep her wits about her, even though she was exhausted and it was a dear friend that the officer was stealing away.

"Two counts of murder, one of attempted."

"Cookie?" Vera almost shrieked. Her face was angry red. "It's ridiculous."

"I don't have to explain myself to you," the detective shot back at her.

Vera's hand went to her mouth.

"Wrong," Beatrice said. "You barged in this house and broke up a lovely party and sent Vera upstairs to look in on her child. You owe us all some kind of explanation."

"Attempted murder?" Annie said suddenly. *Click.* Her brain was suddenly engaged. "Has there been—"

"Yes," he said and suddenly looked deflated himself. He sighed. "You will all need to sit down for this. I imagine it will be out soon enough." He shot Annie a glance of disgust. She glared back.

"The coroner's reports came back a few days ago on

Sarah. She was a mother, a very new mother. Might
have had the baby a couple of months or so ago."

The women stilled.

"Her family wouldn't take too kindly to that,"
DeeAnn said, sitting down.

"No. So, we decided a baby must be around, right?
Either it's buried and dead or someone has it. Maybe
this person knows something, right?" he told them. "So
I sent some guys up there, and suffice it to say, we found
the baby."

"Oh God," Annie groaned, suddenly feeling an ache
that only mothers knew, especially mothers who had lost
babies. DeeAnn's fleshy arm went around her. Annie
was still sore from the emergency D and C; her emo-
tions and hormones were reeling.

"Is it . . . ?" Beatrice finally said.

"A girl baby. Not dead. Very sick from exposure.
She's at the hospital. We're not sure she's going to
make it."

"What does this have to do with Elizabeth?" Vera
asked.

"Maybe nothing, but the baby is also a redhead. And
you had our number one suspect in your living room,"
the detective explained.

Annie felt a chill travel through her. "But why
Cookie?"

"We found this at the scene of the crime," he said and
dangled a plastic Baggie that held an earring that they
all knew belonged to Cookie. "I've seen her wearing
these. Very distinctive, wouldn't you say? I'm betting
DNA tests match Cookie to this earring perfectly."

"That means nothing," Sheila said. "She was camping on her retreat."

"Yes, she could have dropped it, and an animal
picked it up. You know that," Annie said.

He nodded. "Yes. I know that. But this is what I have.

It was right next to the baby. It's all I have. Plus, I have people on my case wanting these murders solved. I need to look further into this."

"That's no reason to jump to conclusions," Annie said.

"I'm not, believe me. How much do you know about Cookie?"

"What do you mean?" Annie asked.

"I mean, do you know much about her past? Have you ever looked her up online, for example?"

Annie shook her head. "No. Why would I? She's a friend."

"I have. And I can't find anything on her. It's as if she never existed."

"Nothing?" Annie said, perplexed, her stomach tightening.

"Good Lord, do you think *everybody* has to be on the Internet?" Sheila said. "Cookie doesn't even own a computer."

"Really? And how strange is that?" the detective said.

"Not very," Beatrice answered. "I just got one myself last year. And I know a lot of people who just don't care for them."

"No disrespect intended," the detective said, "but you are eighty-one years old. I get that. But here is Cookie Crandall, young, probably schooled with computers, and she doesn't own one?"

"This conversation has gotten absurd," Annie said. "You've got no hard evidence against her. An earring? What's that? The fact that she doesn't own a computer? Isn't traceable online? That's lazy police work. I'm sure she will be home tomorrow."

"Doubtful," he told them and placed his hands on his hips. "We've been working with the FBI, and suffice it to say, I'm holding her without bail. Flight risk."

"Now, you've just thought of everything," Beatrice said.

"Believe it or not, I'm good at what I do. This is my job. I am not some kind of hobbyist." He looked at Beatrice, then Annie. "You women need to back off. As I told you before, this is a potentially dangerous situation."

"No chance of that happening as long as you have our friend in jail," Vera said matter-of-factly. "I'm calling Bill right now. He's a lawyer. He'll have her out in no time."

Chapter 31

Beatrice rarely went to the weekly scrapbook crops. First, she had better things to do with her time than sit around with a bunch of women playing with pictures and paper. Second, some of the scrapbook queens irritated her. But tonight she felt the need to be with other people. Besides, Vera took Elizabeth with her, not wanting her out of sight. Everybody in the town—especially the women—was uneasy and frightened even more with the latest news.

The detective had neglected to tell them everything yesterday. The whole story about the baby was disturbing, and Beatrice couldn't shake it. The child was left alone in the woods. She was found naked and filthy. Almost dead from being exposed to the cold mountain air for at least eight hours. At least. The thought sickened and troubled Beatrice, shook her up more than the two murders. Who could do this to a baby? Who would do this? Why didn't the father of this baby step forward, and where were its grandparents? To add to the mystery, the paper had quoted a local doctor, who said the baby was well tended before it was left on the mountain.

She had no idea what kind of sick individual could leave a baby like that, but she did know that Cookie

Crandall had nothing to do with it. She was never sure how she felt about the young woman until last night, when she saw her whisked off by the police. She was odd and had some unusual ideas, but she was no killer.

Beatrice opened Sheila's front door to find the scrapbookers seated around the table, quietly scrapbooking. It felt as if a cloud of doom were hanging over this usually jovial group. Beatrice took a seat and placed her scrapbook on the table in front of her.

"Hello."

A murmur of hellos came her way. Beatrice looked over at Elizabeth, sleeping in a portable crib. *Sweet.*

"So what's the news?" Beatrice finally asked.

"I finally reached Bill. He's on his way back," Vera said.

"They won't let us see her," Annie said and took a swig of beer straight from the bottle. Her dark brown eyes already looked glassy. Beatrice wondered how many beers Annie had downed.

"Evidently, they can hold her without visitors. I don't get it," Sheila said and threw her tape down on the table. "I just can't imagine what she's going through."

Just then the door opened. A slightly disheveled Bill stood there with a key in his hand.

"Bill, how nice of you to grace us with your presence," Vera said, sitting up straighter in her chair.

"I've already been to the station, Vera. Your friend is in a lot of trouble. I can't do much until Monday, but I'll try to get her out on bail. They are saying she's a flight risk. Any idea why?"

"No, Bill. We've no idea. We're all as confused as could be," Sheila said, reaching up to straighten her glasses.

"Here's the key to her house." He handed it to Beatrice. "She needs some personal items. She's written them down." He handed the wrinkled paper to Vera, but all the scrapbookers were already up and pushing their chairs in, going for purses and coats. "Really! Do you all need to go over?"

"What does it matter who goes?" Vera said to him. "Please stay here with your daughter, in case she wakes up. You remember her, don't you?"

He rolled his eyes and sat down in front of the food. "I'll be here," he said, reaching for the last piece of chocolate cake with pink coconut icing, which seemed to call to him.

The women cleared the room in a matter of minutes and were soon standing on Cookie's front door stoop.

Cookie lived on the edge of town, in a tiny one-bedroom cottage on a cul-de-sac. She had few neighbors. It was one of the older parts of town but had been almost forgotten in the town's development and planning.

Not one of them had ever been to her house before.

Beatrice placed the key in the door. It was a little sticky. She jiggled the doorknob around, and it clicked open. All the women filed in behind Beatrice, who walked into the hallway and ran her hands along the wall to find the light switch. When the light came on, the women stood there, hushed by what they saw in the living room. Or what they didn't see. There was no couch. No bookcases with pretty objects and books. No tables to hold glasses of iced tea. No afghans or quilts. Nothing on the walls.

It was unthinkable to this group of women, who all had their homes decorated to the hilt. DeeAnn showed off all her collections of porcelain dogs, which were everywhere in her home; Paige's overdone Victorian decor more than filled the senses; Sheila's penchant for country primitives was profound; Vera's love of French provincial knew no bounds, with florals and color everywhere; and Annie's walls were lined with books and pictures of her children. Even Beatrice, who was not much into decoration, loved art and had several paintings in her home that she cherished, along with antiques and collectibles from sixty years of her life with Ed and Vera.

But Cookie's living room had nothing in it but a yoga mat, a block, some sitting cushions, and belts. A full-length mirror lined a wall and showed a reflection of a poster on the opposite wall of an Indian goddess dancing.

"I guess I know why we were never invited over. There's no place to sit," Beatrice said.

"Maybe she just doesn't have much money," DeeAnn said. "I wish she'd told us. Maybe I could have given her some work at the bakery."

"No," Annie said. "I don't think that's the case. I think she was fine. She was just living as simply as she could. That's all. Let's not read anything into this. Some people just live like this."

"Evidently, she practiced what she preached," Vera said. "She was always talking about living simply. Okay, here's the list. We need her toothbrush and paste, some T-shirts and underwear from her dresser, her hairbrush, and some notebooks in her closet."

The women scattered to find the objects.

Notebooks? Poor Cookie. She must think she's not getting out anytime soon, Beatrice thought.

Chapter 32

Vera found the notebooks on an upper shelf in Cookie's small closet. Two dresses, five blouses, and a few slacks and skirts hung on wire hangers in the closet. That was it. She reached up to grab the notebooks, and a book came crashing to the floor.

She squealed. "Lord, it almost hit me on the head!" she said.

"For such a graceful woman, you can be klutzy," Sheila said and laughed. "What do you have there?"

"Looks like a scrapbook of some kind," Vera said.

The notes of Vera's ringtone on her phone interrupted them. It was Bill, asking that they hurry with the things. He said he'd like to get them to her as soon as possible.

"Do we have everything?" Vera said and gathered the notebooks and placed them in a cloth bag. "We do need to get back."

Before they left, the women took a look around. The rest of the house was as bare and simple as the living room.

"I can't believe how sterile this place is," Paige said. "And Cookie is so creative. It doesn't make much sense."

"I was thinking the same thing," Sheila said. "I mean,

simplicity is one thing, but this place . . . feels cold. Not
at all like you expect Cookie's home to be."

The women piled into Vera's van with a quiet sense
of purpose.

It was odd, Vera had to admit, that creative Cookie
didn't decorate her home. But perhaps Annie was
right—maybe she just preferred the simple life. Vera
had her pegged as independently wealthy. She knew
what Cookie earned by teaching yoga, and it wasn't
really enough to pay rent, let alone feed herself. Vera
figured she didn't have to worry about money.

She mentally sifted through her memories and tried to
remember anything Cookie had said about money. But
the fact was that Cookie was pretty quiet—especially
when they were talking about personal matters, like
money, sex, marriage, or their pasts. Yet she was always
there when anybody needed her to provide a comforting
shoulder without judgment, or a homemade bowl of
pumpkin soup or warm apple pancakes.

She remembered one conversation about shopping. Vera had wanted to take Cookie to the outlets in
Williamsburg, and she'd said she wasn't interested. "I'm
just not into shopping. I'm sorry, Vera. When I'm in the
mood to shop, I shop at secondhand stores."

"Cookie, don't you ever want something new? A
little treat for yourself?" Vera asked.

"Even if the clothes were worn by someone else, they
are still new to me."

Vera now mused over that statement. Then, she
thought it odd. Was she trying to make a point? What
was the purpose? She remembered her saying something
about clothes ending up in the landfill and such. Why
hadn't she paid more attention to Cookie when she said
stuff like that? Now it embarrassed her that she'd been so
dismissive with her. Evidently, either Cookie was in
trouble financially or she was an extremely principled

individual. Vera just wished she knew exactly what those principles were. Vera couldn't fathom someone who could afford nice things and not have them.

She glanced in the mirror as the other women got out of the van and the light went on. Yes, her make-up still looked fine—except her lipstick. She reached into her pocket and smeared lipstick on her lips. A little bright pink never hurt anybody's face.

By the time the women arrived back at Sheila's basement, where they scrapbooked every Saturday night, it was late and they were all beat. It was as if the emotional turmoil over the past couple days had worn them all to a frazzle. First, all the weird murders, then this business with the baby. Now their dear friend Cookie was in jail—and was the only suspect.

"Here's the notebooks she asked for," Vera said, sliding the bag across the table, the large scrapbook falling out of it.

"What's this?" Bill asked. "Not a notebook."

Beatrice sighed. "It's a scrapbook we found, Bill. Somehow it got mixed in with the notebooks."

"Okay," he said, leaving it on the table and gathering the rest of the stuff. "Well, I'm off to the jail." He leaned over and kissed Vera. "You're still mine," he whispered. "You just don't know it."

Vera grimaced.

Chapter 33

Annie had to be sure.

The first thing she did when she went home was head for her bedroom and flip on her laptop and look up Cookie Crandall. Nothing. Was her name even Cookie? Did people really name their kids Cookie? Maybe it was another name, like Catherine? There was a Catherine Crandall . . . an obituary. That couldn't be her. That woman was 102 years old.

Oy. So Detective Bryant was right. Cookie Crandall was nowhere on the Internet. She checked all the information services she subscribed to for journalistic reasons. Was she in any of the government records? Taxes? Social Security? Nothing. *Click. Click. Click.* Birth certificate? Nothing.

What could this mean? It could mean that Cookie was running away from something or someone. It also could mean that she just liked to live "off the grid," and Annie had known people like that. It would make sense. The only thing Annie knew about Cookie's past was that she'd spent time in India, learning yoga. She'd also recently mentioned Eastern Europe. She'd certainly have a passport, then. She'd have to call the passport officials on Monday.

"Why would a witch choose Cumberland Creek? A place that still has the Sunday blue law and is extremely conservative?" The questions Bill had asked earlier nagged at her. Even she and her husband were starting to reconsider their move. If she could afford private school, she'd pull her sons out of the public school so fast. If she thought she could homeschool, she would.

Maybe Cookie was pulled in by the lower cost of living and by the beauty of the area, like she and Mike were. Maybe that was all there was to it. *You think you can manage being different in a place like this, with its bucolic hills and valleys. You allow the beauty and softness of the views to lure you into thinking that the people are soft and beautiful, too. You think eventually you'll find other people like you or that others will learn to like you despite your differences.* But it took Annie over a year to find even one friend. Then, the next thing she knew, she had several—all in the scrapbook club except Beatrice.

Now she was considering leaving again, going back home to Bethesda. She was not sure she was the person to take on the school system about their religious "education" program. She didn't think she had the heart to put her boys through it. She could take anything they dished out. But she didn't want to place her boys in any more sticky situations.

"It's not education if they are teaching just about Christianity," Cookie had said quietly, matter-of-factly, at one of their last crops. "And they are doing the children a disservice by not teaching about the rest of the world's religions. It feels cruel to me."

"They've been doing it for years," DeeAnn said. "Nobody's died from it."

"But religion shouldn't be used as a way to divide. It sends the wrong message. We are all one, no matter how we choose to connect to the universe," Cookie said.

Annie loved it when Cookie spoke up. She was so eloquent and steady about it. Annie herself couldn't talk about religion sometimes, because she was so afraid to offend someone. But how could you be offended by that statement?

Annie's stomach lurched when she thought of Cookie in jail. As a reporter, caught in the thick of investigations, she had spent nights in jail herself and knew it to be an unpleasant place, where it didn't matter how nice of a person you were.

"Hey," Mike said and sat up in bed. "Is Cookie out yet?"

"No," she said, standing up and taking her clothes off. She reached for her nightgown, slipped into it, and crawled in bed beside her husband.

"You smell like beer," he said, wrapping his arms around her.

Mercy, he felt so warm and so hard. Smelled so male.

"Turn you on?" she said and grinned.

Chapter 34

Beatrice was ashamed of herself.

Here she was, a woman who until recently was haunted by her husband's ghost. And a woman who believed in quantum physics, had seen it applied in her own life. She was a national expert; she was quoted in journals and books about the ways of quantum physics. So often, she was the subject of ridicule by the scientists on the other side of the issue—physicists who would not entertain some of her research, particularly her ideas about creating reality, the shifting nature of time, and the possibility of time travel. And yet the minute Cookie started talking with her about witchcraft, she jumped to all the wrong conclusions.

Well, hell's bells, how was she supposed to know that witchcraft was a real religion? And it was a religion that asserted that you could alter reality—which was right up Beatrice's alley. She'd participated in experiments that proved that thoughts and prayer could shift reality.

"You can call it prayer," Cookie had once told her. "I call it magic. It's about connecting with the universe, asking for it to listen, and watching as things unfold. We use different props, that's all, my friend."

And Beatrice had always believed in the possibility

of prayer and had seen its power many times in her life.
Sometimes, when she was alone on a warm night, especially in the hills, and she looked out on the star-filled
sky, she felt like all she needed to do was ask and she
could be lifted into the night.

So, tonight, as cool as it was, she bundled up and sat
on her front porch to talk with whatever entity was listening, to let him, her, or it know that she knew she was
full of hubris and probably had been her whole life, but
that she knew, felt it in every inch of herself, that Cookie
was an innocent woman. Even with her strange, wild
ways and mysterious past. This young woman was good.

Something had brought Cookie to Cumberland
Creek. Whatever it was, Beatrice was grateful for it.
This young woman added so much to their lives.
Elizabeth loved her. *And no matter what you say,
babies, children, they know good people. Yes, they do. So
please, God, Goddess, all, and whatever angels, ghosts,
or demons are around, please help get our Cookie out
of trouble.*

Beatrice knew Annie was upset and had tried to talk
the detective out of believing the evidence. But the fact
that the earring was at the crime scene? That was strong
evidence and really, really bad luck. How to prove
Cookie was innocent? How?

She thought back to the day they found the first
body. Cookie was at Vera's, making pumpkin soup and
bread. She was as shocked as everybody else by the
murder. Beatrice knew that Cookie did not commit that
murder. Goodness filled her—even if it was a kind of
goodness Beatrice could not quite relate to.

Beatrice looked at the stars, the planets, and wondered if Cookie even had a window. She thought about
the look on Cookie's face when she left the room that
night, and was certain that she would not do well in jail.

As strong as Cookie was, there was an underlying fragility in her.

Beatrice stood. She opened her door and turned her back on the night sky, grateful for the heat of her home as it rose to meet her old bones.

Sunday mornings used to be so calm for Vera—now they were filled with the chaos and noise of motherhood. And she preferred it like this. Only sometimes she wished for a moment of solitude.

But this morning her phone rang around ten—still early for a Sunday. She propped Lizzie on her hip and answered it. "Hello."

"Hey there. It's me," Sheila said.

"What's up? Did you go for your run yet?"

"Of course I did. I changed my route this morning, kept close to home. I'm a little freaked out by all the murders. I thought about not going at all, but I try to run every morning. You know that. Might do you some good. Gets your blood moving."

"I chase Lizzie around and dance Tuesdays through Saturdays. That's enough for me, dear," Vera said.

"Are you going up to see your aunt?"

"Next Sunday," she said. "Bill will have Liz. Besides, I wasn't too sure about heading up there this weekend. It's creeping me out."

"I know what you mean," Sheila said. "If you get a chance, why don't you come by? I want to show you this book."

"What book?"

Lizzie was squirming and wanting to get down. Finally, she slid down Vera's body to the floor.

"Cookie's book that we found. It's here, and it's, um, odd."

"What do you mean?"

"Why don't you come for lunch? I'll see what Annie and Bea are doing. I'd like you all to see it."

"Must be a hell of a book."

"There's leftovers from last night, so let's just meet in the basement and I'll show you what I mean."

After she hung up the phone, Vera ran into the living room, where Lizzie was scattering clean laundry all over the carpeted floor. Through the window she could see Beatrice coming up.

"Come in, Mother," Vera said.

"What? Are you psychic now?" Beatrice said, opening the door.

"I wish. I'd play the lotto and win all kinds of money and not have to work a day in my life."

"Now, I hope you'd remember your poor old mum," Beatrice said, giving her daughter a hug before bending down to pick up Lizzie.

"Gran!" Lizzie squealed.

"How are you?" Beatrice said to her, sparking up the way she did every time she saw her.

"Well, Mom, help yourself. There's biscuits and coffee out there in the kitchen. I need to take a shower. Do you mind?"

"Nah, of course not."

"Listen, Sheila called and said she has one of Cookie's books. . . ."

"That scrapbook-looking thing?"

"I guess," Vera said as she started up the stairs. "Anyway, she wants us to come for lunch and to check it out."

"Eh, I don't know. I've got a snoot full of the scrapbook queens these days. You know me. I like being alone."

"Suit yourself, but I'm heading over there to check it out. She said the book is very strange."

"Strange, huh? Maybe I will go."

When she reached the top landing, Vera remembered that Sheila had invited Annie to tag along, and went back downstairs. "Can you call Annie? Sheila wants her there, too."

"Annie's not home. She's off to the prison this morning, interviewing Mary Schultz."

"I thought she was finished with that book?"

"She is."

"Then what—"

"I believe she's trying to get information about the recent murders."

"From Mary? Bill said she's lost her mind over killing her father."

"He pushed her to it, I'm sure," Beatrice said. "Can you imagine?"

Vera turned and walked back up the stairs. Why, she had never thought that there could be a link between Mary and the murder victims. That thought moved around in her brain and both intrigued her and scared her. Poor Mary Schultz had gone through hell, which left her a bit crazy. There was Annie, off to see her. God, she hoped Annie was careful—and she hoped that her friend would unearth what she needed to help get Cookie out of jail.

Chapter 35

Annie sat across the table from Mary Schultz—just as she had done before—but this time was different. First, her friend Cookie was in jail. Second, her family might be in jeopardy. The phone call. The strange symbols. Her boys being singled out in school. The police were always watching her house and following her. Anything else that happened would lead the police to tapping her phone. It was unnerving. She was losing her patience dealing with these backward notions some of the locals seemed to have. If she could just get Mary to talk, she was certain it would help.

"Good chocolate," Mary said. "Thanks so much."

She seemed more alert today, and the guard told Annie that they were trying a new medication on her. Maybe that was why her blue eyes looked so alert and clear.

"You're welcome, Mary," Annie said, thinking she had very little time and so she had to forge a level of trust with the woman quickly. She was pleasantly surprised that the guards let her bring in the chocolates. "You know, I'm not supposed to feel friendly toward the people I visit here. But I can't help but like you. We're a lot alike."

Mary nodded. "I can see that. We're both fighters. I've read some of your stuff. Impressive."

Annie's heart leapt. She had always hated to hear about other journalists playing it this way, but was this *actually* going to work?

"Thanks, and yes, we are both fighters," Annie said. "Sometimes it gets very lonely for me."

Mary slowed down her chewing and looked almost as if she was empathizing. "Me too. It's even harder now. These women in here. They just don't get me."

"I hear you," Annie said. "So, Mary, were you able to find out anything about the Carpenters?"

"Oh yes, Annie. There was a shunning. But my sources don't know why exactly. Just that one morning she was gone. The family—and the whole congregation—turned their backs on her. They just don't talk about shunnings to outsiders."

Annie was stunned. How could your family turn against you? What did it take to do such a thing?

"Annie? You okay?"

"It just makes me so sad to think of it."

"It's hard on everybody," Mary said. "Even the people doing the shunning."

"I get that," Annie said after a moment. "But what would the girl do out in the world? I mean, where would she go? Who would she even know?"

"She probably went to a friend's house, or another congregation could have taken her in. I don't know."

"You mean another Mennonite congregation?"

"I suppose. These days, there are a lot of factions, even up at the Nest. You know?"

"These young women lead very secluded lives, yes?"

Mary nodded—almost with the abandon of a child— as she bit into another chocolate.

"How would she even meet someone from outside of the group?" Annie asked, thinking how frightening it must be for a person who had lived that life to all of a sudden be without the resources it provided.

Mary shrugged, licked her lips. "A market maybe?"

Could be, Annie thought. Maybe she needed to pay more attention to the Wednesday Mennonite Farmers' Market in town.

"What would persuade a family to shun their child?" Annie asked.

"Could be anything. Willful disobedience about anything, like wanting to marry someone outside of the Order or maybe even an unwed pregnancy. Oh Lawd, I remember once a friend of mine knew a girl that was beaten half dead by her daddy." Mary looked down at her hands. "She was pregnant and not married. I reckon she'd have preferred to be shunned."

"I don't know that I could shun my own flesh and blood," Annie said.

"You might be surprised what you'd do if you had a whole group of people telling you this is the way it should be. And if you believe in the common good for the whole group—not just your family. It's simple brainwashing. Some of our brains are easier to wash than others," she said and grinned.

Just then the door swung open; it was Detective Bryant, with several uniformed guards trailing behind him.

"What are you doing here?" he said to Annie. "I want her out of here. She is not to be allowed to visit in this prison until this case is resolved. I thought I told you that."

"I'm sorry. I never got any paperwork on that, sir," the woman behind him said. "Ms. Chamovitz?" She gestured for Annie to leave.

Mary frowned. "We were just visiting."

Annie picked up her bags and handed Mary another bag of candy. "One for the road," she said. "Thanks."

She turned around and glared at the detective, who looked as if he were about to blow smoke straight out of his ears. Okay, now Annie knew that Bryant knew more than he had let on. There was no way a detective would place a ban on visiting a prisoner, unless there was a reason.

Chapter 36

Beatrice had never been moved by scrapbooking. Yes, she had kept some albums throughout her life. But she was always so busy that most of them went unfinished. Her mother, however, had kept several scrapbooks while Beatrice was growing up. There was none of this froufrou, sticker, ribbon, special ink, and paper madness then. The black-and-white pictures were stuck with glue or photo tabs to black or white pages. The older she became, the more Beatrice enjoyed looking at the old pictures of herself when she was younger. Remembering what it was like to have such beautiful, smooth skin; firm, muscular arms and legs; and a mind that never stopped. She also loved looking at the pictures of her parents. She would never give up her wedding album— or Vera's baby picture album. Yes, there was something to be said for nostalgia, the way it could lift a person's spirits in their old age.

But to look at scrapbooking as an art? She'd never imagined such a thing. She'd heard the scrapbook club talking about the artistry of this nationally known scrapbooker or that scrapbooker. She'd blown it off just like any fad. Artistry indeed.

But *art* was the only word that came to her as she

flipped through the pages of the book that sat in front of her on Sheila's basement table. It was breathtaking.

Sheila gazed at Vera with a knowing look in her eye. "Look at these pages. Not the work of an amateur."

Vera glared back at her. "It proves nothing," she said.

What was Beatrice missing? She closed the book.

"I like Cookie just as much as the rest of you," Sheila said. "But this is not the work of a novice."

"No, indeed," Beatrice said, surprised at finding herself agreeing with Sheila. "So?" She looked up at Sheila, then at Vera.

"When she came to us, it was to learn how to scrapbook," Sheila told her.

"This is not really a scrapbook," Vera said. "Look at it. It's more like an altered book."

"Altered books are an outgrowth of scrapbooking. Sort of taken to a higher, more artistic level. But look at this." Sheila took the book and opened it to the title page, pulling back a soft see-through page with bits of gold glitter on it. Rice paper? There, in beautiful hand-scripted silver-inked letters flowing across the page, were the words "Cookie Crandall's Scrapbook of Shadows."

"This hand lettering is exquisite," Beatrice said, looking at Vera. "What do you make of it?"

Vera sat down. "I don't know what to think."

"Something isn't right here," Beatrice said. "The story doesn't add up, eh?"

"If Cookie was lying to us about a silly little thing like her scrapbooking talent, what else is she lying about? I mean, she needed our help with scrapbooking, remember?" Sheila finally said.

"I'm sure there's an explanation," Vera said, turning the next page to reveal a double page painted in azure blue, with golden moon stickers. Each phase of the moon was labeled—new moon, waxing crescent moon, first quarter moon, waxing gibbous moon, full moon, waning gibbous moon, last quarter moon, waning crescent moon, dark moon.

"Oh, look," Beatrice said, pulling out a smaller page, which slid like a drawer from behind the right page of the double layout. "Moon magic. Hmm."

> *New moon: new beginning and projects.*
> *Waning moon: casting out of old ways, banishing of old habits, the removal of troubles and worries.*
> *Full moon: (magic most potent) healing, guidance, completion spells.*
> *The full moon has different names, depending on when it appears. For example, the harvest moon is the moon that appears nearest to the autumn equinox, late September or early October.*
> *A second full moon in any month is a blue moon.*

"I never knew what a blue moon was!" Vera said. "That's fascinating."

"Ladies, you are getting carried away by the beauty of this book," Sheila said. "Let's not forget why I called you here. Either this book was not done by Cookie or she's been lying to us all this time. Which do you suppose it is?"

Vera slid the paper back into place and turned the page and looked at Sheila. "I don't know which it is or even how to go about finding out."

"Why don't you just ask Cookie?" Beatrice asked.

"Then she'll know we've been digging in her things," Vera said.

"She asked you to get her stuff. What's the problem?" Beatrice said.

"I think it's more than that," Sheila said. "It's just uncomfortable. How do you confront a person with something like this? Do you say, 'We think you've been lying to us all this time' and then expect that person to be your friend?"

Beatrice cackled. "If she was your friend, she wouldn't have lied to begin with."

"Does it matter?" Vera asked. "I mean, you're talking about when we first met her, remember? I mean, she could have said she didn't know anything about scrapbooking, you know, just to get invited to a crop or—"

"Why would she do that? That's ridiculous. We've never said to anybody that they could come only if they are new to scrapbooking," Sheila said.

"Well, it's certainly implied," Vera shot back at her.

Sheila gasped. "It is not!"

"I don't remember how she was even invited," Vera said, waving her off. "I had taken some time off myself for a while after Elizabeth was born. When I started coming back again, she was there."

Sheila knitted her brows. "I thought you invited her."

Vera shook her head.

"Well, if you two fools didn't invite her to the crops, who did?" Beatrice asked.

Chapter 37

Vera bristled at her mother's question. Her memory since Elizabeth's birth had been horrible. But she was certain she hadn't invited Cookie to the crops. She sat there, her mind spinning with memories, running her fingers over the moon pages. The words *blue moon* spun around in her head, then the song, as she tried to remember if she had met Cookie before that first crop or if her friends had talked about her so much that she'd felt like she already knew her.

"Look at that!" Beatrice exclaimed, as she leaned across Vera.

Each turn of the page offered a feast for the eye. Pressed flowers and herbs were affixed in neat little rows. The pages had holes cut into them, where the flowers and herbs were displayed in little slips of plastic. Lady's slipper. Foxglove. Henbane. Virginia bluebells. Handwritten descriptions accompanied them. In between the real botanicals were beautifully rendered—yet almost childlike—drawings of fairies.

"Look at that beautiful ink," Sheila said. "It almost shimmers."

"*Shimmer* is a good word for all of it," Beatrice said.

Nothing shimmery about plants, Vera thought. Yet

there was a shimmery, almost alive quality to the page. Was the effect from the ink alone?

Vera looked at one fairy, who appeared to be dancing. How had Cookie drawn her to show such action? The fairy looked like it was ready to dance off the page. Vera blinked, for suddenly it looked like that fairy was leaping off the page and spinning around in the air. Bright, sparkly dust suddenly blew into Vera's eyes, making them burn.

"Ouch!" she said and closed her eyes. The scrapbook fell to the floor with a thud.

"What's wrong?" Sheila said.

"My eyes!" Vera whined.

"What happened?" Beatrice said. "Open your eyes. Let me see."

"I can't! It hurts," Vera squealed.

"Stop rubbing," Sheila said.

"Go get a cool wet washcloth, Sheila. Something must have flown into her eyes," Beatrice said. "I'll rinse them out. It will be fine."

"Fine? The damned fairy blew dust into them," Vera said, her eyes still closed and burning.

"Fairy?" Beatrice said. "Are you having a stroke? Do we need to take you to a hospital?"

"The fairy in the book," Vera said.

Sheila was back in the room now and was laughing. "Fairy?" She handed Beatrice the washcloth.

"You're going to need to open them," Beatrice told Vera.

"No."

"What?"

"It's going to hurt worse."

"Oh, for God's sake," Beatrice said. "First, you're seeing fairies. Now you're behaving like you're two. Open your friggin' eyes. Hold her head."

Beatrice wrung the washcloth over her daughter's

eyes, which were fluttering now, finally opening. Vera reached for the washcloth and wiped her eyes. She pulled the washcloth away from her face.

"Look," she told them. Vera held the washcloth up for them to see. "It's got some kind of fine glitter all over it."

"Well, I'll be," Sheila said, pushing her glasses back on her nose.

"Where did it come from? I didn't see any glitter," Beatrice said.

"It must have come from the book. There's plenty of glitter in there," Sheila said.

"You mean it leapt from the page into my eyes? Just my eyes?"

Sheila shook her head. "No, I mean it just blew into them—"

"With what air current?" Beatrice said, sticking her finger up to feel for one.

Sheila shrugged. "How do I know, old woman? You're the physicist."

"I'm telling you that I saw a fairy leap off the page and fly around. It blew this glittery stuff right into my eyes," Vera said.

"Humph," Beatrice said. "Of all the things that could have happened, I'm fairly certain it wasn't a fairy."

Vera threw the washcloth down. "Oh, really? I saw it! This coming from you? You swear Daddy's ghost was with you for years. And you don't believe I saw a fairy? That's rich."

Sheila crossed her arms. "She's got a point, Beatrice."

"Okay, look," Beatrice said after a moment. "We were sitting right here, looking at the book with you, and neither one of us saw a thing."

Just then the tea kettle went off. "Tea, ladies?" Sheila asked, walking over to the stove in her basement kitchenette. "I've got leftover scones and muffins from last night."

Vera pushed a long strand of her hair behind her ear, her hand shaking. "I just don't know what happened. It looked like a fairy. . . . I don't know. . . . Maybe it was pollen? A piece of a flower?"

"Pollen and glitter," Sheila said, setting a tray with a teapot, cups, and scones and muffins in front of them.

Sheila poured the tea, and Beatrice reached for a gingerbread muffin. Vera noticed her mother's hands trembling slightly. Vera took a sip of her tea. Yes. That was good. Real. Right.

Nothing else seemed to be. She still felt disoriented. Uncertain of what had just happened to her. But as she looked around the room, it seemed like she was seeing things very clearly, with much more vivid hues than before.

"Well, we are still back where we started from," Sheila mused after taking a bite of a scone. "We still don't know what to make of this book or of Cookie."

The three of them sat there, eating, sipping tea, looking around the room. Not one of them picked the book up off the basement floor.

Chapter 38

Annie was trying to focus her thoughts as she drove away from the prison. She was onto a connection that was making the detective nervous. Yes, he was an ass, but he wasn't a stupid man. Mary was probably in the middle of a nervous breakdown, but she knew the events and the people of Jenkins Hollow. He knew that. He was hiding something.

So, the first murder victim was shunned. Which was probably why there was nobody at the funeral. What about the second young woman? Hmm. What was her name? Rebecca. Rebecca Collins. What was her connection to Sarah Carpenter?

She pulled off the road to make a phone call.

"Cumberland Creek Police," a voice said.

"Hi, yes. This is Annie Chamovitz. I'm wondering if visitation has been set for Cookie Crandall."

"No, ma'am. Sorry. No visitors."

"Okay. Thanks."

It was odd that they were not allowing Cookie to see anybody, although it wasn't completely out of the ordinary for someone they considered to be a flight risk.

Absurd. Cookie. A flight risk? That was almost as absurd as Cookie even being a murder suspect. None of it made sense.

She reached into her bag and pulled out her red folder, which had notes and phone numbers from this case. An envelope fell out from among the sheets of paper. She'd scribbled on the back of it. *Yes. There it is, James and Doris Collins.* Their phone number was right there.

Annie keyed the number into her cell phone, wondering if it would work, since the Collinses lived in the hollow. But their place was just on the edge of it, and she might get a call through. It rang. Annie's heart skipped a beat. She hated talking to bereaved parents. What could you say to them? Annie reached over and turned off the radio.

"Hello," a soft feminine voice said.

"Mrs. Collins, I'm Annie Chamovitz. I write for—"

"I know who you are," she said.

Oh.

"I was wondering if we could chat sometime. I know this must be an awful time for you, and I truly hate the imposition. But if there's any information you could give, it might help someone else. Can we perhaps meet somewhere?"

She breathed heavily into the phone, hesitating. "I don't know what there is to say."

"Specifically, I'd like to talk with you about Sarah and Rebecca and their friendship."

"Can we talk over the phone? I mean, I'm not sure I can get out right now."

"The conversation could get a little personal, and, well, would you be comfortable over the phone?" Annie despised phone interviews. She felt she missed something if she couldn't see her subject's eyes, the way they moved, and so on.

"Yes, I think so," Mrs. Collins said.

Okay.

"How long had Rebecca and Sarah been friends?"

"Almost since we moved up here. It's probably been fifteen years. They both loved to play the piano, had the same teacher. They'd get together and practice."

"It's kind of unusual for a Mennonite girl to get close with a Baptist girl, isn't it?"

"Not really. I mean, I guess it depends. They were mostly just playing music together, and I think Sarah's parents trusted us," she said, her voice cracking. "They live so close by, and my husband is a vet. . . . He's helped with their animals."

Aha. A connection.

"Did Rebecca know that Sarah was pregnant?"

Silence.

"Mrs. Collins?"

"You know, I've asked myself that same question. I suppose she did. I wish with all my heart they'd come to me, or some other adult, for help."

"They were both eighteen and probably thought they could handle it. . . ."

"Yes. Except that an eighteen-year-old Mennonite girl is quite gullible. Well, even more so than most eighteen-year-olds."

"What do you mean?"

"I mean they lack experience with men. A handsome young man tells you you're beautiful . . . that he loves you. . . . It feels real and right . . . even if your family and church tell you otherwise."

Well, that sounds like a lot of young women—not just Mennonites.

"I must admit that I'm a little confused about Mennonites," Annie said.

"There's an Old Order here—of the strictest kind. And that's what Sarah's family is. Then you have the others . . . the more modern Mennonites. Several different sects."

"But someone mentioned to me that there's a different kind of Mennonite in the Nest."

"They are not real Mennonites. I know who they are talking about. They dress like them. But they are into other things. It's very secretive."

"Secretive?" Annie asked.

"Yes, in fact . . . Um, what is that guy's name? None of us trust him. What is his name? Oh yeah. Zeb. Strange name. Strange man. Do you know him?"

Annie remembered him vividly, given that she'd just seen him at the funeral. She'd never forget the first time she saw him in person, saw his dark hair, startling blue eyes, incredible physique, and a pistol tucked in the front of his blue jeans. She also remembered his comments about Jews as she was driving him, Bryant, and Tina Sue to the police station. Even more sickening to Annie than the comments from the backseat was the way Tina Sue looked at him as if he were her master, her God. Several times Annie caught that look washing over Tina Sue's face. Childlike. Puppylike. And it was unnerving to see it on a grown woman's face as she looked at her husband. A man whose piercing blue eyes rarely looked at his wife—even as she sat in the station, being questioned, or when he'd sat in the courtroom. The trial had stretched for days. Zeb had shown up only sporadically.

"Yes," Annie finally said. "I remember him from the trial. Someone mentioned that he grew up Old Order."

"Yes, but an awful event happened to his family a long time ago. A horrible murder of some kind. And he left the church. People say he's not been right since."

Annie's stomach tightened. There was no mention

of this when she was researching for her book. Of course, most if it was focused on Maggie Rae and her family—not her in-laws. Could it be that she'd have to talk with Zeb again? Would she have to go back to Jenkins Hollow or the neighborhood there known as the "Nest" for this story? An image of Cookie in prison flashed in her mind. If she needed to prove that Cookie was innocent, she'd do it—but damn, she would not go alone.

"He sort of gave me the creeps," Annie found herself saying. *Oh, great. So professional.* "Um, Mrs. Collins, do you have any idea who the father of that baby was?"

"No," she said. "I wish I did. I keep thinking of it alone in the hospital, with no Mama, no Daddy, not a friend in the world."

Suddenly, a black emptiness overwhelmed Annie. She hadn't even known she was pregnant, had formed no attachment to the baby she was carrying. But the minute it was pulled from her, she was filled with gut-wrenching sorrow.

She and Mike had decided not to have another baby years ago. She should have gotten her tubes tied, or he should have gotten an operation. Just to be sure.

Her doctor had assured her that her feelings were normal. It was hormonal. Even if she didn't know she was pregnant, her body and her hormones did. She took a deep breath. She thought of the baby in the local hospital and wondered what would become of her.

"Did the girls have any other friends?" Annie asked.

"Oh, let me think. . . . There was Hannah," she said. "She works at the bakery. You know which one I mean? It's at the foot of the mountain. Harmony Bakery. Yes. That's it."

"Thanks so much for speaking with me. I can't tell you how much I appreciate it," Annie said.

Yes. She knew Harmony Bakery, which drew in the tourists like flies. It was a bee in DeeAnn's bonnet.

"The tourists just want to go in there and look at all the Mennonites and say they bought an authentic Mennonite pie. If they only knew the markup on that stuff. They are gouging people," DeeAnn would say.

Now that she knew that Hannah worked at the bakery, Annie decided to check it out. It sat at the base of the mountain, so she wouldn't have to venture too far.

Once there, she was surprised to see how big the bakery was compared to DeeAnn's quaint little shop. Cases of pies, bread, rolls, and cakes were lined up in rows. *No trendy cupcakes,* mused Annie.

She smiled at the young man behind the counter.

"Can I help you?" he said, smiling back.

"I'll take a sweet potato pie," she said. "And is Hannah here?"

He placed her pie on the counter. She could smell the cinnamon and nutmeg. It glistened deep orange. If you were going to have a pie, you might as well make it a nutritious one, full of beta-carotene.

His brow knit. "Yes, she just went on break."

"I'd just like to speak to her for a few minutes. That okay?" Annie said.

He shrugged. "Sure. I'll be back."

When Hannah walked through the doorway and saw Annie, she smiled and looked away. "Can I help you?" she said, looking back at her.

"Hi, Hannah. I'm Annie Chamovitz. Remember? We met at Rebecca's funeral."

"Yes, I remember," she said, rubbing her hands on her light blue heavy cotton apron.

She was extremely clean. Her nails were short, and her hair was pulled back in a bun with a prayer cap on top, not a hair out of place. Not an ounce of make-up. Not one piece of jewelry. Simple. Clean.

"Can I ask you some questions? I'm working on a story for a newspaper."

"Me?" she sputtered, her hand to her chest, her face reddening. "Why me? I don't know anything."

"You knew Rebecca?"

She nodded.

"Did you know Sarah?"

She nodded again.

The door to the shop opened, and the bell went off. The young man came back in to wait on the customer. Annie glanced at him. Looked like a tourist, agape over the baked goods.

"Then I'd like to talk with you."

"Well, okay. Can you come back to the break room?" she said, turning.

Annie followed her through the massive kitchen, which was a hubbub of cleaning activity. The huge ovens were being preened over, and two young men were running mops over the floor.

When they entered the break room, Hannah sat down at a table and motioned for Annie to do the same. There were magazines scattered on it—*Taste of the South,* old issues of *Gourmet* and *Saveur. Interesting.*

"What can I tell you? I knew them both," Hannah said.

"I know on the face of things they had several things in common. Jenkins Hollow. Red hair. Their age. They both played piano. What else?"

"Let me think. They both worked here at different points. Rebecca only helped out during the busy season. Sarah was a regular until . . ."

"Until she got pregnant and was shunned."

Hannah's eyes went to her hands as she nodded. This was painful for her.

"Hannah, I'm so sorry that you lost your friends. It must be hard for you," Annie said.

She nodded and looked toward the door.

"Is there anything else you can tell me? Do you know who the father of Sarah's child is?"

"Even if I knew," Hannah whispered, "I couldn't tell you." As she lifted a finger to rub her eyebrow, Annie noticed she was trembling. This wasn't just sadness; it was fear.

"Are you in danger?" Annie whispered back.

Hannah shrugged. "We all are as long as someone is killing out there. Right?"

"Hannah, I can see you're upset. When you feel better about things, give me a call so we can talk more." She slipped her a card.

Hannah nodded as someone walked into the room. She sighed. "Back to work, Ms. Chamovitz," she said and stood and slid the card into a pocket.

After leaving the bakery, Annie sat in her car in the parking lot and called Detective Bryant.

"Bryant," he said.

"I'm at Harmony Bakery," she said.

"Annie? That you?"

"Yes. This is an interesting connection."

"This is a murder investigation. All I can say is, I'm working with the FBI and I don't have to tell you anything."

Annie hung up. *Nice.*

She decided to check her messages. She heard the one from Beatrice about going to Sheila's place, and she decided to stop by. When she walked in the door, she was surprised to find all the scrapbookers there, gathered around the table. Sheila and Vera had goggles on.

Sheila looked up. "Hi, Annie. How are you?"

"What on earth are you doing?" Annie said and squeezed herself into the circle.

"We're trying to see what's in this book," Vera replied. "When I looked at it earlier, something flew into my eye."

"And?"

"For the life of me, it looked like a fairy was flying off the page and threw dust in my eyes."

"Probably a weird illusion with some kind of special ink," Sheila said. "We are trying to figure out what kind of ink this is—without getting fairy dust or glitter or whatever in our eyes."

"Damn thing is probably booby-trapped," DeeAnn said.

"Why would you say that?" Annie said.

DeeAnn shrugged. "I wasn't here when it happened. Sounded kind of freaky to me. Like maybe Cookie didn't want anybody to look in her book. So she set a trap."

"I don't see that at all," Sheila said.

"Yes. That seems kind of mean-spirited of you, DeeAnn," Annie said. "Cookie is our friend."

"Me?" DeeAnn said, drawing back. "It wasn't me who was seeing things and lost her eyesight momentarily." She nodded her head toward Vera.

"Yeah, that's right," Vera responded. "I'm the woo-woo nut in the crowd." She slipped the goggles from her face, looking defeated, tired. "I just can't make any sense of it."

"I'm telling you that there's something in that book Cookie doesn't want people to see," DeeAnn insisted. "First off, she didn't want us knowing how accomplished she is at this—"

"Wait a minute!" Annie interrupted. "Give me the book. I'll take it home and look at it in the morning. Maybe I can find something."

Sheila looked at her, her goggles askew on her face. "I'm not done yet. I'll bring it to you tomorrow. This ink is fascinating. Also, she has an interesting blend of different paper—*washi*, I think, mulberry, and even silk—

on her pages. I'm not even sure I could work with silk. It's very complicated, not easy to work with at all."

Annie suddenly saw the clock on the wall and excused herself. She had no idea it was so late. She needed to stop by Beatrice's place before she went home. Mike's recriminations about her being away from home so much were at the front of her mind. One hell of a day.

Chapter 39

Beatrice needed to think about something other than the murders, Cookie, and that strange but beautiful scrapbook of hers. It was giving her indigestion. She finally had some peace and quiet, so she sat at her computer and checked her e-mail. *Aha.* There was an e-mail from her friend in Paris.

My dearest Beatrice,
How are you? I hope that my e-mail finds you well. I have not heard back from you. Are you okay?
My ankle is healing nicely, and I will be as good as new very soon. The nights in my apartment have been gloomy and cold since you left. Will you come back soon? Next year? There is a place here for you.
Did I tell you about my grandson? He wants to study physics in America. Your field, yes?

Beatrice's heart leapt. Of course he knew that.

I am hopeful to visit him (and you) when he
settles in. We are not sure which university yet.

Well, my dear, I am off to get a bite to eat with
my grandson. Good boy. Very smart. I wish you
could have met him.

No time for that, Beatrice thought and grinned, then
clicked off the e-mail. It was good to make him wait a
little. She didn't want him to think she had nothing
better to do than sit around waiting on his e-mail. She'd
get back to him later. Even though he was in Paris, she
still felt a little restricted by him. She didn't want him to
know that, nor did she want to feel anything for him at
all. It was best for both of them to take their time about
things.

Beatrice heard a car pull up to the front of her house.
Its headlights shone briefly in her window. Who could
that be at nine thirty on a Sunday night? She stood and
looked out the window. *Annie?*

"What are you doing here?" Beatrice said, opening
the door.

"I just need to talk to somebody. Run a few things by
you," Annie said.

"Come in. Sit down. Do you want a drink? Tea?
Water?"

"No," Annie said as she took off her coat and laid it
on the back of the couch. "I won't be long."

"Okay," Beatrice said, sitting in her rocking chair.
Annie still looked pale—along with looking harried and
tired. Circles under her eyes. Hair falling half out of her
ponytail. Annie had never been like Vera, who used to
be perfectly made up all the time, but tonight she looked
particularly unkempt. That old University of Maryland
sweatshirt should be put out to pasture.

"I'm trying to put this all together. I can't stand the thought of Cookie in jail, you know?"

Beatrice nodded.

"So I visited with Mary Schultz today and confirmed that there was a shunning. The Carpenter girl."

"Makes sense," Beatrice said after a moment.

"She was pregnant. That baby is hers, of course."

"Hmm. Well, now. Who is the father?"

"Good question," Annie said, rubbing her hands together. Beatrice noted her fingernails were bitten down to their nubs.

"And what does Rebecca have to do with any of that?"

Annie shrugged. "They were good friends. I spoke with Rebecca's mom, who didn't know that Sarah was pregnant. She said she'd wished that she knew, but Rebecca never said anything to her."

"That's typical," Beatrice said and rolled her eyes.

"Then there's this odd business with this group of people at the Nest—"

"Whoaaa!" Beatrice said. "Who said anything about the Nest?"

"Well, I talked about it with Mrs. Collins today. She said that it's a weird mix of people up there. They are not really Mennonite."

"I'd say." Beatrice had always felt a strange mix of fear and embarrassment when she thought of the Nest, especially when she was around the bright and cosmopolitan Annie. She didn't want her to think badly about the Appalachian people. Annie had already seen some of the worst, and yet she was still here. So she must see the best in them, as well.

"I wouldn't say this to just anybody, Beatrice, but I think there is something big happening. Something more than Cumberland Creek, more than Jenkins Hollow or the Nest. So far, the CDC has been involved, the FBI, and Detective Bryant is not letting Mary

Schultz talk to me. And the murdered girls were onto something. Someone needed to shut them up. Those rune symbols? They mean those girls were a problem to someone, you know?"

"So," Beatrice said, "you have two girls labeled as a problem . . . by someone. They know something. They both show up dead with the markings on them. One has had a baby. And that baby was almost killed on the mountain, left for dead."

"On the same spot where they found Cookie's earring."

The women sat in silence.

"I looked Cookie up online," Annie finally said.

"And?"

"The detective was right. There's not a trace of her anywhere."

"Pshaw. What does that mean?" Beatrice said.

"I mean, I can't find birth records, work records, previous addresses, passports. Nothing."

Beatrice's stomach sank. Maybe she shouldn't have eaten that last slice of chocolate cake. All of the evidence seemed to point to their friend Cookie. Or at least to her knowing more than what she let on.

"But what would Cookie have to do with that mess up in the mountains?" Beatrice said.

"The only time I knew her to even be up there is when she went up for her retreat that day."

"You mean the day we had the flat tire?"

Annie nodded. "And she had that character, Luther, in her car."

Beatrice didn't know what to say or to think. She decided not to tell Annie about the scrapbook—about the suspicions it had created. She'd tell her tomorrow, after she had a good night's sleep. She could see this weighing heavily on Annie—and she didn't want to add to her trouble. Not tonight. It seemed as if Cookie wasn't who they thought she was. But Beatrice knew that very few people were what others thought they were. Look at Maggie Rae, who had quite the secret life. Look at her, Beatrice Matthews, soon to be eighty-two, with a beau in Paris. Who would've thought?

Annie went on. "There's another thing Mrs. Collins mentioned. Remember Zeb? Tina Sue's husband?"

"Of course."

"He's got something to do with that strange group of people in the Nest," Annie said and yawned.

"Tina Sue didn't mention that, eh? I told you she wasn't to be trusted. Hell, I'd have trusted her sister over her any day of the week," Beatrice said.

Annie looked deflated.

"Annie, I think you need to go home and get some sleep," Beatrice finally said to her. "You look tired. Your body has been through hell. Your son was in trouble at school. Your friend Cookie is in jail. Things don't seem to add up. I agree. But we are missing a huge part of this story. We'll come up with a plan, just not tonight. The police will figure it out. It will be okay."

Annie smiled at Beatrice and sighed. "I hope you're right, but this whole thing gives me really bad feelings. I can't even explain the way it makes me feel. The other thing is, Bryant is withholding information."

"No surprise there."

"Seems that both girls had worked at Harmony Bakery."

"There's not many places they can work up there. That may not mean anything at all."

"Except that Rebecca's body was covered in flour," Annie said.

Chapter 40

A great fluttering wind knocked Vera down. What was flapping? A huge bird? As she struggled to stand, she realized the stage was shaky, slippery, odd. One spotlight was beaming on her as she pointed her toe. A screaming violin. A pulsing harp.

She looked up beyond the light and into the blackness of the audience. Was there one?

She prepared for her pirouette, then lifted herself to her toe and spun around into dizziness. How did she forget to find her spot? She preached constantly to her young dancers, "Spot, spot, spot. Pick your spot, glue your eyes there as long as possible, now turn, and whip your head. Find your spot. You won't get dizzy."

A pause in the music. She looked down at her feet. Sometimes a dance was all in the eyes—and a glance downward could be a powerful symbol. But the stage? Was it really a stage? It looked covered in paper. Suddenly, the light shone on a mounded spot on the floor. Vera climbed it—gracefully, of course, for they were all looking at her—her flowing pink chiffon costume brushing against her legs. She peered over the rounded edge onto the other side, which looked like the center of a huge book, where all the pages came together. Where was she? Was she onstage? Was she in a book?

She spun around, feeling her clothing fall to the floor. She was completely naked now. She tried to cover herself with her arms. She heard the audience gasp. So there was an audience—hushed until this moment.

"Dance!" a male voice rang out. It sounded familiar.

"C'mon!" It was a voice with a Brooklyn accent. *Tony?*

Instead, Vera froze, not knowing in which direction to turn, her heart beating so hard that she thought she could hear her pulse throbbing in her ears. She needed to get off the stage. She heard beautiful little bell-like sounds coming from the direction of the crevice. She looked over to it. It pulled her closer.

God, if I could just disappear, she thought.

"You can, my friend," Cookie said to her.

Cookie! She was standing there in her blue robes, holding out a glistening silver robe for Vera, who quickly slipped into it. The audience cheered.

"Don't mind them," Cookie said, holding out her hand. "Take my hand. Let's disappear together."

"Ah," Vera said. "This is a dream, isn't it?"

"Is it?" Cookie said and smiled, taking Vera's hand. "Look, we are inside of a book."

It became clear to Vera then that she was dancing on a book, which she had thought was a stage.

"Well," Vera said.

"Turn the page," Cookie said and held on tightly to Vera. "Jump!"

Vera and Cookie jumped together as the page flipped, but they stayed in the air, hovering above the book, its pages flipping quickly, dusty sparks flying from it, little creatures escaping from it and running off. Fairies? Well, they weren't birds, were they? Vera became mesmerized by one of them and tried to see it more clearly, wanted to run after it.

"You can never catch a fairy. Mischievous creatures. Difficult to harness and manage," Cookie informed her.

"Fairies?" Vera managed to say.

"There's so much about the world that humans never see. So much magic. So many creatures," Cookie said wistfully.

Vera pulled her robe closer to her, loving the soft cloth surrounding her body.

"Do you see?" Cookie said.

Photos were scattered on the pages. Elizabeth. Beatrice. Women that Vera didn't know—but that looked vaguely familiar. They were suddenly in a cave full of a shiny rock. *Quartz?*

"Calcite," Cookie whispered, wrapping her arms around Vera, who was suddenly pulled into a thick gelatinous substance.

"Cookie?"

She was gone.

Where was Vera now? She felt the warm, slimy substance surround her, and a hand covered her breast. A hard male body coming up behind her, his arms enveloping her, his legs wrapping around her. A shot of excitement rose through the center of her body.

"Tony?" she said, trying to reach through the gel, kicking and reaching, their bodies coming together then, sliding apart—until she could no longer reach him.

She awoke in her own bed, tangled in a sweaty mess, blankets askew. She glanced at the clock. Three a.m. *What a dream. Damn.*

Annie was skinny-dipping in a cove. The water was luminous. The moon was full, reflecting on the warm water that circled her thin body. She lay back and floated, letting the moon shine on her as she closed her eyes. The water, the moon, the sky.

In the distance she saw two redheaded young women swimming. Who were they with? Was that Zeb?

Suddenly Annie popped out of the water, the air harsh in her throat and lungs. She was in a cave. She rubbed her eyes—there was some light and shadow playing with them. Was that a candle on a ledge? Was that a book? She struggled to lift herself out of the water, then plodded over to the ledge, where the book appeared to lift itself off of the rock it was on and opened itself.

The pictures appeared to be etchings—a woman running toward a mountain, which morphed into her jumping into a pool of water, with a waterfall in the background. Then the black ink turned purple as a group of masked dancers danced across the page. The page turned, and there were pictures of her boys in their soccer uniforms.

What was this? A scrapbook?

The page turned again—on its own—and there was a beautifully illuminated page. Handwritten. Rich gold. Crimson. Purple. Gorgeous words that shimmered and lifted off the pages and wound themselves around her fingers, spinning, spinning, then traveled up her arms. Oh, these words! What were they? They seemed to seep into the pores of her skin, delivering energy and light to her.

"We are such stuff as dreams are made of, and our little life is rounded with a sleep," a voice said to her from the corner.

She recognized the voice.

"Cookie?"

Cookie stepped out of the shadows. Her hand against the calcite of the cave wall. She looked radiant in her

blue robes, a gold chain around her neck and an
amethyst hanging from it. Her eyes were made up with
thick black eyeliner, slanting upward, giving Cookie
an almost Asian appearance. Funny, Annie had never
noticed that before. Was she Asian?

Cookie nodded.

"What's going on here?" Annie asked.

She smiled. "You are dreaming, my friend."

"That's right. You're in jail. I'm at home in bed with
my husband. I can hear him snore."

His snoring became louder momentarily.

Cookie laughed.

Suddenly, she and Cookie were both in the water,
Mike's snoring getting softer and softer as they swam
deeper and deeper. Annie was mesmerized by the colorful fish swimming around them, some of them coming
up and gently biting her fingers. The colors! Magenta.
Gold. Crimson. And the rocks and sand and plants, with
beautiful exotic-shaped flowers. Oh, that deep orange
strand floating there pulled her in to look closer.

"No!" Cookie said.

But why? Annie could not resist. She touched the
orange strand and pulled it. She felt a heavy awkward-
ness to it and yanked harder. Out popped the head of
Sarah. Eyes wide with fear, mouth gaping open, and still
screaming.

"Annie!"

She was being shaken by someone. *Cookie?* Sarah's
screams were becoming her own.

"Annie!"

She opened her eyes to see Mike's face close to hers.

"What the hell?" he said.

She didn't know what to say. She grabbed her husband and wept into his shoulder.

* * *

Beatrice fell asleep to the sound of rain on the window and roof. Thunder boomed. A blue-silver streak lit the sky. She sighed.

There was a book on a rock, and it was getting soaked in the rain. Beatrice grabbed it and brought it under the shelter of her porch. She was in her bare feet and her favorite nightgown, a poet's shirt nightdress that Ed bought her when they visited Williamsburg, Virginia.

But wait. She hadn't seen this nightdress in years. Was she dreaming?

The book felt heavy with rain in her arms as she laid it down on her table. She took a seat, opened it, and was amazed to find that its pages were dry. Pictures of her mother and father set off by a lacy-paper frame stared back at her. She loved to look at these two; she was blessed with wonderful parents, though her father could be heavy-handed at times.

She turned the page and found a page that held a mirror. She tried to look in it and found her reflection to be nonexistent. What was this? She turned the page again to another mirror. This time, she looked in the glassy, shiny page and found herself staring back. She ran her fingers over her firm, unaged cheek.

Damn, I like this mirror. It makes me look young again.

Her reflection smiled back at her. *I could feel better about giving myself to Jon, or anybody, if I looked this good.*

Suddenly her husband appeared in the mirror. A flash. "You are beautiful. Any man is lucky to have you, no matter how old you are."

She slammed the book shut and stood up to reach for Ed. But he was gone.

Damn him. Coming to me in a whisper of a dream.

Thunder roared. Blankets of rain fell from her porch roof.

She was still in her bare feet, and the wind blew her nightdress against her tight thighs. She had forgotten what firm thighs felt like. She ran her hands over them and then sat back down to investigate this book more closely.

She looked back in the mirror, which was now full of mathematics computations. Mmm. Was this the theory of relativity? It could be—except that piece right there didn't look quite correct.

"It's magic, you see," Cookie said, suddenly standing next to Beatrice.

"Magic? No, dear, it's math. Beautifully done mathematics."

"Your math is my magic."

"I thought you said my prayers are your magic," Beatrice said.

"Yes. Same thing," Cookie said and nodded. "Do you see?" She waved her hand across the crumbling pages, and the numbers began to move. They spun and spun themselves into a wind, flipping the pages back and forth. "What do you wish for, Beatrice? What is your deepest desire?"

When Beatrice was younger, more driven, her first answer would have been for her theory of time travel to be proven, but at this point in her life, she knew it was accurate, knew it in her bones—and it didn't matter what anybody else in the scientific community thought about it. Now she just wanted to be happy, for her family to be happy and healthy, and deep down inside, she knew that somehow her happiness was linked to Jon.

The twirling tornado of numbers sparked into flame. The edges of the pages of the book became singed with the flame, and Beatrice reached for the book to save it from itself and burned her hand.

"Damn!"

Cookie was still there, and as Beatrice looked up into this younger woman's face, so beautiful, so peaceful, the pain in her hand went away. Cookie smiled. She reached for Beatrice's chin and held it firmly. "Stay with us, Bea," she said.

"What the hell does that mean?"

Cookie laughed.

That was that. If there was any meaning in her statement, Beatrice would never know. Cookie vanished—but her laughter lingered in the chambers of Beatrice's ears. Ed had vanished, too. Damn, what was with the people in her life, always leaving her?

Chapter 41

Vera thought she heard Elizabeth cry. She opened her heavy eyes and listened. There was the cry again—but it wasn't Elizabeth. It was something outside. A cat?

A loud banging at her door prompted her to look at her phone on the bedside table. Four o'clock. That couldn't be good. Was she ever going to get some sleep this night? First, that odd dream, and now this. She reached for her robe, and her pulse quickened. She flew down the steps after reaching for her cell phone. It felt cold and hard in her hands. The blue light from her phone seemed more than enough to illuminate her way. She pressed the button for her mother's phone number. She had yet to hit SEND when she heard a voice.

"Vera! Open up! It's me, Bill."

She unlocked the door. "What the hell are you doing here?" she whispered. She took one look at his red face, bloodshot eyes, and swaying body and knew he'd been drinking.

"Vera, darlin', there's a baby on your porch," he said.

Behind him, a police car with flashing lights went by.

"What?" Vera wondered if she was still awake or if she was dreaming.

"Look," he said and pointed.

Vera cricked her head out the door and saw something move on her porch swing. She stepped out into the cool November air. Everything held a blue cast, even the grass. Between the streetlights and the night sky, blue light imbued her surroundings. She could see dust—or was it insects?—flying in streams beneath the streetlights. But mostly she saw a small baby wrapped in a white blanket, one fist poking out toward the moon. Was that a hospital bracelet? It cried again. She reached for the baby and scooped it up to her chest. It was ice-cold. She opened her robe, placed the baby close to her skin, and ran back in the house.

"Bill, don't just stand there. Call the police," she said. "When you're done with that, get a fire going and make yourself some coffee. You better get sobered up quick."

Vera reached for an afghan that had been thrown across the couch and sat in her rocking chair next to the fireplace. She could hear Bill on the phone in the kitchen, rattling around the coffeemaker.

The baby fussed, as if she was going to cry a bit, but remained mostly quiet as she nuzzled into Vera, who was rocking her gently. She slid her hand over the baby's arms and read the hospital bracelet—BABY JANE DOE, EVIDENCE. The baby was warming up quickly. Bill quietly wandered into the living room and started working on a fire. The fire ablaze in the fireplace, the room lit up from the glow, and the baby's eyes closed. Her breathing was slow and steady.

Vera looked at her cherubic face and nearly melted from the sweetness.

It took only ten minutes for the police to arrive. Bill met them at the door and asked them to proceed quietly because there was another child upstairs, asleep.

"As I said, I was walking by and heard this crying noise. I thought for a moment that Elizabeth had gotten out," Bill told Detective Bryant.

"And you picked up the baby and brought it inside?" Bryant looked at Vera.

"Yes," she said, not looking away from the baby.

"Probably no evidence now," he said, almost to himself.

"Sorry about that, but the baby was cold," she said. "My first instinct was to warm it up."

"It was a good instinct," a slightly graying man told her, coming toward them.

"Hey, Doctor," Detective Bryant said.

Vera thought she recognized him. Was he the ER doctor that worked on Beatrice's neck?

"It's cold enough for any baby to die of exposure outside, let alone this one. She did the right thing."

"Yep, well, whatever," Bryant said. Turning to Bill, he added, "I can smell you from here."

"I was trying to walk it off," Bill said. "And I was walking, not driving."

The doctor came toward Vera and unwrapped the baby. He felt her pulse, listened to her heartbeat and lungs. "She seems fine," he said with relief. "This poor kid. But I still don't know how she got out of the hospital."

"We have police looking over the security tapes," Bryant said. "We were already out looking for her. One of the nurses realized she was gone."

"I suppose I should take her back," the doctor said reluctantly. "She's a ward of the state, until things shake out."

"What things?" Vera asked.

"Her parentage, for one. Who's the father? And is her family capable of taking care of her? I mean, they've had nothing to do with this baby, as far as I know," the doctor responded.

"Can't you just run some of those DNA tests?" she

asked, surprising herself that she was this sharp at this time of day, having been awakened in the wee hours.

The doctor chuckled. "Yes. But this isn't some television show. And which man in Cumberland Creek should we get DNA from? Besides, it takes a lot longer than you think—especially when there's no insurance to speak of—since so much is up in the air. Hospitals. Insurance. What a pain. I remember when you could really practice medicine, back when my dad was still working."

"Mine too," Vera said. "He worked right down the street."

The physician's head tilted. "That's right. You're Doc Matthews's daughter."

"You knew my father?"

He nodded. "Of course, and my father practiced in Bluestone."

"Dr. Green? Yes. I vaguely remember him," said Vera. His father was one of the few physicians her father had befriended. Her father thought very highly of Dr. Green and his family. They were similar to her own family, if she remembered correctly. They had only one child, and it also came later in life. Doc Green's wife was a chemist.

"Maybe we can break this little reunion up and get out here and leave these good people to get some rest," the detective said sarcastically, leaving Vera to wonder where his "bedside" manner was—or if he even had any.

"Why don't you leave her here?" Vera said. "I mean, she's sleeping so soundly, and I still have a bassinet in my room."

"She's a ward of the state," Bryant replied.

"I think it would be fine, as long as you bring the baby back later this morning," the doctor said. "Medically speaking, I think sleep is the best thing for her. I need to get some vitals, but I don't think that's even going to wake her up. She seems to be sleeping so soundly."

"The doc's orders trump mine," Bryant said, looking at the sleeping baby. A softness came over his face that almost left Vera breathless. "Bring her to the hospital later this morning."

Chapter 42

After finally falling back asleep, Annie dreamed of
Detective Bryant again. It was an unsettling dream.

They were searching for a map, looking through piles
of papers and books. The map was a life-and-death
matter.

"Don't worry," he said more than once in the dream.

When the alarm buzzed and she opened her eyes, she
was surprised by the light. Her dream was set in a dark
and dusty place. A cave? A basement? Her arm reached
across the bed and hit the alarm. *Okay, shake it off,* she
told herself. *It's time to get up and get breakfast going
for the boys.*

"Late night, huh?" Mike said when she entered the
kitchen. He was sitting at the table, drinking coffee and
eating toast. He'd make himself breakfast, but make the
boys breakfast without being asked? Well, that never occurred to him.

She grunted, reached for a cup, and poured herself
some coffee. She sat down at the table. "I stopped by to
see Beatrice last night. I had quite a day."

Obviously not paying any attention, he lowered his
newspaper. "What did you say?"

She looked at him and rolled her eyes. "Never mind,"

she said and smiled. "I should just keep my mouth shut until I have at least one cup of coffee, especially when you're reading the paper."

She saw movement out of the window on her front porch. It was Sheila in her bright red jogging suit, her hair needing to be brushed, and her lipstick smeared. Annie opened the door.

"Good morning, Sheila. What's up?"

"Vera has the baby," she said.

"What baby?"

"Sarah's baby. They found it on her porch last night. Someone took it from the hospital. And they don't know if they put the baby on her porch specifically or if the person who took the baby became scared when they saw the police."

"The police?" Mike said, coming up behind Annie.

"Yes," Sheila replied. "Someone stole the baby from the hospital, and the police were out last night looking for it."

Mike looked at Annie, eyebrows lifted.

"No," Annie said. "I didn't know anything about this one. My eventful day had nothing to do with this incident. I was visiting Mary, then interviewed Rebecca's mother, stopped by Sheila's, then went to visit Beatrice. I was out late, but I don't recall seeing any police."

"Oh no, you wouldn't," Sheila said. "This was at three in the morning. Can you believe it? If you want to see the baby, you should go on over there. She's got to take it back this morning."

"At three I was waking up from a nightmare," Annie said.

"You too? Vera had a doozy last night about dancing on a stage that was a book. Or something. See you," Sheila said and started to leave. "Come to think of it, I had a strange dream, too. It just came back to me. I'll tell you about it later."

That was weird. That three women all had strange dreams last night. Was there a full moon?

Mike sighed.

Annie cringed.

"We agreed that this job would be perfect because it was freelance and wouldn't take too much of your time. Damn, Annie," Mike said.

"I know, Mike. But it comes in fits and spurts, and there doesn't seem to be a way to gauge it." Annie paused. "I'll go over after I get the boys off."

"Oh," Sheila said. "Of course. And here's some muffins DeeAnn sent over."

"You've seen DeeAnn already today?"

"Oh yes," Sheila replied. "And I bought you this to look at." She walked in the house and placed a cloth bag on their kitchen table, just as Sam was making his way to the table. "Good morning," Sheila said to him. "Muffins?"

He smiled sleepily and reached for a muffin.

"Chocolate raspberry," Sheila said and smiled.

"Miss you, Mommy," Sam said, attaching himself to Annie and pulling on her already divided heart. Mike's eyes connected with hers—she knew what he was thinking.

"What's in the bag?" Ben said as he tumbled in, looking over the muffins.

Sheila handed him one. "And this is for your mama."

"What is it?" Annie said, reaching into the bag.

"It's Cookie's scrapbook," Sheila said. "We gave up our investigation. It led to nothing."

"Oh, I'll look at it later," Annie said. The next thing she knew, Mike was kissing her good-bye, the boys were yammering for juice, and Sheila was gone—back to her daily run around the neighborhood, though Annie wondered how much running she actually got done between muffin stops and delivering news and scrapbooks.

Suddenly it was just her and her chocolate-smeared boys.

"Chocolate for breakfast?" she said and smiled.

"I think we should have it every day," Sam said.

"Me too," Ben said.

"Don't get used to it. Tomorrow it's back to eggs or oatmeal."

Later, after the boys left for school and she emerged from the shower, feeling like she could face the day, she spotted the bag on her table. What was so special about the scrapbook? she wondered, and glanced at the clock. She better get moving if she was going to meet the baby.

Chapter 43

Beatrice awakened with a book spread over her chest. Oh, bother, she had fallen asleep with *Leaves of Grass* again. The phone rang—and she let it ring. Whoever it was would surely leave a message if it was important.

She felt the hard edges of the book and reached for her glasses. She vaguely remembered taking them off at some point. She sat up a bit on her pillow. Where had she left off?

Just then the phone began to ring again. She sat up all the way. "Damn," she said, reaching for her bedside phone, then seeing Vera's number on the display.

"What?" she said into the phone.

"That's no way to answer the phone," Annie said.

"What's going on? Why can't people just leave me alone?"

"Have you had your coffee yet?" Annie said, ignoring her question.

"No, I'm just getting up."

"There's plenty here, at Vera's. She has Sarah's baby."

"What?" Beatrice's heart leaped, and she hung up the phone. *Hmm.* Where was that blue sweater? And where were her sneakers? She desperately wanted to see that child.

* * *

When she finally arrived on the scene, Beatrice smelled the undeniable scent of buckwheat pancakes. Pungent. Delicious. She couldn't wait to taste some. She was pleasantly met with a fresh stack of them on the table. Bill was cooking.

"Help yourself, Bea," he said, smiling at her.

"Don't mind if I do," she said, grabbing a plate and heaping pancakes on it. "Now, where's this baby?"

"Here she is, Mama," Vera said, coming up behind her.

Elizabeth was toddling beside her and reached up for her grandmother. Beatrice placed the plate on the table and held Elizabeth. "Good morning, sweetie." She buried her head in the mess of little girl in her arms. When Beatrice lifted her head from Elizabeth, she saw the baby looking up at her out of the cradle of Vera's arms. She gasped. "Lawd," she said. "I've never seen such blue eyes."

"I have," Annie said, coming up beside Vera. "On Luther."

"Humph," Beatrice said. "You don't think that . . ."

"Who knows, Mama? You never know. We'll surely find out after the DNA tests are done."

"DNA?" Beatrice said, sitting down at the table, in front of the plate of pancakes. She spread butter over them, then looked back at the baby, who had an unnervingly mature look to her and seemed to like watching Beatrice.

Annie nodded. "Yes, they're testing so they can find out the parentage of this baby."

"You know, I had the weirdest dream last night," Vera said after a minute. "I think it was all related to that scrapbook."

Annie's head cocked. "You know, I did, too."

"I always have odd dreams, and the older I get, the worse it gets," Beatrice said. "Last night was a doozy."

"So we all had weird dreams last night about the scrapbook?" Sheila said, looking them all over. "I dreamed a wild dream about being back in art school, and Cookie was there, talking to me about art one minute, and the next minute I was absolutely naked in a cave and being chased by a huge scrapbook. The cave was so lovely, with lush moss and sparkly rocks."

"Sparkly rocks? Calcite?" Beatrice said, remembering that there was calcite in the caves she loved in her youth.

Bill walked back into the room just as DeeAnn and Paige were coming in the front door, loaded down with breakfast food, murmuring hellos.

"What I want to know is what any of it has to do with the murders," Bill said while pouring a cup of coffee.

"Any of what?" Sheila said. "We're talking about dreams."

"I thought we were talking about this baby and DNA?" Bill said.

"Keep up," Sheila said.

Annie said to Bill, "Maybe the father of this baby knows who killed her mother. Or worse. Maybe he's the one who killed her."

"But why would he kill Rebecca and then try to kill the baby? It doesn't make any sense to me," Bill replied.

"Murders rarely make sense," Beatrice said. "And most criminals are not very bright, in any case. That's why lawyers make such a damn fine living."

He rolled his eyes.

"How is Cookie?" Beatrice asked him.

He looked away from her.

"Bill?"

"I don't know, Bea. I've not seen her in a while."

"What? You're her lawyer!"

"Yes, but she's refused to see me for the past several days."

"And they are not letting anybody else in," Annie said.

"I'm sorry, ladies," Bill said after swallowing some coffee. "It doesn't look good. I can't defend her if she won't talk to me."

"I agree, Bill," Sheila said after a few minutes. "Cookie is not the person we thought she was."

"Now, hold on," Annie said over the baby's fussing. "Why would you say that, Sheila?"

"She doesn't know," Beatrice said to Sheila. "She doesn't know about the scrapbook."

Sheila said, "We found this scrapbook—"

"The one you were looking at last night? The one in the bag at my house?" Annie said.

"Yes. It's beautiful. Obviously not done by a newbie," Sheila said, crossing her arms.

"So, do you think that proves anything about Cookie being a murderer?" Annie said. "Honestly, I don't believe you could turn on Cookie so quickly because of a stupid scrapbook."

"Now, wait a minute. Nobody's turned on her," Beatrice said. "We'd all like to prove her innocence. But things don't add up. That scrapbook is a work of art, and she claimed to know nothing about scrapbooking."

"There could be a thousand reasons for that," Annie said.

"Like what?" Bill said.

"Maybe she just wanted to fit in," Annie said.

"Unlikely. She doesn't seem to care about fitting in, walking around claiming to be a witch," Beatrice said.

"What are you saying, Bea? Do you think she's a likely suspect?" Bill said.

Beatrice paused and thought about it. "No, I don't. But I'd bet my life that there's more to her than what we know."

"That could be said about anybody," Sheila noted.

Beatrice thought that was an odd statement coming from the Scrapbook Queen of Cumberland Creek.

"Indeed," Annie said. "Everybody in this room has had secrets or has one now. Cookie is human. She is entitled to a private life, just like the rest of us."

Annie looked around the room at the other women. Sheila looked away; Beatrice looked straight at her, white eyebrows lifted; Vera looked at the baby; Paige, at the table, was looking deep into her pancakes. DeeAnn shrugged as she sipped her coffee. All of them had gathered this morning to get a look at the mysterious baby.

Sheila finally said, "Annie, I think you're not seeing things clearly—"

"What is there to see?" Vera interrupted. "Who cares about the scrapbook? Okay. It's odd. But we know Cookie. We know she didn't kill anybody. That's the important thing."

"We don't know her," DeeAnn said, standing closer to Sheila. "I'm sorry. Just because she's hung around here for about a year doesn't mean we know her. We have no idea where she's from or who her people are."

Beatrice groaned. God, she hated that turn of phrase.

"Well, you know what? You could almost say the same thing about me," Annie said, then turned and walked out of the house.

"Annie!" Vera called to her and followed her to the front porch, but as far as Beatrice could tell, Annie was gone. Beatrice turned back to her pancakes and looked back up at the baby. Annie was right about one thing. The baby had eyes just like Luther's.

Chapter 44

Annie's cell phone abruptly interrupted her placing her key in the car's ignition.

"Hello, Annie," the voice said. "This is Zeb McClain. I hear you want to talk with me."

After days of trying to track him down, she'd finally heard from him. A surge of fear ran through her. What was he up to?

"Yes," she said, shocked that he had actually returned her call. She was unprepared for this.

"I'm in town today. Do you want to meet somewhere?"

"Sure, let's meet at the bakery downtown," she suggested. DeeAnn's Bakery, right on Main Street and one of the morning busy spots. She was not going to meet him in some far-off location. The man freaked her out.

After stopping by her house to pick up her recorder, Annie found her way to the bakery, where Zeb was already sitting at a table. An obviously curious DeeAnn was behind the counter.

"Hello," Annie said. "Can I just get a cup of coffee?"

DeeAnn nodded.

Annie took a deep breath. Talk about facing your fears. This man was blatantly anti-Semitic and walked around with a gun tucked in his jeans. He was the nightmare she never knew existed. She turned around to place the cup of steaming coffee on their table, and a man sitting at the corner table lowered his newspaper. It was Bryant. What was he doing here?

"He's watching us," Zeb said and smiled. "Please sit down."

Zeb exuded charm in this moment. Hard to believe that he was the man spouting anti-Jewish statements in the backseat of her car last year.

"Sorry," Annie muttered. "It's probably me he's watching."

"Why?" His brow knit.

Annie smiled. "Let's not get into that, Mr. McClain."

"Zeb, please," he said.

She looked over at DeeAnn, who was wiping the same counter over and over again, trying not to be obvious. She made a mental note not to take her on any undercover operations.

"Thanks for seeing me," she said, clicking on her tape recorder. "I was wondering if you could answer a few questions about Sarah Carpenter."

"I barely knew her," he said after a few moments.

"And her friend Rebecca?"

"I know her family. That's why I went to her funeral," he said, then took a bite of a cinnamon scone.

"How did you know them?" She stirred her coffee and could feel DeeAnn trying not to stare.

"Rebecca's father is a vet. He came to our farm a lot when we still had beef. We used to farm beef."

Farm beef? Odd turn of phrase, Annie thought. As if it weren't a cow—just the end product, beef.

"So you just went to the funeral to pay your respects to the family."

He nodded.

"So what can you tell me about Luther Vandergrift?"

He shrugged. "Nice guy. Very smart. A little lost. But I think he's found a home on the mountain. That's pretty much it."

"I read that his mother was an ancient language scholar of some kind."

He blinked. "I don't know anything about that. Sorry."

"I just thought it was odd—since there were rune patterns carved into the young women who have shown up dead," Annie said and slurped more of her coffee.

"Is that so?" he said, lifting an eyebrow. "Sounds fascinating."

He looked out the window.

"I'm not from around here, Zeb," Annie said, leaning her elbows on the table. "So forgive me if I seem ignorant to local ways. But why do you dress like a Mennonite now when you are not a Mennonite?"

He sat back in his chair, placed his scone down on the napkin. "Some of my people were Mennonite. I admire their fortitude."

"So you are dressing out of respect for them?"

He nodded.

Detective Bryant coughed. Annie looked up at him and saw him looking like he was going to strangle someone.

"But that doesn't answer my question. There seems to be a group of people surrounding you, dressed the same way. What's that all about? Some kind of local tradition?"

He didn't squirm, twist a napkin, or start to sweat. He was cool, confident, and met her eyes. "Not really. We are a group of people that get together and hike and meditate, pay homage to our ancestors."

"Is that group open to anyone?" Annie asked after a

moment, then took a big gulp of her coffee. Damn, it was good. And damn, so was Zeb. He was composed, which made her wonder about how much he really knew. Perhaps he knew nothing. Perhaps it was true that this group of his just got together to hike and such.

"No," he said. "There are certain requirements."

"How about someone like me?" Annie asked, one eyebrow cocked. She just couldn't help herself.

He leaned back in his chair and grinned. "Now, Ms. Chamovitz, you know you ain't qualified. We are a non-Jewish group. If you wanted to convert, that's another matter."

"But I was born a Jew," she said, meeting his composure with her own. "Why would I want to do that?"

He flinched, just a half second. He wasn't used to being challenged.

"Why would that stop me from joining you to meditate and hike?" She gave him her best smile. "I don't understand."

"My, my, my," he said. "You are certainly no shrinking violet."

It was good that he thought so, but her heart was racing, and even though she didn't like to admit it, the fact that Detective Bryant was in the corner gave her a bit more courage. Still, her body was betraying her. Heart. Stomach. Sweat.

"Do you know that preventing me from joining on the basis of my religion is illegal?"

"It's not. We are a spiritual group, and you can only join if you believe the way we do. That's all."

"What is the basis for this group?"

"I didn't come here to talk religion with you," he said. "But if you want a primer on what I'm doing on the mountain, you're welcome to visit." He lowered his voice. "I'd love to *have* you," he said.

She was as surprised as he was at the loud smack of her hand across his face. He stood up, the detective standing behind him, and made for the door. Annie looked at her red hand as the stinging brought her attention back to the table. Had she just smacked Zeb McClain? A tickle stirred in her stomach, erupted as a nervous laugh.

"Annie?" DeeAnn said, coming from around the counter, opening her arms.

Chapter 45

So many bad memories at this hospital—starting with the loss of Vera's father over twenty years ago. It was just after they had upgraded and built a new wing, and her father was brought in for heart surgery, which was successful, but an infection set in quickly afterward. Then he was gone. Too soon.

Her mother's grief had scared her. Her own grief had shaped her life in ways she was only beginning to understand now, as a mother, and staring at midlife without a partner. Fear. Death. It had all shaped who she was. But even though she was alone now, Vera was finding it not so bad. What was she afraid of? Actually, she liked being alone. Of course it would be easier if Bill were sharing her life with her. But it wasn't worth the sacrificing of herself.

She held on to the baby she was carrying, felt its heat, smelled its newness. Nameless child. Motherless child. Fatherless. What kind of life would she have?

Vera looked at the doctor, who came toward her with a smile. A nice guy. But he wasn't the father of this baby. Nor was she the mother.

Yes, she hated this hospital. And she hated giving the baby back to the doctor and the staff there. She had no blood tie to this child. Still, her heart broke as the doctor took her from her arms. Suddenly they felt cold and empty.

"Is it okay if I visit from time to time?" she asked the doctor, holding back tears.

It wasn't her baby, she told herself. Her own child was with Beatrice today. But still, once she became a mother, her heart seemed to open even more to children and babies. She knew the love that each child brought into the world. *We are born with such a capacity to love. What happens to us?*

"I don't see why not," the doctor said, smiling, revealing deep dimples on either side of his mouth.

"What will happen to her, Dr. Green?"

"Call me Eric, please," he said. "And I don't know. Once we figure out who the father is, things might start to fall into place. The mother's family appears to not want the baby. The police are still looking over the security tapes, and the DNA tests are still pending."

"I hate the thought of her going into the system," Vera said. She handed him a business card. "Can you call me if you get a chance, if there's a break in the case? Or . . ."

He read the card. "So you're a dancer."

"Sort of. Now I teach. Have my own studio," she said. "Speaking of which, I better get going. Nice chatting with you."

"Likewise," he said, flashing a smile.

Wow. Was *he* a handsome man. Why hadn't she noticed that earlier this morning—or before? What a beautiful, strong jawline he had and the warmest brown eyes. She was certain he was the same doctor who operated on her mother last year.

She worked her way through the long, shiny-floored corridor and hit the elevator button. She should probably take the steps, but she was in a hurry. And she was teaching two dancing classes this morning. That would be plenty of exercise.

The elevator doors opened, and a couple of Mennonites exited. The woman didn't look her way at all. The young man looked at her and smiled. His blue eyes met hers right before he exited. Now, where had she seen him before?

She finally made it to her car through the maze of cars in the parking lot and glanced in the back at the infant car seat. It was a good thing she'd kept that. She sat behind the wheel and thought about her lesson plans as she drove to the studio.

The man in the elevator had left her with an uneasy feeling—but where would she have run into him before, and why? She switched on the radio and kept driving.

As she drove, she thought over the course of events this morning and wondered if Bill was still sleeping it off on her couch. She hoped he'd be gone by the time she returned. She briefly thought of Tony and wondered how he was doing, feeling a twinge of longing. It would be another few weeks before she could get up to the city to see him. He had promised a special evening, which aroused her curiosity.

She walked into her studio, thinking of Tony, the baby, and the Mennonite man she saw on the elevator, and remembered. *Aha.* He was the young man who had helped change their tire the day they were up in Jenkins Hollow. What was his name again? She suddenly felt sick. Luther. His name was Luther.

Chapter 46

When Annie reached into the cloth bag and pulled out the scrapbook, she felt a sudden stinging pain. She pulled back her hand. "Damn," she said as she looked at her bloody finger. Paper cut. Very deep.

After running cold water over it, she found the antibiotic cream and Band-Aids—a chore in itself in her disorganized house. Finally, she sat down at her table with a cup of coffee and the scrapbook that she'd heard so much about. She quickly flipped through it, the book opening to the center-page layout. The left-handed page was a key to the meaning of runes, which were drawn in black on the gold paper. Annie ran her fingers over it. It almost felt like cloth, it was so smooth, and the paper weave was so fine. What kind of paper was this?

Looking over the drawings and handwriting, Annie had to agree the scrapbook looked artistic—not something a newbie had done. She flipped the book around. It did say "Cookie Crandall's Scrapbook of Shadows." So it *was* Cookie's book. *Hmm.*

She went back to the centerfold and untied a ribbon that was on the opposite page. It was wrapped around a shimmery button that had a moon face on it. She unwrapped it and lifted the paper. It was a pop-up—

intricately cut, painted colorfully. A mountain range. Flowers. People. Trees. Cows. Horses. And caves cut into one of the mountains. There was a small bubbling in the paper, and Annie ran her fingers across it, found a slip of paper tucked between the page and the pop-up.

She pulled it out carefully—the paper seemed brittle and yellowed. She unfolded it to reveal beautiful script written in cobalt-blue ink.

The Legend of Starlight Mountain

In the deep ravines of the three mountains, which look like sleeping sisters, is a cavern where energy shifts and warps. This place is a gathering spot and has been from the beginning of time. People have sat together in the hollows, in the warm pools of water, on top of the mountains, and have journeyed together.

The Lady of Starlight walks here. She is the guardian, caught in a web of time. Caught in dreams. She is a woman of heart, spun with beams of moon, stars, and sun.

Lovely. Annie folded the paper back up and slid it into its socket. Evidently, Cookie was a writer, too.

She was mesmerized by the pop-up. It was so precise. She thought of the charming legend and looked at the mountains. What would this story have to do with Cookie? Anything? Or was it a flight of fancy from a creative mind? And why would it be in her scrapbook of shadows, which Annie thought was a sort of spiritual journal for witches. She gazed at the pop-up and thought she saw a sparkle of light coming from the biggest mountain. *So charming.* She reached inside and felt a tiny, hard object and pulled it out. A clear, shiny rock. Calcite? Annie held it up to the light and reveled in the beauty of the light shining and reflecting from the little stone. She placed it back inside the paper mountain and closed the page, wrapped the ribbon around the button, and turned the page to find more cobalt blue.

What was this? She ran her hands over it—a plush velvet pocket stitched perfectly onto the page. She could almost see why her friends were suspicious, given the perfect stitches, the gold-embroidered pentacle, all placed on a scrapbook page. It took skill she didn't know Cookie had. But still, that didn't mean she killed those young women—or that she tried to kill the baby. Annie slid her fingers inside the pocket and pulled out several objects. A delicate yellow feather. A bit of lace. A cameo pendant. The pendant looked old, Annie thought, but she wouldn't know. And another envelope—milky-yellow vellum. Inside the envelope was a strand of bright red hair, some rattlesnake skin, and a tiny claw. *An owl's?*

Annie's hands opened, and the envelope drifted to the table.

She turned the page to find two new pages made of old, slightly frayed silk. In the center of the left-hand page was another document made of some kind of parchment. She opened it, and it splayed out like an accordion with pockets. Inside each pocket was a card. Annie had seen tarot cards before, but these were exquisitely hand-drawn and painted cards, and she was unsure that they were indeed tarot cards. But still, there was something similar about them and the tarot cards she had seen.

A beautiful young woman kneeled over a creek in the first drawing. The water and rocks shimmered from a special ink. The word *Star* was scrolled across the card. Annie counted seven tiny crystals glued onto the card, which definitely looked like little stars. Two urns had been drawn on either side of the woman, who was dressed in a three-tiered hippie skirt. Annie turned the card around. On the back of the card, it read:

I am refilling this pool so that those who are thirsty may drink, and I am also watering the earth so that, come spring, the seeds will grow. Come. Drink. The water tastes wonderful, like liquid starlight. Follow your star and have hope.

Evocative. Annie had never paid much attention to things like tarot cards. Were they all like this? Or was this a special deck? These cards must be special to Cookie. There were only five here. Weren't there supposed to be whole decks? *Hmm.*

The next card represented the moon. The drawing showed a huge full moon against mountains and sky. Two wolves were in the foreground and appeared to be howling, heads turned up, mouths open. They were standing next to a stream. Annie turned the card over and read it:

Here are the dark mysteries you seek—the most primal and ancient powers. Poetry, art, and music stem from this terrifying, alluring place. Don't lose yourself in this desolate, primal land of madness and illusion. Trust the river. Trust the moon. Harness the power. Don't get pulled under.

Interesting and kind of scary, though why should Annie feel fearful of a card?

The next card was blue, white, and black and read "High Priestess" across the top. Were those pomegranates . . . or apples? *Hmm.* A woman had been drawn there with a crown on her head, which was a beautiful trinket embellishment—a crown with a crescent moon etched into it, attached to a veil. Only her eyes were visible on her face. Lotus flowers. Pillars. Scroll. She turned the card over:

> *Knowledge; instinctual, supernatural, secret knowledge. Behind the curtain a path leads to the deepest, most esoteric and secret knowledge. Possible illumination.*

The next card was the hermit, which Annie had always assumed to be a male, but the drawing clearly depicted a robed woman carrying a lantern. It was sort of a plain card. She turned the card over and read:

> *Introspection, analysis, and virginity. A desire for peace and solitude. Always out wandering and searching.*

Which reminded Annie of the story she'd read earlier about the wandering woman. What was that line again?

> *She is a woman of heart, spun with beams of moon, stars, and sun.*

These cards did say something about Cookie. She felt alone. But it was her choice. And she had a purpose. But what was it?

There was only one card left, and it was the chariot. It was so full of images that Annie's eyes didn't know where to look. Chariot. Armored warrior. Sun. Moon. MapsSphinxes. Lions. Horse. A canopy of stars. Annie flipped the card over.

> *Struggle. Obstacles. Movement from one plane to the next (water to land and back again)— conscious and unconscious, earthly and spiritual.*

> *It succeeds by attacking from the side, rather than*
> *straight on. On the one hand, loyalty and faith and*
> *motivation, a conviction that will lead to victory*
> *no matter the odds. But the chariot can also signal*
> *a ruthless, die-hard desire to win at any cost.*

Since this book was a spiritual book of a sort, Annie wondered if what Cookie thought she had was a purpose. It was clear that she meant to achieve it.

Annie placed the cards back in the paper pockets.

It all rolled over in her mind. If it was true that Cookie picked the cards to place in her book because they had some meaning to her, it made sense. But exactly what was Cookie's mission?

On the opposite page was a deep berry-brown booklet, similar to the document made of parchment in that it folded out like an accordion. On the front page of the booklet, written in silver, was the word *charms*. She lifted the booklet slightly—the sleeve of her sweater had gotten caught beneath it. A manila envelope slid onto the floor. She reached down to pick it up, and the sound of the school bus's squeaky brakes at the end of the block snapped her to attention. Had she been sitting here all day? Where had the time gone?

Chapter 47

Even though it wasn't Saturday when the croppers received Annie's call, they all decided to meet in Sheila's basement. Even though it was last minute, Sheila laid out a bit of a spread of snacks.

"I've been looking at Cookie's scrapbook of shadows," Annie began as the others gathered around, glasses of wine in their hands. Plates of cheese and crackers were sitting on the table.

"And did you get something in your eyes?" Vera asked.

"No," Annie said. "It made me wonder if any of you know anything about Cookie's scrapbook of shadows. I mean, what has she told you about it?"

DeeAnn shrugged. "The only thing she said about it to me is that it was like a witch's journal. They keep notes and such in them."

"I think that's all I know, too," Sheila said.

Paige nodded in agreement.

"That's pretty much what she told me, too," Annie said. "And that all makes sense . . . except for this. I found this tucked in it."

"What is it?" Paige asked,

"It's an envelope full of clippings."

"About what?" Sheila asked.

"About this town. About Jenkins Mountain and the hollow," Annie revealed.

"And look at this," Paige said, reaching into the envelope. "A brochure about the caves."

"Oh, that's just the public ones," DeeAnn said. "Not the good ones. They're too distant."

"And here are some clippings about Luther," Annie said. "She either knew him before she came here or researched him after. It's all pulled from the Internet. Turns out he was a brilliant medical student in Pittsburgh, then lost his family in a car accident and never went back to school. Get this. His mom was a linguist, and his father was a physicist."

"Well, well, well," DeeAnn said. "Isn't that something?"

"Here's a census report," Sheila said. "About the town, what the median income is, what the agricultural crops are. There's a lot of information here."

"Cookie researched this area before moving here," Annie said.

"That's not unusual," Paige said, then bit into a hunk of yellow cheese.

"No," Annie said. "But with all the stuff in her scrapbook and now this, I'm beginning to think that Cookie came here for a reason."

"What do you mean?" Paige said.

"I have no idea what I mean," Annie said and smiled.

"Like a spy?" Sheila said, her eyebrows lifted.

"What would she possibly be spying on us for?" Vera asked and waved them off.

"Not us," Annie said. "Someone else. But who? Luther?"

"Oh!" Sheila said as DeeAnn tipped over a glass of wine onto Cookie's scrapbook.

They scrambled around to save the open page with the

painted photo of the beautiful auburn-haired Victorian woman.

"Shoot," DeeAnn said when the page came off in her hand.

"Let's put it up on the window. Maybe if the sun gets to it . . . ," Sheila said, but as she placed the page on the windowsill, she noticed something odd about it. "Well, I'll be. There's something hidden beneath the picture."

Sheila carefully pulled out two folded slips of paper and unfolded one.

"A map," Annie said.

"A gorgeous hand-drawn map," DeeAnn said.

"It's Jenkins Hollow," Paige said. "There it is. . . . I don't know what all this is."

"That's beyond the hollow. I've never visited that way. Who knows what's beyond the ridge?" Sheila said.

Annie reached for the other slip of paper and unfolded it. "Lady Jenkins, four generations."

"What?" Paige said. "Could she be a Jenkins, as in—"

"This looks very Victorian," Sheila interjected. "I guess if she were four generations from the original Mary Jenkins, it might make sense."

"But why would Cookie have her picture?" Annie said.

Chapter 48

Beatrice listened to her daughter ramble on about Annie finding clippings in Cookie's scrapbook of shadows and then about seeing Luther at the hospital and calling the police on him. By the time they arrived, he was gone. So they were heading to Jenkins Hollow to try to find him tomorrow, just for questioning.

"He may be perfectly innocent, but I swear, that day he gave me the creeps, when I saw him standing there at the hospital. And Bryant did tell us, if we saw anything out of place, to let him know. And yesterday Annie found all these clippings about him. I think he's certifiable."

"Good work," Beatrice said. "Let's hope it means something. Let's hope it gets Cookie out of jail and that justice is served." She smacked her lips.

"Mother, are you eating? You know I hate it when you eat on the phone," Vera said.

"Land sakes, can't a woman have a bite while her daughter's mouth goes a mile a minute?"

"Oh, Mom," Vera said. "You can be so rude."

"I'm old, and you're my daughter. Why do I need to be polite? Besides, these peanut butter cookies are to die for. I love them warm out of the oven," she said.

"We'll be right over," Vera said. "Don't you dare eat them all."

Beatrice smiled and sat back in her rocker. Vera was easy. It was so joyous to see her daughter eat after all these years of dieting. A few years back, she just stopped and gained about twenty pounds—and she filled out beautifully. Beatrice would never understand the desire for extreme thinness. Ed used to say that he liked to have something to hold on to.

But when she thought of thinness, she thought immediately of Cookie, who had said she ate as she pleased, but never seemed to gain an ounce. She wondered how she was faring with jail food, given that she didn't eat meat and liked only local, organically grown food. She and all the other townsfolk had been eating locally for years. Now it was a movement. That always made Beatrice snicker. Still, it was a good movement.

She rocked and looked out on the gray skies. Thank goodness for the fall. The summer was way too hot. Very little enjoyment in that. Before she knew it, it would be Thanksgiving. She couldn't believe how fast time was moving.

Time. Ah yes, Beatrice had pondered the issue of time her whole life, but the older she became and the less of it she had, the more she thought about Richard Feynman's theory of time reversibility. *Quantum electrodynamics. Oh, let it roll around in your head,* Beatrice thought. She loved those words.

Richard's assistant, Jewel, had called her one night to discuss his "diagram," which represented the interaction of two particles as the exchange of a third particle.

"Let me run this by you, Bea," Jewel had said.

She remembered the day perfectly. Vera was sitting on her lap. She had the flu and was burning up with fever. Ed was making a few house calls and would be home shortly.

"Time is on one axis and space on the other, and the interaction is viewed as happening both in forward and in reverse time," she'd said to Beatrice. "Do you have it pictured?"

"Hold on," Beatrice said, reaching around Vera for a tablet on the phone stand. She drew the diagram as Jewel spoke.

"An electron on its way from point A to point B can bump into a photon, right? You can see that it can be drawn as sending it backward not just in space, but also in time. Then it bumps into another photon, which sends it forward in time again, but in a different direction in space. In this way, it can be in two places at once."

She hadn't understood it right away. Then she'd seen the paper on it, and it clicked.

So theoretically, if photons behaved this way, one had to wonder about bigger objects. Like people. Ah, if she could go back in time, would she? There was no doubt in her mind that if she could figure out a way, she would go back to when she had just married Ed. Just to experience the newness of their love once again. She'd always love the man—even if she was attracted to another man. Love was love.

And would she go forward in time? *Hmm*. She didn't think so. If she had to be without Ed for the rest of her life, she'd choose here and now and Vera and Elizabeth.

Chapter 49

Saturday night at Sheila's crop Vera was thinking about the hummus and the freshly made pita she was eating. Fresh pita made by an expert baker, Vera thought, was so much better than what was in the stores.

"Damn, this is good," Sheila said after a bite of the pita dipped in the hummus.

DeeAnn leaned across the table and picked up a piece of the flat, round brown bread. "Thanks," she said.

"I like what you're doing with your book," Paige said, leaning over DeeAnn's shoulder. "I've always wanted to do one."

"What are you doing?" Vera asked.

"I'm making a scrapbook of recipes, stories about the food, and pictures of it. Even have some pictures of people," DeeAnn said. "Like, look at this. She's my grandmother, and she's holding the peach pie that I have the recipe for. And there was this story about the neighbor's dog getting into the pie one day. She left it on the windowsill, and the screen had a little tear in it. Somehow that dog ripped the screen and got ahold of the whole pie!"

"What kind of dog?" Sheila asked. "Big?"

"I think it was part German shepherd and part

wolf, and it was huge. In those days, there were wolves everywhere—or at least it seemed like it," DeeAnn said.

"I think that the idea of a scrapbook of recipes is a good one," Vera said. "Your kids will love that. Someday."

"Someday is right," DeeAnn grumbled.

The sliding glass door opened, and Annie walked into the room quietly. Everyone muttered hellos, barely looking up from their projects. Paper and pens were scattered all over the table, along with ribbons, lace, and glue. Plates of cake, hummus, bread, pretzels, and cookies sat in between the scrapbooking supplies. There was a cleared spot. Annie's spot. Next to it was Cookie's spot, also empty.

"Hey," Annie said, dumping her bags on her chair and walking to the refrigerator. She pulled out a beer and opened it with a hiss. She set the bottle down on the table after taking a drink.

"Just so you all know, I'm back from talking with Bryant. The police have yet to find Luther," she told them. "Evidently, they think they saw him in the security tapes. He might be the one who kidnapped the baby. And when Vera called, they were already out looking for him."

"Those hills go deep out there, and the people are not apt to be helpful to the police," Paige said.

Sheila piped up. "And there's caves, too. I remember going in some of them when I was a kid."

"Mama has always talked about those caves," Vera said. She shrugged. "I'm sure the police know about them."

"I'm surprised you're not with them," Sheila said and looked at Annie.

Annie looked surprised. "Why would I be with them?"

"To get the story, of course," Sheila answered, setting down her glass of wine.

"I'd rather not go out to those mountains," Annie said. "Sorry, but it scares me out there. I've got a family. A husband. Two boys." Her voice caught in her throat. She cleared her throat. "I've got too much to lose by walking into a possible trap of weirdos out in the middle of nowhere. "

"Oh, Annie, they're not all like that," Vera said, her heart beating faster. Annie looked away, into her box of photos. "Besides, the police are there. I'm sure they'd protect you."

"I don't know about that," Annie said. "I don't know if they are capable of it."

"Well, now," DeeAnn said, "I'm sure they'd try."

"Two girls dead. Obviously, whoever is doing this has nothing against killing people," Annie said. "And then there's Zeb."

"You let him have it," DeeAnn said. "I don't think he'll be bothering you again."

"Don't be so sure," Annie said.

Vera wanted to change the subject. She was increasingly uncomfortable with these murders, and she was uncomfortable with Annie's dilemma—that she was Jewish in this small community and seemed always to be fighting psychic battles, even some very physical ones. Always having to be ready when the questions came: Why don't you celebrate Christmas? Why don't you come to our church? And now her boys had to fight battles that no child should. Religion should not be used as a way to divide people. Vera had stopped going to church years ago, when the gay issue came up.

"How is Ben doing?" Vera finally said.

"He's fine now," Annie said. "Though I'm not sure he'll be fine for the whole time he's in school."

"Where are the parents of these other children?" Sheila almost yelled.

"The kids are just spouting their parents' viewpoints,"

Annie said, setting out her scrapbook. "Those views seem to be more popular than I imagined."

"I don't believe it," DeeAnn said. "I don't believe that the people in the community hate witches, or anyone, for that matter. I mean, here we are. We disagree all the time. We're all of different backgrounds. And we set that aside."

"Not everybody feels the way you do. I mean, look at this business with Cookie. Don't you think some of us here at this very table suspect her because she's a witch?" Annie said.

"Now, hold on," Paige said. "It has nothing to do with that. It has to do with that book. I don't give a hoot if she's a witch or a wizard. Facts is facts."

"What about the person? Not the book. Not the religion. The person!" Annie said.

The room was silent, except for the music playing.

Sheila turned the music up a bit. "I love this song."

"Nice beat," DeeAnn said, and stood to dance around a bit at her chair. She was a large and curvy woman. Watching her move to the music was like watching the earth move.

Vera laughed. "You missed your calling!"

When the song was over, and all had calmed down, Annie cleared her throat.

"I brought the scrapbook," she said quietly. "Does anybody want to see it again?"

Chapter 50

Annie pulled a few of her own pages, as well as Cookie's scrapbook, out of her bag. "Here it is."

"Well," Vera said, "I've already seen it."

She continued to sit in her chair while the other women gathered around as Annie sat the book on the table at Cookie's spot, placing her own pages-in-progress in front of her.

"By the way," Paige said, "I looked up Mary Jenkins to see if there were any traceable progeny. It doesn't seem like it. I still need to check census records. So I have no idea who that woman in the picture is."

"It's odd that you couldn't find anything. I mean, you know so much local history," DeeAnn said. "Now, this book is amazing," she said, turning back to Annie.

"It's remarkable," Annie said. "I've never seen anything like it. There's a beautiful pop-up. A story. A blue velvet pocket. Silk pages. Books within books. A bunch of stuff."

DeeAnn folded her arms. "It's hard to believe that Cookie could work any of that stuff. She could barely cut a photo out when she first started."

"I know," Annie said. "It's odd. There must be an explanation. But I can't get in to see her."

"Neither can Bill half the time," Vera said.

"What?" Sheila squealed. "He's her lawyer."

"She doesn't want to see him," Vera said and shrugged.

"Oh, look at this, this recipe tag, with these moon embellishments," DeeAnn said.

Paige reached her hand to the page and felt the tag. "So smooth and rich," she said. "Recipe for mugwort tea . . . hmm. Look at the beautiful ink and lettering."

Annie's attention shifted to her own page. Ben's soccer page. His sweet face looking at her from the page. She was considering where to place the soccer ball sticker.

But Sheila's innocent words stuck in her gut.

I'm surprised you're not with them. . . . To get the story, of course.

What had she turned into? When she lived and worked in Maryland and D.C., she covered several dangerous stories—everything from a cocaine ring to a dogfighting ring. Those were some dangerous men. Sure, she was a little afraid, but she was smart and figured they were not. She outsmarted them every time with her careful research and methods. Why was this case any different?

"Isn't that beautiful?" Paige said, pointing to a page.

"Beautiful and strange," DeeAnn said. "How did she do that? Get that color?"

"She painted the paper and the photo," Sheila said. "Interesting."

"There's a strand of red hair in the blue velvet pocket. I'm assuming it belongs to the woman in the picture," Annie said. "Whoever she is."

"Hmm," Sheila said, barely paying attention. The three of them were immersed in the scrapbook, with all its beauty, its weird images, and information.

"What did you think, Annie?" Vera said from across the table.

"When I first saw the strand of red hair, it startled me. I immediately thought of the dead girls," Annie said, then took a long drink of her beer.

The women mulled over the clipped red hair and sat silently for a few moments.

"Have you tried the hummus?" Vera said to Annie.

"It's good, "Annie said and went back to her page.

Yes. She had always been a good journalist. Careful with her facts and research. Willing to take calculated risks. But maybe this risk was too much. There was a murderer out there—a troubled person, carving runic symbols into young redheads, perhaps painting them on houses, someone who perhaps had it in for her and her family simply because they were Jewish. There was that mysterious call. Then Beatrice's house being painted. But it had started before then—the day she'd driven Beatrice out to Jenkins Hollow and she'd seen the swastika on a barn. Since then, Detective Bryant had told her it was more than kids playing pranks. Hadn't he?

She thought about her grandparents and the people they knew who were in the Holocaust, and an overwhelming sense of awe came over her. How did they survive? What kind of strength and fortitude did they have? What was her problem? Why couldn't she face this ignorant group of locals?

"My God," DeeAnn said. "Is that Elizabeth?"

"What?" Vera stood up. "Where?"

"Here, in this picture."

Vera walked around the table. "Yes. It's a picture of Cookie with Elizabeth."

"It's so odd-looking," DeeAnn said. "Look how old it looks." She held up the picture.

"Oh," Sheila said, "you can age any picture with the right techniques."

"Sure," Vera said and sighed. "But I wonder what this picture is doing in this scrapbook of shadows."

Sheila shrugged. "Oh, you know Cookie isn't the most organized person. It could've come from anywhere."

"Wow," Paige said. "Look at this pop-up. Amazing."

"That's exactly what I thought," Sheila said.

"You know, from this angle it looks like our mountains," Vera said.

"What are you talking about?" Annie said.

"You know . . . I think you're right. Look," Paige said. "The center mountain is the shape of Jenkins Mountain. This looks like the hollow. And here is the cave. . . ."

Annie's stomach churned, and the hair on the back of her neck stood up, something it had done only a few times in her life.

"Okay," Vera said after several minutes of utter silence, each woman deep in thought and looking at the scrapbook. "It's a model of a section of the local mountains. So?"

Just then Annie's cell phone went off. *Damn.* When she saw the call was from her editor, she momentarily thought of not picking up. "Excuse me, ladies. I have to take this."

"Annie Chamovitz."

"Annie, this is Steve," her boss from the paper said. "How are you doing? They find him yet?"

"I don't know. I don't think so. The last I heard, they were looking for him in the mountains."

"And?"

"And what?"

"Is that where you are?"

"No. I'm at a friend's house. It is Saturday night and—"

"Listen, Annie, should I send someone else?"

"No, of course not," she said. "It's just I'm not sure I

have to be on the ground for this. If they find him, Bryant will let me know."

All the women were now looking at Annie.

"Are you kidding me, Annie? I want you on that guy's case. Maybe I should send a staff reporter. I want us to be the first one on this story."

"That doesn't make sense. Murder in a small Virginia town? That doesn't make headlines in a Washington paper, even online. You need to tell me what you know, or you can find someone else to cover this. And you can bet your sweet ass they'll get lost for days up there."

Her friends' eyes widened.

"Okay," he said after a minute. "We've gotten an anonymous tip that there may be some major drug trafficking moving in and out of that area. You in?"

"Now you're talking, and I'm on my way," she said, hanging up the phone and gathering up her things. Should she call Mike, wake him up, or just wait to fill him in tomorrow?

"I'll put on a pot of coffee," Sheila said.

"I'm going to call Mike and tell him I'll be late," Annie announced.

"What are you doing?" Vera said. "You're not—"

"I'm going to Jenkins Hollow. I need to be covering this story," Annie said.

"Tonight?" Vera said. "I don't think that's a good idea."

"Why not? The cops are up there tonight, still looking for Luther," Sheila said, switching on the coffeepot. "Let's all go. We'll be safe. Now, go call your mom, Vera. Tell her you'll be late."

"She has Lizzie for the night. I don't need to call her. They are probably both sound asleep."

"You don't have to come, Vera. None of you need to come. I'll be all right. This is my story," Annie said, thinking that it was time she followed her gut instincts.

From the minute she met Luther, she'd felt ill at ease. She'd allowed her fear to get in the way. What was she turning into? She'd been seriously sidetracked by trying to prove that Cookie was innocent.

"Are you kidding?" Paige said. "I know those mountains like the back of my hand. You don't. You're going up there to get lost. I won't have it. I want to get to the bottom of this as much as you do. Besides, this is exciting. I wouldn't miss it. I'm always up for an adventure." She closed her scrapbook and then reached for her purse.

Chapter 51

Beatrice couldn't believe her ears. "Come again," she said.

"Beatrice," Bill's voice said on the other end of the phone. "It's Cookie. She's asking for you. Look, I didn't want to mention this to Annie or Vera or anybody. But Cookie is not doing good. She's not eating, and she's lost weight. I've tried talking with her. All she will tell me is that she didn't kill those girls. She won't open up to me at all."

"But why me?" Beatrice said.

"I don't know. But can you do it? I've talked to the police, and they will let you see her tonight."

"I have Elizabeth tonight, and she's here asleep. I can't wake her. How about tomorrow?"

"Nah, I've gotten special permission for tonight. They won't extend it for tomorrow. How about I come and stay with Elizabeth?"

"Well, okay," Beatrice said. "I'm glad to help."

But now, as she sat across the table from Cookie, Beatrice sort of wished she hadn't come. *Thin* wasn't the word. She was emaciated. Had she eaten or slept at all? She almost didn't even look like herself, even as she managed to give Beatrice a little smile.

"Cookie, dear, you must eat something," Beatrice said. "You look awful."

"Bea," she said, her voice barely a whisper, "we don't have much time, and they are watching us, you know? Let's not waste it with you lecturing me. I simply have no appetite. You have to believe me. I will be fine. But you need to listen to me with an open heart and mind."

Beatrice was slightly taken aback by Cookie's candor. She didn't look like she could sit up, let alone put a sentence together. Still, Cookie's delicate beauty shined through, with her scrubbed-clean face and those intriguing green eyes of hers. In fact, she was much prettier this way. But how could she look so tired and hungry and still be beautiful? Beatrice wondered. Even the young woman's bony fingers held a certain beauty in them.

"Okay," Beatrice managed to say, still feeling confused as to why she was there. Why hadn't Cookie called one of the other women? She tapped her fingers on the table. "What's up?"

"Bea, I've wanted to tell you things from the start. There's never been a right time. . . . But your research into quantum physics and time . . ."

Beatrice focused. Cookie was speaking her language. But it was surprising.

"In a way, it's what brought me to Cumberland Creek, along with the huge calcite deposits in the mountains."

Calcite? How odd. Vera had dreamed about the stuff, and now Cookie had mentioned it again.

Beatrice knit her brows. "What do you mean? My research has been out there for years. And still has yet to be proven. Also, most physicists think I'm a twit."

"They are wrong."

"How do you know? What are you? Are you a scientist?"

Cookie laughed. "Of a sort. But I want you to look at me, Beatrice." She lowered her voice even further. "We come from the same bloodlines. It's all I can say right now."

A fire lit in Beatrice's brain. *Quantum physics. Same bloodlines.*

"Are you a time traveler?" Beatrice blurted out.

"Oh dear, I thought I could explain this to you, but you're getting the wrong idea," she said and smiled. "I suppose you could think about translocation and invisibility like time travel. But it's not time travel—more of a shifting from one plane to the next. Yes, it has happened that I've gained or lost a year or two . . . but it's not time travel as you imagine it. Part of my ability has to do with the calcite. My robe is made from it, which helps to make it look like I'm invisible. You can read about that. Just a few articles out about it. But there's so much more to it."

Beatrice sat back in her chair. Had she just heard that? Was she having another crazy dream? Some sort of episode?

"Invisibility? Time travel?" Beatrice managed to say, while feeling the blood drain from her face. Was this young woman mad? One of the reasons time travel had yet to be accomplished was that even though they were somewhat successful with quarks and other subatomic particles, there was always a change at the molecular level. Too dangerous for people. Beatrice knew that.

"It's not exactly safe . . . or easy. We are still working on that. And let me reiterate. It's not really spiritual time travel. It's more of a shift between—"

"Jesus," Beatrice said. "It can't be correct. It can't be

that you are one hundred percent okay and are traveling through time. It has disturbing relevant—"

"It's going to take you some time to sort through everything I've just said to you and decide whether or not to believe me. I know it sounds crazy. Maybe it would be better for you to think of it as magic. In any case, we need to act quickly."

"Act?" Beatrice said, sitting forward on the end of her chair.

"I'm in trouble here. I need to get out of here, and you can help me."

"First, I'm expected to believe you are from the future or are time traveling or something. Then I'm told my theory is correct, just a little off, and now you want me to help you escape?" Beatrice pushed her glasses back on her nose. Damn, she would have to get them fixed again.

Cookie nodded and met her eyes.

Beatrice was finding it all hard to believe, but then again, why not? She'd never believed in ghosts before she lost her husband, and yet she'd been haunted by him for years. She had believed with all her heart that waves of time could be penetrated, manipulated, traveled through—and here sat, perhaps, living proof. But Cookie, of all people? On some level it made sense. She was so different from anybody Beatrice had ever known—the kind of difference that she'd normally pooh-pooh. But there was an underlying quality to her character that Beatrice found compelling and likable. Now it made a strange kind of sense—especially if they were family. Or was Cookie just disturbed?

In either case, Beatrice decided to go along with it. What the heck. It couldn't hurt. What else did she have to do?

"First, this is the most important thing. You have to promise not to tell anybody," Cookie said.

"Oh."

"I've kept your secret about your boyfriend. Will you keep this one?"

"Sure," Beatrice said. "It's too bad, though. There's a couple people I'd like to call and rub their noses in it."

"Be patient."

"Well, okay," Beatrice said reluctantly.

"I have the robe made of calcite, so that's taken care of on my end."

"What? How?"

"One side of the fabric of my robe is a calcite compound. The other side is a terry-cloth robe. This is technology that is known about now, but there's more to it than what the general population knows. Anyway, they let me have it here. This isn't a high-security prison."

"Oh, right."

"There's a book on my closet shelf at home. A scrapbook of shadows. You need to get it," Cookie said.

"Oh dear," Beatrice said. "Hmm. I think Annie has it."

"Damn," Cookie said. "I hope you all don't mess with it much. It's a powerful book that also works with the calcite. But, listen, can you get it?"

"Sure. Why not?"

"I just need for you to get it and take it to a spot on . . . What do you call it now? Um, yes, Jenkins Mountain."

"What? How can that help?"

"It has a device in it that will open a portal of energy for me. Can you do it?"

"Sure. But don't you need to be there?"

"No, I have a matching device implanted in me." She pulled back her hair and pointed to what Beatrice would have thought was a suspicious-looking mole.

"Oh."

"It doesn't matter where I am. Its energy will be enough for me to get home," she sighed. "You've got to be very careful, Bea, to see that nobody catches you or takes the book before you have it in place."

"Why?"

"Because a group of people at Jenkins Mountain are messing with this. The group at the Nest is creating dangerous rifts, but they don't know how to manage it. If they figure it out, there will be big problems. This book is the key. You must guard it."

Beatrice's heart leaped. This was getting more interesting—and more strange—by the minute.

"There's one more thing. If my calculations are correct—and they usually are—you have three days."

"Three days?"

"Yes. Everything has to be just so. The moon, the season, the planets. Everything aligned."

"I think I can manage that. But, Cookie, what about you? Will you be okay? You look dreadful, I'm sorry to say."

"I'll be okay. I've been here before, believe me, and suffered the consequences. I know what I need to do. I just need to get that book to the cave," she said. "You know the one I mean."

Suddenly Beatrice knew exactly what she meant. A crystal-clear picture came to her mind. A cave deep in the hills, one she used to play in as a child sometimes. She and her cousins played house there. Pretended it was a castle, with its calcite crystal walls. Goodness, she hadn't thought about that place in years.

On the drive home, it occurred to Beatrice that they hadn't even discussed the murders for which Cookie was being held on suspicion. Lord, she was exhausted. Here she was, out at ten o'clock on a Saturday night. Well, since she was up, she'd stop by the crop at Sheila's to see if she could get the scrapbook from Annie.

When she pulled up to the basement side of the house, she noticed that Vera's van wasn't there. *Snack run? Beer run?* It was too early for Vera to go home. Beatrice slid open the sliding glass door, and all the lights were on—but nobody was there. Had they all gone to get some food? *How odd.*

She poked around on the table. *Plenty of food here. Drink, too.*

Then she saw the scrapbook of shadows sitting on the table.

Good. One problem was solved. She placed it under her arm and dashed out to her warm car.

Chapter 52

By the time the four women found the center of the police search, it was close to midnight. Vera was glad for the coffee she had downed on the way to the hollow. She'd forgotten both how tiring it was to drive these windy roads and how dark it was in the hills. There were no streetlights. They passed the middle of the Nest, where the church sat, and there was one streetlight in its parking lot.

"There's some lights up ahead," DeeAnn said. "I bet that's where the search is."

"The question is, what's taking them so long? They've been up here for days," Paige said. "A bunch of cops can't find one man? Something is wrong with that."

"Maybe they are looking in the wrong place," Annie said as they approached a roadblock.

"Jesus," Vera said under her breath. "Now what?" She rolled down her car window as a fresh-faced police officer approached. "What's going on?" she said and smiled sweetly.

"Don't I know you?" the officer said, looking at Vera. "Aren't you Beth's dancing teacher?"

"Why, yes, I am." She flashed her best smile. "Your daughter is just the sweetest thing. And talented, too."

Impatient sighs from the backseat.

"What are you doing up here?" the officer asked.

"We brought Annie Chamovitz, you know, the reporter. She needed a ride."

He looked over at Annie, and his smile faded. He nodded. "Nobody's allowed past this point, I'm afraid. Not even reporters. We're on a manhunt. Can't have you underfoot."

Annie pulled out her identification and showed it to him. "Can you get Detective Bryant? Is he here? I'm sure he can vouch for me."

The officer's face hardened. "Detective Bryant gave me orders. You ladies need to turn around."

"Now, hold on," Annie said. "Here's my press pass, my ID. This is my story. I've been working on it for weeks. I have high-security clearance."

"Ever hear of obstructing justice?" the officer said. "Ladies, I can't let you through."

"It's okay," Paige said from the back. "I'm tired and want to go home."

Vera knew Paige was lying through her teeth just by the tone of her voice.

"Sounds good to me," Vera said. "Sorry to trouble you, Officer."

"But—" Annie began to protest. DeeAnn reached up and pulled her hair. Annie whipped her head around and looked at her. "What the— "

"I'm warning you," the officer interrupted. He looked at Annie. "No shenanigans."

Vera started pulling away to turn the car around. Annie mumbled in her seat after they had pulled far enough away.

"I ought to whip your butt for pulling my hair," Annie said to DeeAnn.

"I'd like to see you try, honey," DeeAnn said, and they all laughed. "Besides, you may want to be a little more respectful of me. Since we're here, I'm going to show you a place where we might be able to look down over everything. All the police hubbub. I doubt they know about it. And if you're lucky, the stars will be out tonight. Now, it won't take long. I know the back roads."

"Back roads? You mean *this* road isn't a back road?" Annie said.

"No," DeeAnn said. "It does have a little pavement to it."

Annie rolled her eyes. "Good God."

"Turn left up here," DeeAnn said.

"Left?" Vera said, straining to see. "Oh yes, I see. Are you sure? It looks like a cow path."

"It is," DeeAnn said. "But you can drive it."

"I hope so," Vera said, looking over at Annie, who was holding on to the dashboard to keep from sliding around but had a huge grin on her face.

The road bumped and twisted. Trees, bushes, and grass barely made way.

"Thank God I filled up the tank," Vera said.

"We won't be driving much longer. You see that old barn up ahead? That's my husband's Uncle Josh's barn. Um, er, at least it used to be," DeeAnn said. "You can pull up right there. We need to get out and walk the rest of the way."

"Walk?" Paige said, pulling her blond hair behind her ears. "I'm not sure I've got the right shoes for walking far."

"We may not have far to go," DeeAnn said, unbuckling her seat belt. "Just up the hill a little ways there's a great view."

"What on earth would we do if we ran into one of the murderers?" Vera spun her head around to look in the backseat.

"What are the chances of that?" Annie said. "I'm

more concerned with bears and bats and God knows what else. This doesn't seem very safe."

"Of course it's not," Sheila said. "It's an adventure. You in?"

Annie grinned. "Do you have a flashlight?"

Vera couldn't believe it. "Annie, are you crazy? You know what these people are like. Why would you go out in the mountains this time of night, in the middle of what is a dangerous manhunt, surrounded by a group of weirdos and bears? What on earth is wrong with you people? I'm not going anywhere. And I suggest you don't, either."

"I'm with you," Paige said, crossing one of her long legs over the other one. "I'm not dressed for a midnight mountain hike. My feet are already killing me from these new shoes. Lunatics, all of you. I think we should go home."

But even as she said those words, DeeAnn, Sheila, and Annie were getting out of the van.

"Listen, if we are not back in an hour, just follow that dirt path right there. You see?" DeeAnn pointed to a barely there trail surrounded by undergrowth and looming trees, which cast long shadows. "And be quiet if you come up the trail. You don't want to scare the bears," she said, pulling out a flashlight.

Chapter 53

Annie's heart was pounding so hard that she could hear it in her ears and she wondered if the lumbering DeeAnn could. Evidently not. She pushed on through the brush and the weeds, with a fit Sheila right behind her. The moon was shining brightly, and they could see their way through the shadows of the trees and rocks, saving their flashlight batteries in case.

The rock path snaked ahead of them at a steeper grade. An owl screeched into the night, and Annie jumped at the sound of thrashing leaves. She grabbed on to Sheila, who was right in front of her on the narrow path.

DeeAnn turned and looked at her. "It's okay," she whispered. "Just an owl."

Annie swallowed hard. *Just an owl. Okay.*

"The caves are not much farther," DeeAnn whispered. "Just up around that hillside. Can you see it? I tell you, the cops don't know their way around up here."

"Yes," Annie said, looking up and suddenly feeling off balance, though she kept going. Her feet tangled beneath her, and she fell on her knees, narrowly missing Sheila as she plummeted to the rocky ground. "Damn," she whispered. "Ow!" She sat on her behind.

"Annie, are you okay?" Sheila said.

"I took a bit of a fall," she said. Her jeans were torn, and her knees were stinging and bleeding.

"Can you get up?" DeeAnn asked and leaned over to help her stand.

"Oh yes, I'll be fine," Annie said, but she struggled to stand and, man, it hurt to walk. She'd just have to take it a little slower.

"Shh!" DeeAnn suddenly said, crouching down. "I hear voices."

She pulled Annie and Sheila behind a large boulder.

The only thing Annie could hear was animal sounds—the owl again, night birds—and she thought she smelled something like smoke. Was it smoke?

DeeAnn still held her finger up to her mouth. Sheila looked at Annie, wide-eyed, wild haired.

First, Annie heard the soft thump of a foot on the ground, then the definite rattling of rocks sliding around underfoot, then the voices. Definitely male. Definitely coming closer. From the same direction in which they were heading. The hair on the back of Annie's neck stood at attention. Maybe Annie's clumsiness and aching knees had saved the day. Maybe. But these men, now just visible, coming down the hillside, dark figures outlined in the simple lines of Mennonite hats and coats, were heading straight for the van if they kept on the same path. *Shit. Now what?*

The men stopped a few feet from the boulder.

"I can't believe how well the calcite boulders are working," one man said. "I mean, you hear about these theories, but to see it working like that? Unbelievable."

"I just wish we could've gotten this side of the caves done before all the sacrifices were made and the law came up here. I hated that we had to do that."

Sacrifices? Did Annie hear that right?

She looked at DeeAnn's wide eyes, noting that the rest of her face was wrapped in a green wool scarf, her eyebrows lifted, holding back panic. The men were heading down the path. They didn't speak as they went by the women crouched behind the boulder. Annie didn't breathe. DeeAnn didn't move. Sheila was biting her lip. It was as if time stood still. Each of them was thinking the worst and afraid to make a move.

DeeAnn whispered, "They are definitely not cops."

"No," Sheila said.

Annie had tried to get a good look at the men's faces, but it was too dark—even with the moonlight so bright. The trees all cast long, menacing shadows, and the men were dressed in black, with hats on their heads. Too shadowy. It seemed like they were not far from where the police actually were. How could these men be so close and not be found by them? What were the calcite boulders they were talking about?

Annie turned and leaned back quietly on the boulder. Her knees were killing her.

"What are we going to do?" DeeAnn said.

Annie thought a moment. "We are going to have to follow them back down the hill. They are heading for the van. Who knows what they will do if they see Vera and Paige?"

"*If* they can actually see," Sheila said, pointing to the clouds moving across the moon. A gentle breeze was circling and shaking the leaves on the trees. Leaves scattered around them.

DeeAnn stood up and offered Annie her hand. "Let's go," she said, pulling Annie to her feet.

Annie marveled at DeeAnn's strength. *Bakers and their arm strength,* Annie mused.

Sheila was already up, with her hands on her hips.

They walked as slowly and as carefully as they could, mindful of the noise level. The wind blowing around leaves helped. Annie tightened her scarf around her neck and buttoned her hood for more warmth. Was it getting colder, or hadn't she noticed the mountain chill before?

Annie had learned a few tricks over the years to keep her mind calm and cool and thus prevent herself from panicking. She took some deep breaths and looked around. So many of the trees had already shed their leaves that twisted branches were all that she could see as she headed down the path. Such interesting shapes, too. A nearly perfect five-pointed star. A pointy witch's hat. The outline of a bird.

All of a sudden, DeeAnn's arm snapped in front of Annie as she heard a loud sound, like a rocket or a single firework, and something stung her and rippled through her back. Sheila flew off to the side of the path and into a bush as Annie's body lurched forward onto DeeAnn, who cast her off like she was nothing more than a kitten. Annie, lying facedown in the dirt, waves of searing pain moving through her back, tried to lift her head but could twist it only far enough to see, through blurring, heavy eyes, DeeAnn knocking someone to the ground. What was going on?

Don't pass out, Annie told herself. *Don't pass out. You need to write about this.*

Chapter 54

It was 4:00 a.m. when Beatrice's phone rang.

"This better be good," she said into the phone.

"Mama," Vera's raspy, tired voice said. "I'm in jail."

Beatrice sat straight up in bed. "What?"

"Bill's not answering his house phone or his cell phone. He needs to come down here to the jail."

"He's here," Beatrice said. "I'll get him up. We'll both be there."

"No, you need to stay with Lizzie. Please."

Beatrice could hear voices in the background.

"All right, all right," Vera said haughtily. "I'm getting off the phone."

"What on earth?" Beatrice said.

"It's DeeAnn, Sheila, and Paige. They need to call their husbands, and these police are just the most impolite group of people I've ever seen. Obstruction of justice, my hind end," Vera said.

"Where's the fifth musketeer?" Beatrice suddenly wondered out loud.

"Oh, Mama. She was shot. She's in the hospital." Vera's voice cracked. "They won't tell us a thing."

"Shot?" Beatrice said. "Annie was shot? What nonsense were you into tonight?"

"I have to go. Bye." *Click.*

Beatrice struggled to get her old body out from the tangle of blankets. She reached for her robe. Never thought she'd see the day that she'd be waking up her ex-son-in-law to go bail her daughter out of jail. *Obstruction of justice?* So, that was why they'd all left the crop. They were out messing around with the investigation. *Good for them.* The police didn't seem to be getting anywhere. But then again, apparently, neither were they.

Bill awakened quickly and was out the door before she knew it.

"Now, don't dawdle," she yelled after him. "I need to get over to the hospital and see Annie."

He turned and looked at her. "What?"

"Annie was shot," Beatrice told him.

"What were they all doing last night?" He flung his arms out in exasperation.

"Your guess is as good as mine," she said and shut the door to keep the cold air from getting into the house.

She walked into her kitchen and went straight for the coffeepot. After she wrestled with it and got the coffee brewing, she sat at the table. There was Cookie's scrapbook of shadows, with its shiny metallic cover gleaming in the dim light. *Damned thing.* Now Beatrice had to figure out how to get it to the mountain, to the cave, to the exact rock—the diamond-shaped rock inside the first passage.

She still considered Cookie's story. Wasn't sure she believed it. But just in case, she'd do her part. In the meantime, she remembered she had some egg custard pie in the fridge and decided to finish it off. Fortification and comfort all in one smooth, sweet, creamy pie.

She knew she had a hell of a day in front of her. Her daughter was in jail. Annie was in the hospital, and her nephew was coming to pick her up around noon. She'd called her cousin Rose to ask her to help her out with the scrapbook. Rose never came off the mountain, but her sons did, and one of them would happily come and get her for a visit. She'd packed her bags before going to bed last night.

She could trust Rose. She'd promised Cookie that she wouldn't tell anybody. She knew that Rose would help her and not ask many questions. After all, Beatrice had done the same for her. They were family. The bonds were long and deep.

By the time Bill came back, Lizzie had eaten her breakfast and was watching *Sesame Street*. Beatrice was pacing the floor when her daughter walked in. Of course, she went right to Elizabeth and loved her up.

"Mama, miss you," Lizzie said. "Dad, miss you," she said, lifting her arms to her father.

"Want to go in the backyard and swing?" he said.

She squealed in delight.

"There's some muffins on the table," Beatrice told her daughter. "You look like hell."

"Thanks for staying with Lizzie," Vera said and wandered into the kitchen. "Thank God you've got coffee."

"Of course," Beatrice said. "Have a cheese muffin. Want me to make you some eggs?"

Vera sat at the table and drank her coffee, reached for a muffin. "Mama, what's that doing here?"

"I wanted to look at it," she replied. "Now, what happened last night?"

Vera told her mother what she knew. "Paige and I were sitting in the car, and we heard the shot. We took off up the path and ran smack into Zeb and Luther. The next thing we knew, the cops were there—"

"Where?" Beatrice asked.

"They followed us."

"What about Annie?" Beatrice said.

"I called the hospital on the way home, and she's in critical but stable condition. Some man shot her. Nobody knows who he is. Not Zeb. Not Luther. But they do have him."

"How did they get him?"

"DeeAnn strong-armed him, knocked him down, and he hit his head on a rock."

Beatrice couldn't help but smile at the thought of sweet, round-faced DeeAnn pushing the shooter to the ground. *Well, if that don't beat all.*

Chapter 55

Vera canceled all the classes at the studio for the next day. *Damn.* She hated doing that, but her assistant was on vacation, of all weeks. But she could barely crawl up the stairs to bed at her mother's house—she was certain she couldn't teach dance.

"Where are you going?" Beatrice said.

"To bed. I'm exhausted."

"I'm leaving at three. Who will stay with Elizabeth?"

"I'll go into the office and wrap up some things. I can be back by then," Bill said.

"Make sure you are. I have plans," Beatrice said.

"Where are you going?" Vera said.

"I'm going to spend a few days with your—"

The doorbell interrupted her.

Vera wondered if she'd make it up the stairs—and if she did, if she'd actually be able to sleep. She turned around and started to go back down the stairs, just in time to see her mother open the door and clutch her chest.

"Jon!" Beatrice exclaimed.

What? Who was Jon? She rushed toward Beatrice to see a striking silver-haired man standing in the doorway, dressed impeccably in a dark blue suit, suitcase beside him, flowers in his hand. He reached out for Beatrice; then they kissed each other like Europeans, once on each cheek.

"Jon! I can't believe you're here. What a surprise," Beatrice said, pushing Vera out of the way as she led him into the living room.

"Bill, can you get Jon's bag?"

Bill had Elizabeth on his hip, and both he and Vera looked bemused as they stood looking at this dapper gentleman holding Beatrice's hand as she led him to the couch.

What on earth was going on here?

Lizzie slid down her father's body, and he went to get the bag and she went to her grandmother's side.

"This is Lizzie," Beatrice said, introducing them. "Lizzie, this is Jon, a friend of mine from Paris."

"Hi," she said shyly.

"Pleased to meet you, mademoiselle. Your grand-mama has told me so much about you," he said with a slight French accent.

Lizzie buried her face in her grandmother.

Vera cleared her throat.

"Oh," Beatrice said, as if she just remembered her grown daughter was in the room with her. "This is Vera, my daughter."

Vera came forward to where Jon stood, placed her hand in his, and shook it.

"Very nice to meet you. The dancer, yes?" he said.

His smile spread across his attractive face. High cheekbones. Lovely olive complexion and soft, heavy-lidded brown eyes that sparkled as they met with Vera's. So this was why her mother never talked about Paris.

Vera nodded, unsure if she could actually speak to this charismatic man, who was obviously as taken with Beatrice as she was with him. She'd never seen her mother glow like this.

"This is Bill," Beatrice said.

Bill stretched his arm across and shook his hand.

"The husband," Jon said.

"Ex," Beatrice said.

"Oh, I'm sorry," Jon said.

"What are you doing here, Jon?" Beatrice said, delighted, after he sat down.

"I wanted to surprise you!"

"Well, you have," Beatrice said and sat down.

"Besides, I was a little concerned that I'd not heard back from you."

Vera sat in the closest chair she could find. She could sleep later.

"I'm sorry, Jon. I've a very busy life. And lately, it's worse than ever. We've had a series of murders in town, and it's pretty crazy."

"Murders?"

"Nobody we know, yet, but a friend of ours is a suspect. We've been trying to prove her innocence."

"I see. So busy that you can't e-mail me?" he said, smiling.

Vera watched her mother awkwardly finger the button on her sweater.

"Look, Jon, do you think I sit around on the computer all the time? Besides, I have gotten back to you . . . once, I think. Right?" Beatrice squirmed a bit on the couch, wrapping her arm around the unusually still child sitting next to her.

"Yes, once." He shrugged. "Anyway, I'm here now, and I've a room over at the Blackberry Inn."

"I've got a room here you can have," Beatrice said.

Vera sank back into her chair.

"Stay here. There's plenty of room," Bill said.

Vera shot him a look of reproach.

"I insist," Beatrice said. "After all, I stayed at your place in Paris, and it was so nice."

Surely not, thought Vera.

"Well, okay," he said.

"Great! But there's one problem," Beatrice said. "I have plans to be out of town until tomorrow. Will you be all right alone?"

He sighed and looked at Bill and Vera. "I've come all the way from Paris, and this woman, she still makes me wait for her."

Chapter 56

Annie vaguely remembered the bumpy ambulance ride. Good thing there was already an ambulance close by. Mostly, she remembered wanting to sleep and the paramedics asking questions over and over again: What's your name? What's your birth date? Do you have any children? What are their names? Ages? Turned out that was a technique to keep her awake—because not only had she been shot, but she had also suffered a concussion from DeeAnn and Sheila trying to pick her up and get her to the van, then stumbling over themselves and dropping her. Annie was glad she didn't remember that at all. But it was a weird feeling to have only spots of memory about an incident. She hadn't even realized she was shot until she was in the ambulance.

"No," she'd managed to say. "Not shot. I just . . . just . . . fell down . . . again."

The paramedic had laughed. "No, honey. You were shot in the back."

Mike was asleep in the chair beside her when she opened her eyes. Where were the boys? She wanted to wake him. She reached for him and found she was heavy with wires and tubes. Her arm fell back down on the bed. Her eyes felt heavy, and she closed her lids to the murky depth of a fitful sleep, where she dreamed of giant Mennonites chasing rabbits and Hasidic Jews dancing around a bonfire. At first the heat drew her in. God, she was so cold. Then the firelight mesmerized her—the way it flickered and shapes would move around within the center of it. A bird. A witch's hat. A star. But the light started to hurt.

"Annie?" Mike's voice called out to her.

Where was he? She looked around the bonfire, didn't see him.

"Annie!" he said, touching her.

She opened her eyes to the harsh light. She squinted.

"Does the light bother you?"

"Yes," she managed to say with a dry mouth.

She watched him close the heavy curtains.

"Sweetie?" he said as he came back to her bedside. "How do you feel?"

"Thirsty."

"You can have some ice," he said, turning around and reaching into a bucket. "No water yet. You just came out of surgery, you know. They don't want you getting sick."

"Surgery?"

"Yes. They removed the bullet," he said, then placed an ice cube in her mouth.

It felt so good, so cool and wet. Such a relief on her dry, thick tongue.

He smiled. "You know a lot of guys would never imagine saying that to their wives. I've imagined it a thousand million times."

She chewed the ice, relished the feel of the cool little chunks sliding down her throat. "Sorry," she said.

"I'm just glad you're okay," he said, his voice cracking. "I thought moving here . . ."

"I know," she said with a sinking feeling. "Where are the boys?"

"With Sheila today. They want to see you, but let's, ah, give it one more day," he said.

"What's happened? I don't remember much."

"Everybody is safe, though your friends spent some time in jail," he said.

Annie smiled. She couldn't imagine.

Mike placed another ice cube in her mouth.

"The police had a couple of men at the station. The guy who shot you claims you were trespassing, so they let him go." He rolled his eyes. "The police will be around soon enough to see if you want to press charges and all that. But I figure that's hopeless. They are still questioning this Luther character, though, last I heard from Bill," he said.

"Luther? But what about Zeb?"

"They questioned him and let him go."

"What about Cookie?"

"Nothing. You can't do anything but rest now," he said. "So I wish you would."

Man, her head hurt. She looked around the room and suddenly saw all the flowers.

"Flowers."

"Yes. How about that?"

"Oh, look at those beautiful yellow roses," she said.

"Yes, those are from Beatrice. She dropped them off on her way out of town."

"What? Where's she going?"

"To stay with her cousin Rose."

"Rose?" Annie said. Damn, her brain ached, and it felt like there was cotton in it. Who was Rose? Why did that strike a chord with her? *Oh, damn!* Beatrice was heading up to Jenkins Mountain! What was she up to?

Annie tried to sit up.

"What are you doing?" Mike said, gently pushing her back down.

"When did Bea leave?"

"A little while ago. Why?"

"I think she's heading up to Jenkins Mountain."

"So?"

"She's up to something."

"You know what? She probably is," Mike said and smiled. "But it's not your problem. You can't do anything about it. You just got out of surgery. Got it?"

Annie's brows knit as she nodded, not meeting her husband's eyes, unable to get the image of Beatrice, with her handgun, traipsing around Jenkins Mountain out of her achy, fuzzy brain.

Chapter 57

Rose had insisted over the phone that Beatrice bring her new friend with her. "We've plenty of room here," she'd said. "You can't leave him alone with Vera. She'll make mincemeat of him with all her questions."

Beatrice had agreed, so she and Jon made the trek up to the mountain, driven by Samuel, Rose's youngest son. Jon was tired from his flight and napped most of the way. Beatrice didn't mind. Bluegrass music filled the car, and she relaxed and let the music lift her spirits even more. Samuel had never been much of a talker, so the trip was mostly scenery and music, which suited Beatrice just fine.

When they arrived, Rose had laid a table for them. They ate a late supper of wild turkey, mashed potatoes, green beans, pickled okra, and biscuits.

"I've not had wild turkey in years," Beatrice said. "I've forgotten how good it is. How different."

"It's a magnificent feast!" Jon said, lifting his wineglass. "My compliments to the cook!"

"Thank you," Rose said, blushing.

Beatrice laughed. She took another bite of her gravy-soaked mashed potatoes and swore she couldn't take another bite of anything, until Rose brought out a pumpkin pie.

"Made from pumpkins out of the garden," she said, smiling at Beatrice.

"You know me. That's my favorite. Lord, I can barely stand canned pumpkin these days," Beatrice said.

Jon's eyes grew wider. "I've never seen this kind of pie before."

"You're in for a treat," Beatrice said.

While Jon was working on his third piece of pie, Beatrice sipped her tea, more satisfied than she had been in quite some time. Homemade mountain cooking from her cousin always soothed her. But this time was different. She looked at Jon, and a warm rush of acceptance came over her. Now she felt able to admit how she felt about him to herself. He and Rose had taken to one another like family already. The food of home, the good company, and the surrounding autumn hills, trees ablaze in crimson, gold, orange. Yes, she was home.

"How is the murder case going?" Rose asked her.

Beatrice filled her in.

"And Cookie?"

"She is still in jail, as far as I know. Speaking of which, I have to take care of something for her tomorrow. I promised I'd take this scrapbook of hers and place it in the caves. It's going to help her somehow."

"Really? That's an odd request."

"You'll have to trust me on this. Maybe someday we can talk about it. But for now, I can't tell you much more than that."

Rose's gray eyes lit up as she lifted her eyebrows. "I love those caves. We had such fun there as kids. Remember?"

Beatrice nodded, looking at her cousin, a few years younger than herself, wrinkled, a little hunched over, with heavy lids, but still Rose as a girl was in Beatrice's memory as clear as day. She still had the same smile, the same mannerisms. Beatrice thought about how time was not a friend to our bodies—but to our spirits, if we were lucky, it was the best thing.

"You know, there are all sorts of stories about those caves," Rose noted.

"I sort of remember . . . ," Beatrice said.

"The creek that runs underneath them, along with the calcite, and their exact coordinates make it a wonderful place for meditation, prayer, ritual. We used to have the best midsummer rituals there."

"Do you go there often anymore?"

"No," Rose said. "I've stopped. A few years back a new group started holding rituals and things up there. Moving rocks around. Taking too many herbs and plants and not reseeding. Bad energy." Rose was a practitioner of what was frequently called PowWow, which was a combination of old German wisewoman beliefs and Christianity, blended with Native American precepts. Rose saw no irony in this belief system. It made sense to her to blend it all together.

"What do you mean?" Beatrice asked.

Rose shrugged. "I used to go up there and collect herbs and mushrooms. The mushrooms stopped coming. The herbs left there are not quality. I've found evidence of ritual, but not earth-friendly ritual. They leave their trash. Also, the calcite is disappearing."

Interesting. Didn't Cookie mention calcite?

"Will you stop mincing words with me? What's going on up there?" Beatrice said.

"It's a group of people who call themselves the New Mountain Order. Zeb McClain has set himself up as some kind of guru. I don't know what they are up to. Some folks say they are Mennonite. Some say they are pagan." She stopped and looked at Beatrice. "But they are neither," Rose said.

"How do you know?" Beatrice said, feeling a little scared now about taking Cookie's beautiful scrapbook up there and leaving it. She had said. 'You've got to be careful, Bea, to see that nobody catches you or takes the book before you have it in place'."

"I was talking to some people about them. What they are doing is making up a religion based on some other religions. They claim they are going back to their German roots and practicing an old Germanic paganism called Asatru. But they seem to be blending some Mennonite precepts into it and, from the looks of it, neo-Nazism," Rose said.

"It's stupid young people wasting their time," Beatrice said.

"Oh, Bea, I wish that was so," Rose said. "But there seem to be new people coming here as their 'followers' all the time. And they know enough about magic and the elements to be dangerous. Lawd, have mercy."

Cookie's words came back to Beatrice. Cookie was telling the truth. . . . At least this part of her story held up.

"Magic? Humph," Beatrice said.

"Call it magic or call it prayer. Call it whatever you want."

Beatrice's brain clicked. "Do you think these folks would know anything about the baby? Or the murders? You know, that Luther boy was questioned, and his DNA was taken to see if he was the father."

"Land sakes, Beatrice, everybody up here knows who that baby's father is. It's Zeb."

"What? He's old enough to be Rebecca's father!" Beatrice sat back and crossed her arms.

"And that's who she was living with, off and on, during her pregnancy."

"Why don't the police know this?"

Rose sipped more of her herb tea. "I should think

they do by now. All they'd had to do was talk to anybody in Jenkins Hollow about it."

Beatrice sighed. There was Annie and Vera and all the scrapbook club trudging around on the mountain the other night, among all these crazy people! They could've been killed. Oh, the stupidity.

The next morning the alarm went off at four. Beatrice was loath to rise from her bed of quilts, but she could smell the coffee brewing and was hoping for a piece of pie before they went up to the caves. Sure enough, Rose had the pie there—along with biscuits, gravy, and scrambled eggs.

Beatrice was grateful for a full stomach and a thermos of herb tea as they took off through the woods. She was surprised to find that Jon kept up with two old, strong-legged mountain women. It was a slow and steady climb compared to their youthful jaunts.

Once, while taking a break and sitting on a boulder, Jon looked out over the quickly fading fall-colored landscape and marveled at the beauty of it. "No wonder you never want to leave here," he said.

"I don't get up here often enough," Beatrice told him.

"C'mon, you two. Let's go," Rose said.

The caves were almost exactly as Beatrice remembered them, but the entrance looked smaller. Huge mountain laurels grew around the craggy opening. She found herself grateful that they'd not be going far inside today. When they were kids, they had no idea what dangers were inside. These caves were wild and not some tourist attraction.

Beatrice clutched the scrapbook as she watched Rose enter the cave opening. The caves had grabbed her by the heart from the first time she'd entered them.

As Beatrice grew up, she had learned about the mystical meaning of caves. In literature, caves represented many things—the womb, a place of safety and creativity, a sanctuary, a mysterious or unexplored part of ourselves. Of course, mythology was rich with cave references. Zeus was raised in a cave by Rhea. Somnus, the god of sleep, resided in a cave where the sun never shone and everything was in silence. And the great Oracle at Delphi was deep in a cave. Beatrice loved great stories—whether they were about myths, mathematics, love, or crystals.

"Every time I enter this place, I think of Jesus being buried in a cave," Rose said once Beatrice and Jon were at her side.

"That was more common than you think," Beatrice said.

"Many people worshipped in them. Before . . . anything . . . caves were recognized as the womb of Mother Earth," said Jon.

Beatrice smiled and turned back to look at him. She ran her fingers along the rocky walls and breathed in the cool, damp air. The three traveled together in single file, Beatrice in the center, until she spied the diamond-shaped rock.

She blinked hard. Was she seeing things, or did something give off a little spark? She remembered her murky childhood dreams of this place. She was often mesmerized by the sparks coming from the calcite that was all around and by the light from small openings here and there. It bounced and created an otherworldly effect, depending on the time of day.

"Here it is," she said. "The rock I need to leave this thing on."

She placed the shiny, thick book in the center of the dusty gray-brown rock and was relieved to have shed its weight. She glanced down in the ravine next to the rock. She'd dreamed about that spot, too, about falling into it. One of her mother's fears and admonitions.

"Shall we go a little farther?" Rose asked.

"Certainly," Jon said.

Beatrice hesitated. "Why don't you two go without me? I'll catch up or catch you on the way back."

Rose shook her head. "Now, Bea, we can't leave you here by yourself. Against the rules. You know that. We stick together."

Beatrice knew she would say that.

"Jesus, Rose, I've been coming up here since I was a child. I'm not going to do anything foolish. I just want to sit here with the scrapbook a few more minutes."

"I'm not going to argue with you. We'll stay together until you're ready to move on." She looked at Beatrice with a firmness in her jaw, which, Beatrice knew, meant she was resolved to stay.

"Suit yourself," Beatrice said, sitting on the ledge of a rock that was there. Jon sat beside her, reaching for her hand. She looked down at their hands touching like this. Such a human gesture. She thought about the generations that came before her and what the simple act of holding a hand could mean. She wondered who the first human was that discovered how important touch was to life. How important this one gesture was.

Yet she dared not look at her cousin, or else they would burst into fits of schoolgirl giggles. So she kept her eyes lowered. Then, suddenly, the sparks in the cave became more vibrant, and she lifted her eyes to see her cousin looking at them and smiling in awe at the little lights everywhere.

The light was bluish, then white, and it seemed to get brighter. All three of them were spellbound by the lights and shadows. It felt like time was standing still. Beatrice wanted to imprint this moment on her brain so she would never forget the beauty.

And just as suddenly the lights faded, and Beatrice swore she could hear something scuttling. A rat? A bat? A bear?

"I've never seen that before. In all the years I've been coming here," Rose finally said.

Beatrice nodded. "Me neither."

"Extraordinary," Jon said in a hushed tone.

Beatrice glanced at the diamond-shaped rock, where she'd placed the scrapbook. It was gone. Vanished. She walked over to the rock and ran her hands along it. Yep. Gone.

"What happened to the scrapbook?" Jon asked.

"Maybe it fell," Beatrice said, shining her light into the crevice. Even with the flashlight, it was hard to see, for the hole reached farther into the mountain than her light could reach. "I don't see it."

"Well," Rose said and placed her hands on her hips, "it couldn't have disappeared into thin air. It must have fallen. We can't do anything about it now."

Beatrice thought a moment. Could it be that everything Cookie had told her was true? Up until this moment, she had entertained the possibilities but hadn't exactly believed any of it. Did the scrapbook of shadows disappear into a time warp?

Beatrice shrugged. "I guess we will never know." As a quantum physicist, she was used to such conclusions and accepted them readily, but Rose was not and took off toward the entrance.

"Now, either someone took the damned book while we were stargazing or it fell. If someone took it, we damned well are going to find them," Rose declared.

When they came out into the open air, it didn't look like anybody was around. But Rose pointed to a boot print in the dirt. "Was that here before?"

Beatrice and Jon shrugged.

Chapter 58

"It's a damned shame they won't let us bring you any food," Sheila said, ignoring Mike's explanation of how the doctors wanted to keep Annie on a bland diet for a few days. "Everybody knows there's nothing that will make you heal faster than homemade food—even if you still are in the hospital."

"I agree," Annie said, smiling weakly and shrugging.

"They didn't say anything about booze, did they?" Vera said and smiled, pulling out a bottle of white wine from her bag.

"Now, wait a minute," Mike said. "Annie's on all kinds of medication. I don't think that's a good idea."

"When did you become such a party pooper?" Annie said.

"Since my wife was shot while she was on some damned foolish escapade," Mike said.

It could have been a mean statement, but it came out so softly and with such care that Vera found herself envious of his concern. But Annie didn't look pleased. Of course, she was not herself. Annie's surgery went well, but she still didn't remember a lot of what went on that night. Vera wished she could erase it all from her mind. She wished she could go back to Saturday night and talk them all out of going to Jenkins Mountain. None of them had realized the depth of the depravity they would be walking into.

Annie could have been killed. Shoot, any of them could have been. These people were not messing around. They probably had killed the two young women and tried to kill the baby. Lord, what had they been thinking, going up there?

"So . . ." Vera sat down on the bed. "How are you feeling?"

"Weird," Annie said.

"Uh-huh. Of course," Sheila said.

"Did you hear the big news?" Vera asked.

Annie shook her head.

"Mama has a boyfriend," Vera said, looking at her pink fingernails, thinking she'd need another manicure soon.

"Yep," Sheila said, pushing her glasses back on her nose. "And he's French."

"French?" Annie grinned. "Really? Beatrice?"

"I know," Vera said. "It's so out of character. But you should have seen her blushing and smiling and, um, sparkling."

"That's so wonderful," Annie said.

Vera frowned. "I'm a little worried. I mean, who is this guy?"

"Obviously, she met him in Paris and had a bit of a fling," Sheila stated.

"My mother has never had a fling in her life. My father was her only boyfriend, her husband, and she hasn't had any interest in men since he died."

"Maybe it's about time," Annie said. "Why are you so concerned?"

"I guess it's because I don't want her to get hurt," Vera said after a moment.

"There are no guarantees," Annie said. "But Beatrice can take care of herself."

"I hope so. It does explain a lot about her trip, why she's been so secretive. I'm going to investigate a little further."

"What is she doing on Jenkins Mountain?" Annie asked.

"She goes up there every now and then to visit with Rose."

"Is that all she's up to?" Annie said and yawned.

"Of course," Vera said, looking at Sheila, who was deep in conversation with Mike about soccer. "What else?"

"I don't know. I just thought it odd that now—after everything—she would choose to go up there."

"It's a big mountain," Vera said. But her stomach flopped around. "She won't be anywhere near where the investigation is."

Just then a series of noises erupted from the hallway and the door to Annie's hospital room flew open.

"Where is she?" Detective Bryant said.

Sheila stood; Mike walked stiffly around to the other side of Annie's bed; and Vera squealed, her hand clutching her chest.

"Whatever do you want?" Vera said, spreading her arms in Annie's direction. "Annie is right here."

"I'm not talking about Annie," the detective said, out of breath, uniformed officers coming in behind him.

"Who are you talking about, then?" Mike said. "I mean, really, barging into this room after Annie's surgery! What do you think you're doing?"

Detective Bryant shrank back into himself and drew in a deep breath. "Sorry, Mr. Chamovitz. We're looking for Cookie Crandall."

"Cookie?" Annie tried to sit up even farther in her bed, her hospital gown pulling on her. "What's going on?"

"Cookie is gone," the detective said.

"But I thought she was in jail," Vera said, her heart racing.

Bryant nodded. "She was."

"Then what are you talking about?" Vera said.

"She escaped from the jail," he said reluctantly. "We thought she might be here."

Vera's mouth dropped open.

'Well, now," Sheila said with a grin. "How did she manage that?"

Annie went white. Unfortunately, the detective noticed it.

"What do you know?" he said.

"Excuse me," Mike interrupted, "but I've about had enough of this. My wife has been in the hospital for two days. She knows nothing about where Cookie is."

"I'm sorry, Mr. Chamovitz. But this is a serious matter. We have a murder suspect who has escaped from jail. Could you or your wife—or anybody in this room—be harboring a fugitive?" The detective placed his hands on his hips, revealing his gun and his badge perched on his belt.

They sat in silence for a few minutes while the officers looked in the hospital room's empty closet, under the bed, in the bathroom.

Annie looked at Vera. "I'm sorry, Vera. But do you think . . ."

"What?"

"Do you think Beatrice knows anything about this?"

"What?" Vera said. "My mother? Oh no, I wouldn't think so." She shook her head.

"I wouldn't be surprised," Sheila offered.

"She loves Cookie. And Beatrice was the one visitor she would see. Remember?" Annie said.

"Why d-didn't I think of that?" the detective stammered.

"Well," said Sheila, "you're obviously not as bright as Annie."

Mike smirked. "Nobody I know is, Sheila."

Vera stifled a giggle while watching the detective's face turn all shades of red.

"C'mon guys. Let's get over to Ivy Lane," Detective Bryant muttered.

Annie, Mike, Sheila, and Vera sat quietly as they watched the police officers go. After they left, Vera reached into her purse for her cell phone. It was time for a call to Aunt Rose.

Chapter 59

Annie's head was spinning, but there was nothing she could do about it. She was stuck in a hospital bed and couldn't get up and go home on her own if she wanted to. But the truth was, she wasn't sure that she did. She felt terrible. Even with all the pain meds. She still ached everywhere, not just her lower back. When she tried to move her arm, it felt like she was moving through heavy water. Her head throbbed, and her mouth felt cottony. And, worst of all, her brain was foggy.

Amid all the turmoil, pain, and confusion, she was getting weird vibes from her husband. He was ticked off. Sure, he was kind and considerate and he loved her. . . . She was lying in a hospital bed. But he had also let her know that he wasn't happy that she was here. She never should have gone to the mountain—or at least she should have gone with the police. She knew that. So did her editor—also not happy.

She knew that Mike had grown tired of not having his wife around for days when they lived in D.C.—and of not knowing if she was safe. When they moved to Cumberland Creek, he thought that part of their lives was over. But Annie had gotten sucked into it again.

Nothing like a bullet in your back to shift your focus

back to where it belongs. Actually, the bullet was more in her ass—thank God it was good and fleshy there, or else there might have been some damage to her actual spinal cord.

She sifted through the memories of the past few days and shuddered. They still had no idea who murdered Rebecca and Sarah. The police were combing the mountains looking for someone, but who? And would they ever find them in the vast and dense geography that was Jenkins Mountain? She had some murky memories surfacing. Words like *sacrifice* and *calcite.* Was she dreaming? Was she remembering?

She wished she could turn over on her stomach to sleep. She managed to roll over on her side and look at the pattern on the wallpaper.

"Would you like the TV on?" the nurse said as she entered the room.

"No," Annie said.

The woman lifted Annie's arm and wrapped the blood pressure cuff around it. Then she took her temperature. "Your temp has gone up. Let's give you a little more Tylenol."

Annie downed the pills and curled back into a ball on her side.

Could Beatrice have helped Cookie escape? Well, why not? Maybe she sneaked something into the cell. What? A key?

How did Cookie manage to get out of the building without anybody noticing? The courthouse and jail were right smack in the middle of town. How could she have left without anybody seeing? Was it at night? Early morning? Damn that Cookie. If she were innocent, why would she escape from jail?

Just then someone entered her room. She could feel a breeze, looked up and saw Hannah, Rebecca and

Sarah's friend, standing by her bed. A smile spread across her face.

"Your story is all over the paper," Hannah said. "You're going to be okay?"

Annie nodded. "I'm too rotten to die. And you?"

She nodded. "But he's still out there somewhere, isn't he?"

"Yes. I'm sorry," Annie said.

"You are so . . . brave," Hannah said and sat down on the chair next to Annie's bed, reaching down to the floor for something. "I'm not sure I'd have gone to the mountain in the dark. And I live there."

"Brave or stupid," Annie muttered.

Hannah laughed, her face lighting up, beaming.

"You should do that more often. You're so pretty when you smile," Annie said. "Thank you for coming to see me."

"My parents are waiting for me in the hall. They thought it would be okay."

"You can come and visit me anytime," Annie said. "You don't have to wait until I'm shot."

"Lord willing, that won't happen again," Hannah said, suddenly serious. "You know, Rebecca was in the bakery late on the night she died," she said with her voice lowered. "When I left at ten, she was still there. It wasn't usual. She kept watching the clock, as if she were going to meet someone, and I caught her looking in the mirror a few times. I thought maybe she had a date."

"Did you ask?"

"No. I wish I had. I was in a hurry to leave. She said she'd close, and I left," she said.

"Thanks for telling me that," Annie said.

"I have to go." She stood and reached for Annie's hand, held it firmly. "I'm going to pray for you."

Usually, Annie would have some snarky remark

about that. But Hannah was sincere—she believed what she was saying had meaning to Annie and that it was the best thing she could do for her. Goodness emanated from this young woman.

As she turned to go, the nurse walked in the room, followed by two friendly-looking men, obviously not from the area.

"Mrs. Chamovitz?" said the nurse.

"Yes?" Annie sat up more.

"These doctors are from Eastern Psychiatric Hospital. They want to chat with you."

The nurse raised Annie's bed.

"What? Why me?"

"Calm down," the nurse said. "They're not here to evaluate you."

"Okay," Annie said, looking over at the doctors as they approached her bed. "How can I help you?"

"Thanks, Mrs. Chamovitz. I'm Dr. Greenberg, and this is Dr. Stanley." He pointed at the other doctor. "We, ah, sometimes work with the FBI on missing persons cases. And we received this e-mail today from the FBI."

He handed her a sheet of paper.

FBI Alert
Wanted: Cookie Crandall

Underneath was a picture of Cookie.

"What do you think? You know her, right?" Dr. Greenberg asked.

Annie didn't know if it was the news or if she was just feeling worse, but her stomach lurched and waves of heat emanated from her skin. She could barely nod. Was it Cookie all along? Had Cookie murdered those young women and tried to murder that baby?

She should have known it—between her weird scrapbook and all the other coincidences. . . . Annie should have known it. No. She wasn't thinking clearly. Cookie was not a murderer.

"We've just come from the jail and learned of her escape," Dr. Stanley said. "It's a pattern with her. She moves from town to town, gets into trouble, and escapes. She's brilliant. But quite dangerous."

"Dangerous? Cookie?" Annie said.

Dr. Stanley nodded. "Yes, she suffers from countless delusions. In lay terms, she has a split personality disorder, of sorts."

"I've spent a lot of time with her. I don't understand it. If she was that sick, why wouldn't I have picked up on it?" Annie said.

"Which personality did she use? The artist? The witch? The time traveler?" Dr. Greenberg asked.

The blur in Annie's head was taking over.

"I'm sorry. I'm not feeling very well," she said.

"Sure," Dr. Greenberg said. "We're sorry to bother you, but we've been here a few days already and we're heading out of town tomorrow. We wondered if you had any idea where she could be."

Beatrice, Annie thought, but shook her head no. Her head sank back into the pillow. She turned back to face the wall with its weird wallpaper. The patterns reminded her of those damned runes. *Women who cause trouble.* Beatrice had to know something about where Cookie had gone and how she got there. Annie was certain of it. But she was too damned tired to even speak.

Before she finally closed her eyes, one question formed in her mind: Did he say time traveler?

Annie dreamed of mountains and tunnels and caves. Runic patterns written into rock. Lights and shadows. Finally, Cookie, in what appeared to be the center of a cave, surrounded by beautiful waterfalls and rocks. She smiled at Annie, reached out and lifted Annie's chin.

Such a soft touch. Such a loving gesture. So much friendship and warmth.

How could Cookie have killed anybody? Was she mentally ill, like the doctors said? With these thoughts entering her dream world, Annie awoke with a start, surprised to find her face wet with tears.

Chapter 60

"There you are, Ms. Matthews," a tired-looking Detective Bryant said as he entered the small room at the police station. "You've led us on quite a little merry goose chase today."

"I did no such thing," Beatrice said, trying not to smile.

After the police had left the hospital, they had gone to her home to question her. Of course, she wasn't there. And after they waited around for a little while, they figured she was out and was not coming back. So, they called Vera to ask if she knew where her mother was. She told them she was visiting Rose. So the police went to Rose's house—an hour away from Cumberland Creek proper. And by the time they got there, Beatrice was already back home, having a nice hot bath while Jon was taking a nap.

"So where is Cookie?" the detective said, sitting down on the chair across from her.

"I don't know," Beatrice said, looking at him in the eye. And it was true. She was amused to find that Cookie had escaped from jail. She had no idea if it had something to do with the scrapbook she'd placed on the rock or not. But she was gone. Apparently, she'd left her clothes behind—except for her robe. So, if she had slipped into some kind of time-travel tunnel, she was out there running around in her robe. And if she was out on the street somewhere? Beatrice shuddered to think of the possibility. "I'm kind of worried about her. I mean, they told me she doesn't have clothes, just her robe. She could be anywhere. In trouble."

He looked at her and squinted. "I think you know more than what you're telling me."

"Humph."

"Ms. Matthews. This is a serious matter."

"I know that."

"Can you help me out here?"

"I can't. I've told you that I don't know where she is."

"How did she get out?"

"How would I know that? I've not been in town, even."

"You spoke with her the day before she escaped. And you were the only one she wanted to talk to."

He had her there. But still, she had no idea where Cookie was—or how she'd gotten out. Beatrice took a sip from the paper cup that held her tea.

"I don't know what you want me to tell you."

"Tell me what you talked about."

"That was a personal conversation. Now, I'm losing my patience. Where's my lawyer? I don't need your badgering, young man."

"Bill's on his way," he told her. Then he got up from his chair and left.

Beatrice took another sip from her tea. She was trying to contain herself. But she felt like bubbling over with the news of it. Of course, the only way Cookie could have "escaped" was if everything she'd said was true. The device within the scrapbook had worked and had allowed Cookie's "magic" to work for her escape. Her "invisible" robe had helped. All this, coupled with Beatrice's placement of the scrapbook in the cave, had provided an escape for Cookie. Somehow. That made Beatrice's heart and mind race.

Her years of study on time and the possibilities of travel through time and space were not wasted flights of fancy.

Bill entered the room, looked at Beatrice, and shook his head.

"What's going on, Beatrice?"

"They think I helped Cookie escape."

"Did you?" he said, eyebrows lifted, hands on his hips.

"Oh, for God's sake," she said.

He sat down. "You talked to her the day before she escaped. Did she say anything?"

"Bill, what Cookie and I talked about . . . it was personal," she said, tripping over her words. She was lying to Bill, her lawyer and her ex-son-in-law. For the first time a pang of anger shot through her. *Cookie!* She had placed Beatrice in an untenable position.

"I know you very well, Beatrice. If you're not going to be honest with me, maybe you should hire another lawyer," he said.

Beatrice squirmed in the seat. Of all the things she was, a liar did not top the list. Lying to the police and lying to her lawyer, even if he was just Bill, was serious business. But she certainly could not tell him the truth.

"I'm hungry," she said at last. "You got anything to eat? One of those chocolate bars you carry around?"

He dug around in his jacket pocket, pulled out a chocolate bar, and handed it to her.

After fooling around with the wrapper and finally opening it, Beatrice took a bite and looked up at Bill, who was watching her intently. Well, there was nothing they could do to Cookie now. And most of them already thought she was a half-crazy old woman.

"Bill, the only thing I know is that Cookie asked me to take a book up to the caves in Jenkins Mountain. And I did that. When I came back, she was gone."

"A book?"

"Yes. Her scrapbook. She called it her scrapbook of shadows."

"What does that have to do with anything? Christ, Bea, you could be in a lot of trouble. Do you want to spend the rest of your life in prison?"

"Just because I took a scrapbook up to the cave?"

"You didn't bring anything *in* to Cookie?"

"No. Like what? A key? How would I get a card key?"

Bill stood up and paced the room. "I think the police are pretty certain she had one. They've been looking at the security tapes, and it looks like she, uh, just opened the door."

"Looks like?"

"Actually, the film skipped. They see parts of it, but not her actually taking a card key and sliding it into the door. One minute she's there, and the next, gone."

"Interesting."

"I'd say."

"So . . . ," Beatrice said, clearing her throat. *Damn, this chocolate is pretty good.* "Have they looked at the security tapes from when I was there?"

"Some problem with those tapes, too," he said.

Beatrice cackled. "Virginia's finest."

He nodded. "They've not brought charges against you yet, Bea. But I'm afraid they will. They are going to try to prove you helped her escape. This is quite an embarrassment to them. They need someone to pin it on. You know?"

"I'll be damned if it's going to be me," she said, smacking her lips.

Chapter 61

Vera pulled into the police station parking lot.
Honestly. These police have no manners. Why would
they hold a soon-to-be eighty-two-year-old woman for
questioning about Cookie's escape?

Just then, through her rain-splattered windows, Vera
saw a police car pull around the corner of the lot. It
looked like it had a crowd in the backseat. Vera couldn't
resist. She sat in the car and waited. The police were
bringing in three Mennonite men. All of them were handcuffed. She couldn't see their faces. They were keeping
their heads low and were wearing wide-brimmed hats.
Who were they? It was so odd to see Mennonites in
handcuffs. Vera collected herself and looked in the
mirror. Her hot pink lipstick was still in place. And she
loved her new chestnut-brown hair color.

She grabbed her umbrella and opened the car door
and clumsily tried to manage her umbrella and her bag
in the downpour and the wind. When she entered the
station, she placed her umbrella against the wall. Her
feet had still gotten wet, and she hated the feeling.

"Can I help you?" the man behind the counter said.

"Yes. I'm Vera Matthews. I'm here to collect my mother, Beatrice Matthews," she said.

"Just a moment." The man turned and said something to another officer who was sitting at a desk.

The three Mennonite men were walked back into the corner, where Vera couldn't see them.

"I'm sorry, Vera. Your mother is still being questioned," the officer said. Vera and this particular officer, Dan Reynolds, had gone to high school together. His daughters had danced at her studio for years.

"Can I see her, Dan?" Vera said.

"I don't know, Vera," he replied. "I'm not sure what's going on back there."

"Well, it's just Mama," she said and smiled.

"I think it would be okay for you to go back, Vera. Go ahead. It's the second door on the left. I'll let them know you're coming," he said and turned to the phone.

"I'm sending Beatrice's daughter in to see her," Vera heard him say as she walked through the door and into the office area, where there many other doors off to the side. She remembered being brought in and questioned here, and it was most unpleasant. She grimaced and lifted her bag to her shoulder, then opened the door to see her mother, with chocolate smeared on her cheek, sitting next to Bill.

"Hello there. Come to see your dangerous mother?" Beatrice said and smiled.

"You've got chocolate on your face," Vera said and handed her a tissue from her bag. "Right there. So what's the deal, Bill? Mama?"

"We're waiting on Bryant," Bill said. "Where's Lizzie?"

"With Sheila," she replied, sitting down. "So is anybody going to tell me what's going on?"

"They are just questioning your mom about Cookie's disappearance."

"They have no proof of anything," Beatrice said, folding her arms across her chest. "I'm innocent."

"Well," Vera smirked, "I'm not even sure *I* believe you. I'm sure they don't."

"Now, ain't that something? Even my daughter—"

"Spare me the diatribe," Vera said. "If you know where Cookie is, you need to tell them. Tell us." She lowered her voice. "She could be in trouble."

"Of course she's in trouble," Bill snorted.

"I'm really worried about her," Vera said.

"If Cookie Crandall has gotten this far in her life, I'm sure she is going to be just fine," Beatrice said, then changed gears. "Have you ever been able to remember how you met Cookie?"

No. Vera was sure of their first meeting. Cookie had a shirt on that said NAMASTE across the chest, and Vera asked her what that meant, and the next thing she knew, she had hired Cookie to teach yoga at the studio. Cookie made a person feel at ease right away, and she had a kind of calming charisma.

"I remember Annie telling me about her," Beatrice said, before giving Vera a chance to answer.

"Annie?" Vera said.

"Yes. Annie said she met her at the library and she was reading an interesting book. They struck up a conversation," Beatrice said.

"Yes!" Vera said. "I think it was Annie who brought her to the first crop. But what does that have to do with this, Mama?"

Beatrice's face went blank.

Vera could see that her mother wasn't budging. Call it intuition or years of dealing with the old coot. She leaned back in her chair and thought a moment.

"What were you doing up on the mountain, anyway?" she asked Beatrice.

"I told Bill this story already. Cookie asked me to take her scrapbook up there."

"And do what with it?"

"Put it on a rock."

"Why? Whatever for?"

"That's what she asked me to do," Beatrice said. "And so I did it. Jon, Rose, and I took the scrapbook and placed it where she asked me to."

"Where was that?" Detective Bryant said, entering the room.

Beatrice sighed. "It was in one of the caves."

"But what does that have to do with anything?" Vera said. "Really? Why would that help Cookie to escape?"

"I don't know, but it must have something to do with it," Bryant said. "Did she say if someone would be picking it up there?"

"No," Beatrice said.

"I guess I should send someone to have a look around. Which cave is it? The big one?"

"No, it's the smaller one," Beatrice said. "But you won't find a thing. So save yourself the trouble."

The detective squinted. "What do you mean?"

"The book is gone. It must have fallen into the crevice there."

"Pretty deep?" he asked.

"Yes," Beatrice said.

"What happened, Mama? Did you drop it?"

"Not that I can recall," Beatrice said after a moment.

"What kind of answer is that?" Bryant said, exasperated.

"It's an honest one. You see, I looked away from it. We all did. The calcite and the lights were glowing. You know how they sometimes do? We sat and watched. And when it was over, it was just gone."

"Just like that?" Vera said after a few minutes.

Beatrice nodded. "None of us saw it slip. But we did hear noises. I thought it was an animal or something."

Detective Bryant leaned across the table, getting in Beatrice's face. "Am I supposed to believe this? How gullible do you think I am?"

"Whoa," Bill said, standing up. "You need to charge her or let her go. Right now your case is looking pretty flimsy."

"I ought to throw her in jail and get rid of the key. She knows something, and she's not telling us. She's lying," Bryant barked.

"Are you calling me a liar?" Beatrice said, her voice raised.

"Bea—" Bill began.

"Yes, I am," the detective said.

"Sit down, fool, and I'll tell you the truth," Beatrice said.

"Mama!" Vera said.

"Hush, girl!" Beatrice said. Now she would give them all something to think about. "Cookie is a witch. You know that. Evidently, she's more than that. She's learned how to travel through space and time, kind of like a time traveler. I took the book up on the mountain because the coordinates are exactly right. She reached out to me because of my research into quantum physics. Told me all about it."

"Humph. She's a time traveler? What she is is an escaped mental patient. We've had doctors here looking for her," Bryant said.

"Oh my," Vera said. "But she always seemed so together. I don't get it."

"It doesn't surprise me," Beatrice said. "She told me she had been here before and it was unpleasant."

"Ms. Matthews, if you believe she is a time traveler,

you are sitting in the wrong kind of institution," Bryant said with a sly grin on his face.

Beatrice folded her arms and set her jaw firmly. "When can I go home?"

That damned Cookie.

Chapter 62

"So, as I was sitting there, another officer walked in the room and announced a break in the case, and they just let us go," Beatrice said after she sipped her tea.

Annie's heart skipped a beat. "What happened?" She sat up a little more in the hospital bed.

"There was a confession," Beatrice said. "Evidently, the police were getting ready to make an arrest, and this other person—not the man they were going to arrest—steps forward and confesses. Do you remember Luther? The man who helped us with our tire?"

Annie shivered. "Yes. The man with the rune earring."

"It was him," Beatrice said.

"I need to get out of this bed," Annie said. "Can you hand me my laptop and my cell phone?"

Beatrice handed her the items. Annie clicked on the computer and saw the story was breaking all over the Web. *Damn.* Here she was, scooped. This guy had been under her nose all along. She'd missed it.

Luther Vandergrift walked into Cumberland Creek Police Station, Tuesday, November 12, and confessed to the murders of Sarah Carpenter

*and Rebecca Collins, along with the attempted
murder of Sarah's infant child, now in the custody
of Sarah's parents.*

*According to the police report, twenty-eight-
year-old Vandergrift has been a drifter since the
loss of both of his parents eight years ago. A one-
time medical student, Vandergrift relocated to Jenkins Mountain from Ambridge, Pennsylvania, after
connecting online with a group called the New
Mountain Order, led by Zeb McClain.*

*"We get together, hike, and meditate," Zeb said
offhandedly during a phone interview.*

*But according to the Federal Bureau of Investi-
gation (FBI), members of the group have records
for various crimes. "We've not been able to find
any concrete evidence that these folks, as a group,
are up to no good. But you have to ask yourself
why a young man would come all the way from
Ambridge, Pennsylvania, to hike and meditate,"
said federal agent Roger Delvechio.*

Indeed.

*"Vandergrift has a record of violence," Detective
Bryant of the Cumberland Creek Police Department added. "He spent some time in jail for assault.
And one crime involved sexual assault. That's all I
am at liberty to say."*

I wonder if she had red hair, Annie thought.

*Other than Vandergrift's history of violence, his
brief stint as a medical student at the University of
Pittsburgh, and the loss of his parents in an accident, there doesn't seem to be anything else on
record about him.*

"Ah, well," Beatrice said. "There's still more reporting to be done, I'd say."

"Well, sure. And I've been on the case this whole time."

"When are they going to spring you?"

"I don't know. I still have a bit of a fever, and the doctors are afraid there's an infection somewhere."

"How do you feel?"

"Seriously? I feel, like, awful." She couldn't keep a clear enough head to piece one sentence together on her laptop.

Beatrice took another long drink of her tea. "You need to take care of yourself. I'm all for women following their passions, dear, but your health needs to be a priority. They have a confession. There's nothing you need to do right now. And it turns out that we were right about Cookie. She wasn't a killer, after all."

"But you said that they were getting close to arraigning her."

"What? Oh no, that wasn't Cookie. It was someone else. I'm not sure who it was. Oh, wait. I think it was Zeb. I guess it doesn't matter."

"It matters to me. I mean, just because this guy confessed doesn't mean he actually did it."

"Why else would he confess?"

"A lot of people have confessed in the past and were completely innocent."

"I heard they even had DNA evidence on this guy. They found one of his hairs somewhere or something. Sounds like a pretty tight case."

"I'll have to check all that out," Annie said, mentally listing the interviews she wanted to line up. Hannah. Zeb. Luther. Roger Delvechio. Detective Bryant. If she could stomach that.

Chapter 63

Jon's dark eyes lit up as he looked at Beatrice over a breakfast of eggs, biscuits, and gravy.

"I didn't invite you," she said.

"Beatrice," he said, "we are both too old to worry about invitations, yes?" He smiled. "And we are both too old to worry about what other people think of us. Surely."

"I never did," she said and laughed. "But there will be questions."

"Life is full of questions. We'll answer them on our own, eh?"

"Yes," she said after a moment, feeling her heart give way. "I suppose you're right."

But here she was, soon to be eighty-two, feeling like a teenager or a newlywed. One moment she felt like a ridiculous old fool. The next, she allowed the feelings to wash over her and reveled in them. She had never imagined another man would come into her life. She and Ed were so well suited, and she had loved him completely.

She'd known many women who had lost their husbands, and all of them had remarried. Most of them lost their second husbands, too. Tootie buried three of them before she whispered to Beatrice as she hugged her at the funeral, "Never again. I can't take any more." And she herself died four months later.

It was a risk always to get close to anybody at any time in your life—a careful line to walk between being open enough to allow the good in and to recognize the bad. But at her age, the risk felt sharper. She had found her place in the world as a widow and had occupied it for years. The other side of that sharpness was the sweetness of finding love again.

Here he was. Sitting in her house. At her kitchen table. Eating biscuits and gravy. Drinking from her coffee cups.

Cups that Cookie adored. They were purple, her favorite color.

Funny, Beatrice should think of her now. Beatrice was caught between hating and loving her. Maybe feeling sorry for her. Was she an escaped mental patient? She would have thought so at one time during their brief time of knowing one another. She'd always thought there was something not quite right, sort of out of time about her. Or was Cookie Crandall exactly who she claimed to be? A magician–time traveler sort of person from the future who had come back to set something right? Or maybe that was not what she had said to Beatrice at all. She'd said it was like time travel or some such thing. But Beatrice liked to think of her that way. Of course, it almost vindicated her life's work. But perhaps she was as delusional as Detective Bryant thought she was.

She laughed at that. Nah. She was not delusional. She looked across the table and saw Jon plainly, clearly, just as she saw Cookie that day, leaning across the table in the jail, spilling her secrets.

Life was getting even more interesting in her town. There were murders and weird religious cults. According to the FBI, they had been watching that group for a while—and still were. They claimed it was for tax evasion. The group had been trying to set up a nonprofit religious organization that was full of ex-convicts. Turned out Rose was right about shenanigans on the mountain.

Blissfully unaware until Rose had filled her in. Beatrice realized that even then, it was just a blip on her radar screen. Land sakes, she couldn't keep track of everybody. There were people moving into Cumberland Creek all the time. There was a new person sitting across the table from her.

And as she thought about Cookie and Jon, their appearance in her life, it just confirmed her belief, which sharpened as she had gotten older: Science could accurately predict some events, but the most meaningful things in a life often held no prediction, no explanation. The universe could be completely, delightfully random.

She started to get up from the table, reaching for the spent breakfast plates.

"Let me get that, *ma chérie,*" Jon said, beating her to it.

"Well, now," she said, sitting back in her chair, "I could get used to this."

Chapter 64

Vera's train ride stretched in front of her as she looked out the window at the snowy landscape. Snow in November, the week before Thanksgiving. Could it be that she hadn't seen Tony in two months? During this time, so much had happened to steal her time away—she'd even been in jail. And then there was Annie, who still was in the hospital, now being treated for pneumonia.

Vera hated to go away—even now. Even though they had the murderer in custody, it still felt unfinished to Vera. Just a nag she felt pricking away at her.

And then there was her mother's romance with Jon. Why, before Vera even knew it, he was moving in without any explanation from either of them. Good God, didn't he have a home in France? Vera didn't like it. They should have at least consulted her about it.

"Why should they consult you?" Tony had said during a phone conversation. "They are grown-ups."

"She is my mother," Vera had said. "Why has she been so secretive?"

"But do you need her permission to come and visit with me?"

"No. That's different. I'm not eighty-one years old. What if he's after her money?"

Tony chuckled. "You're a mess, Vera."

"Okay," she admitted. "I'm a mess."

She saw his face immediately when she stepped onto the train platform. The eyes. The grin. The dimples. All heading her way. His arms encircling her, then reaching for her bags. He led her to the cab he had waiting for them.

"You're a little late. I was starting to worry," he said, handing her bags to the cabbie, who placed them in the trunk.

"You know how these trains are sometimes. And we have a little weather," she said, trying to get her bearing. It always took awhile to get used to the speed of things when she first got into the city.

They entered the cab. It would be a short ride, but with her baggage, it was easier to take a cab to Tony's place. They sat quietly for several blocks, holding hands, as she watched the buildings and people on the busy streets.

"I'm coming for a visit to Cumberland Creek. I want to meet your daughter, your mother, and yes, even Bill. Maybe those scrapbooking friends of yours, too. I want to come for Christmas," he said, after a while.

Vera didn't know what to say. She felt as if all the breath had been knocked right out of her. He didn't ask her if it was okay. He just told her he was coming. This felt a little forced. She felt like a cat being back into a corner—almost felt her back hunch over in a protective stance. She breathed, counted to ten.

"I don't know why that's so important to you."

He looked at her, astounded.

"We're here, folks," the cabbie interrupted. Tony took out some cash and gave it to the cabbie.

His apartment building loomed in front of her. A man came out of the building and smiled. He recognized her.

Why did she feel like running the other way? She stopped in her tracks.

"Vera? What's wrong?"

"Listen to me, Tony. Don't push me. Do you hear me? I've been pushed around my whole life. Felt like I was living someone else's life for the first half of it. I'm not ready to commit to you. I'm not ready to bring you into my daughter's life."

"God, Vera, we've been seeing each other for over a year like this. When are you going to be ready?"

Vera suddenly realized that they were still standing on the sidewalk outside his apartment building. The man was politely looking away. Who ever said that New Yorkers were impolite?

"Do we need to talk about this here?" she said quietly.

"No, let's go upstairs."

But as soon as they arrived in his apartment and he kissed her, her anger with him almost melted away. They went at each other like sex-starved newlyweds. Afterward, when she was lying in his arms, he grinned shyly at her.

"Whatever you want, Vera. I will wait for you."

Her stomach flipped. Was that what she wanted to hear? His feelings for her were growing. And she felt nothing but lust. All she wanted to do was sleep with him. That was not a good thing on which to build a life-long relationship. She kept thinking it would fizzle out. But it hadn't. Sometimes she would lie awake at night remembering the way he touched her, the way he made her feel—like a vibrant, sexy, whole person. She was a middle-aged mother. Her feelings of lust should be set aside with her youth. But it was what it was.

But she had never totally considered his feelings and now wondered if she was being fair to him by considering him only as a lover, nothing more. She'd always wondered if you could have sex without love—if you could actually ever enjoy it. Good Southern Baptist girl that she was, she'd never truly considered that yes, you could enjoy sex with a man and not be in love with him.

Which was exactly what Bill had tried to tell her when she found out about his cheating on her.

Chapter 65

When Annie opened the unlocked door of the little house Cookie had lived in, she was surprised that the heat was still on. It was so nice and warm, in contrast to the cold November air. She walked into the empty living room, wondering what had happened to Cookie's yoga things that were in there. Did her landlord take them? She was hoping to find something of Cookie's. Anything.

Out of the hospital several days, Annie had just filed her latest story. During her research, she had been floored when she spoke to the FBI agents, who confirmed her suspicions—that the group of people on the mountain was a cult of sorts, that it was more than a front. Many outsiders were coming into the area to study with them. When she asked one of the agents about the anti-Semitism, he confirmed that he thought it was one of the precepts of the cult. She shivered, thinking about being on that mountain with a bunch of people who hated her because she was Jewish.

"These folks are very clever. They know the legal system and are working it. Until one of them steps out of line, there's not much we can do about it," the agent had revealed.

"Murder is out of line," Annie had pointed out.

"Yes, but that had nothing to do with the cult. It was one individual."

"It seems like the murders had a ritualistic element, with the runic patterns cut into the victims. I even heard them mention the word *sacrifice* when I was out on the mountain the night I was shot."

He'd sighed impatiently. "Many murderers have a ritual. We don't think it has anything to do with the group," he'd said in a clipped voice, leading her to believe the case was closed.

But what about the word *sacrifice,* which she'd overheard that night on the mountain? Why was he ignoring that?

Why can't I leave this alone?

She looked out Cookie's sliding glass door at the mountains. She'd never known that Cookie had such a beautiful view—no wonder her scrapbook pop-out so accurately reflected the shape of those mountains. She saw them every day in all their glory. In fact, it was almost a straight line from her house to the mountains. *Interesting.*

She walked into Cookie's bedroom, where it seemed to be even warmer. The warmth circled Annie as she took in the empty room. Even the closet was empty.

Where was Cookie? Annie felt the sharp, cutting pang of friendship loss, and she leaned against the wall, suddenly sobbing. It was almost as if Cookie had died. Annie had been so busy getting better, spinning her stories, that she hadn't allowed it to sink in.

She slid down the wall and sat on the floor. A sudden heaviness came over her. Ah, maybe she'd pushed herself too hard. She had played with the boys earlier in the day and wanted to leave for the crop early, so she didn't get a chance to take a nap.

Cookie was gone.

And nobody knew where to even start to look. There were the doctors who claimed she was an expert at escaping and reinventing herself. Didn't she care about the people she left behind, if that was the case? Annie wondered if they were real doctors. Were they FBI? She had no idea and made a mental note to try to track them down.

And then there was Beatrice's story that she told the police—that Cookie was traveling through time, or was adept at making herself invisible and moving through space? The police had shrugged her off as an old fool who'd finally lost her quantum physics marbles. But Annie knew better. Still, it didn't help in trying to make sense of anything, and maybe it didn't matter. Because Cookie was gone—and that was how she wanted it to be, or needed it to be.

Annie felt herself give way to weariness, lifted her knees, and draped her arms over them. She laid her head down. Closed her eyes. Man, she'd nearly lost her mind over this thing. Didn't see things clearly at all. It was almost as if the whole thing were a misty dream. Maybe it was time to stop being a reporter.

"No," a feminine voice said. "You must continue. There's more for you to do."

She struggled to lift her head up. Did she really hear that? Or had she slipped into sleep and was dreaming? She looked around and saw nothing. "Cookie?"

The windows in the bedroom flew open, and yet more warmth surrounded Annie. She watched as the brown leaves blew around, and she stood up to latch the windows. She turned around to a pile of leaves in the room. Oh well, it simply didn't matter. Nobody lived there anymore. She shoved the leaves over to the corner and realized there was a piece of paper in the middle of it all. A picture. Annie brushed away the dirt. It was a photo of Cookie holding Elizabeth. A smile spread across Annie's face, and her heart lifted.

* * *

"That picture looks old," Sheila said as the group gathered around to see it.

"It was outside for a while, I think," Annie said. "I'm just glad to have it. I'll make copies for everybody,"

"I had seen another picture like that in her book, remember?" Vera said. "Whoever Cookie is or was, I believe she loved my girl."

"Indeed," Sheila said. "Does anybody know what happened to the baby?"

"She's with her father now," Annie said. "Zeb. Can you believe that? That beautiful little baby belongs to Zeb McClain, Tina Sue's husband. He lied to me, obviously, when he said he didn't know Sarah. At first, Sarah's parents were keeping her. I'd feel better about that."

"I wonder how Tina Sue feels about that," Paige said.

"I bet I know," Vera said, sitting down to her own scrapbook project, picking up her scissors. "It's not pleasant. It's not the first time he's cheated on her."

DeeAnn held up a recipe card embellished with pie stickers. "I can't imagine a younger woman wanting to sleep with my husband. In fact, I can't imagine anybody wanting to sleep with him." She howled with laughter.

The other women joined in.

Annie took a deep breath, taking in her friends. Even with all the weirdness in this community, she guessed these women made living here completely worthwhile. Although her children's schooling would need to be figured out with this Weekly Religious Education program. She had just begun to fight that.

And then there was this group of neo-Nazis living on Jenkins Mountain. She vowed to figure all that out. She knew there was more to it than the authorities were leading her to believe. But how to find out?

"At least one murderer is off the street," Paige said.

"Make that two murderers," DeeAnn reminded her. "Two murderers in a little over two years."

"Interesting," Vera said after a moment. "Both of them have connections to Jenkins Mountain and the Nest."

"That's no big deal," DeeAnn said. "Most of the people at this table could say the same thing. Whether it's us or our husbands."

Everybody, perhaps, except for Annie.

"I just can't get over Zeb McClain as a guru. Jeez, what's the world coming to?" Sheila said.

Something clicked in Annie's brain. She'd known gurus before—both the real kind and the phony kind, the ones who wanted nothing more than their followers' money or sex, or were on some ego trip, or just plain mental cases. Zeb definitely had charisma—just as other gurus had. She'd known women who appeared to be sane and intelligent, who would sink into submissive roles to be close to a guru. She'd known men who had sold their homes and handed over the money to their gurus. She'd known children who grew up in communes under gurus, never knowing who their father was or the outside world.

"Does anybody know who the police were getting ready to arrest when Luther confessed?" Annie asked.

"Wasn't it Cookie?" Sheila said.

"At first," Annie replied. "But didn't someone say that they were getting ready to arrest someone else? I was in the hospital, and I kind of remember a conversation about this."

"That's right," Vera said. "I was in the station with Mama when they brought the men in."

"Men?"

"I couldn't see their faces. It was pouring down rain. I was in my car. But once I was inside, sitting for a while with Mama and Bill, Detective Bryant came in, told us to leave, that they had just gotten a confession."

"Okay, so if it was Luther that you saw, who else would have been there?"

Vera shrugged.

"Maybe it was Zeb," Sheila said. "Makes sense. After all, he is the *guru*," she added with a smirk.

Annie needed to hear someone else say that.

Would a man confess to murder to protect his guru? Oh, now. She was leaping to a conclusion, but her gut was telling that Luther's confession was not exactly right. Did she believe he could kill somebody? Yes. Did she believe that he killed Sarah and Rebecca and tried to kill that baby? She wasn't so sure. Nah, it was too crazy, even for her. And besides, they had Luther's DNA all over the place—even on the baby's clothing from the night he, evidently, dropped her off at Vera's place. Annie's brain was still foggy after her hospital stay. But her gut had a mind of its own.

Chapter 66

Annie left the crop a little early. She was still feeling a lack of energy and needed to chill on her couch and sort through some of her bizarre memories of the shooting and her hospital stay. As the blue lights of the TV screen flickered in the otherwise dark room, she sank into the couch cushions and noticed the stack of cards brought over from the hospital. She reached for them, thinking she really had not gotten a chance to look over them.

She heard the toilet flush and wondered which of her boys was roaming through the house. Soon Mike padded into the room.

"Hey, you're home early," he said and sat down next to her. "Something wrong?"

"Just tired," she said. "Not myself."

She opened one of the cards and laughed. That DeeAnn always made her smile. The next card was from her editor—very conservative blue. The card after that was thicker than the others.

"Give yourself some time, Annie. You've been through hell," he said and placed his arm around her as she was opening the next card. A note fell out. It was from Hannah Bowman.

Please help me. I am afraid for my life.

Annie gasped. Tears stung her eyes. "Hannah," she could barely say.

"What?" Mike said and reached for the note. "Good God. We need to call Bryant."

"Wait," Annie said. "She didn't ask the police for help. She asked me."

"Annie, I love you, but there is no way I am allowing you to go traipsing off to a godforsaken place to help a young woman who may be in danger. Besides, they've caught the murderer. He confessed."

"Did you just say 'allow' me, Michael Jonathon?"

"Annie!"

"For God's sake, Mike, do you think I'm a different person because I'm a mother now? Do you think that gives you the right to be in charge of me? Since when do you *allow* me to do anything?"

"Are we going to discuss semantics now? Because you damn well know what I mean. I mean I don't want you putting yourself in danger. We moved here for you to be safer, for us to be here for our boys, remember?"

"I know, Mike," she said and sighed. "But it looks like I'm still a reporter. And more than that, I am a person. This young woman has reached out to me, and it might already be too late."

"The police have—"

"I don't believe that young man killed those young women," she said for the first time, even though she'd felt it for some time.

"I'm confused. Luther confessed, right?"

"People confess for all sorts of reasons. Not always because they are guilty."

"What makes you think Luther didn't kill those women?"

"It's just a feeling I have, Mike. And this whole case doesn't make sense to me."

"So you're going to risk your life because of a feeling you have? Okay," he said, running his fingers through his dark hair. "So, what if your feeling is right? What if you go up to the mountain to rescue this girl and get hurt again, or worse . . . ? Annie, what would I and the boys do without you?"

His brown eyes were filling with tears. This wasn't just a power play. He wasn't simply trying to tell her what to do. He was genuinely concerned. Every once in a while, Annie was struck by the feeling that she didn't deserve this man. He loved her and wanted to protect her. Why was her first inclination to be angry with him?

"I mean, you were just shot. If that didn't scare some sense into you, I just don't know what the problem is," he went on.

She took a deep breath.

"Okay, Mike. I am scared. I don't want to go back to Jenkins Mountain. But Hannah is in danger. And maybe there's a reason she asked me and not the police."

"Yes, but you can't risk going up there. Let's call Bryant."

"Bryant!" If steam could come out of her ears, it would have been filling up the room.

"What's your problem with him?"

"Where do I start? He's sexist, for one thing, a smart-ass, for another. Not helpful. A liar. Shall I go on?"

Mike grinned at Annie. "So he just sounds like most

of the cops you've known. C'mon. He's a cop. He's got to be a good guy, basically. Right?"

"Okay," she said, hesitating. "I'll call, but you have to promise you will let me handle it."

"Pinkie swear," he said and kissed her.

Chapter 07

Chapter 67

By the time Bryant came to the door, it was close to
midnight. Annie had not calmed down, even though
Mike had made her some chamomile tea, which usually
helped soothe her.

"Can I get you some tea or something?" Mike said
to him.

The detective looked at Annie. "I'll have what she's
having. Thank you." He sat across from Annie at the
kitchen table. "What's going on?"

"I went to the crop tonight, came home a bit early,
started going through cards, and this slipped out of the
one that Hannah Bowman gave me."

"Whoa," he said, reading it over.

Mike sat a cup of steaming tea in front of him.

"But we have the killer now," Bryant said.

"She gave this to me after Luther confessed."

"Are you sure?" His eyebrows knit. "I mean, she may
not have known about the confession at that point."

"No, I can't be sure," she said. "Everything was
foggy for me. I was on all this medication."

He sipped from his cup. "Interesting," he said.

Annie wasn't sure if he was talking about the tea or
what she'd just said to him.

"I was shot," she told him. "It's taken a while for me to sort through this. But nothing has made sense from the beginning. It's one of the strangest cases I've ever covered."

"What do you mean?"

"The rune symbols are one thing, but the other things go in this order. The CDC showing up quickly during the second murder sighting, the FBI sending undercover agents here, and the way Cookie was held so long without being charged."

The detective nearly choked on his tea. His eyes met hers as her husband sat next to her.

"Flight risk, my ass," she finally said, glaring at him.

"What do you want from me?"

"I want answers, and I want you to help me rescue Hannah."

"First, Hannah is in no danger. We have the killer. And second, why would I tell you anything? This is police business."

Mike's arm went around her in a protective stance.

"I'm a crime reporter, Bryant. I've worked on a lot of cases, but nothing like this. At some point everything comes together and makes sense. The more I think about it, I think we're missing a huge part of the puzzle. But you know what? I can live with that. I don't need to do your job for you. If you feel like Luther is your man, then fine. But how difficult would it be for us to go and check on Hannah?"

"Us?" Mike said. "I don't think so."

"I agree with your husband, Annie. Let's not rush into anything. You're barely healed from your wound. But here's what I'll do. I'll give the bakery a call in the morning to check on her, okay?"

"Let's call now," Annie said.

"It's almost one a.m."

"The first shift is probably getting in now," Annie said, handing him the telephone.

"Nah, that's okay. I got it," he said and pulled out his cell phone.

Annie's heart was racing. Was Hannah in trouble? Were they too late? Why hadn't she looked at her cards earlier?

Within moments Bryant ascertained that Hannah hadn't been to work in two days. Her parents didn't have a telephone, so nobody from the bakery was able to call to see where she was. If her parents knew she was missing, they would deal with it in their own community.

Bryant clicked his cell phone off. "Son of a bitch. She's missing." His face was an angry red.

Annie's stomach clenched, and her head dropped to Mike's shoulder. "I didn't want to be right about this," she said.

Chapter 68

After making a deal with Bryant about getting an exclusive, Annie caved in and stayed at home, next to the computer and phone. She slept off and on while lying on the couch, until Sam and Ben got up and her day began with fixing breakfast for her boys. She made pancakes, feeling the need to start the day with a sturdy meal.

When the phone rang, she jumped, but it was Beatrice. When Beatrice heard the news, she called the others. By noon, Annie's house was filled with food and people. She still had no word from Bryant.

"It seems like there's something we could be doing," Sheila said, waving her arms around.

"That's foolish. You need to leave these matters to the police," Beatrice said.

"Humph," Vera said, shoving a spoon of sweet potato baby food into Elizabeth's mouth. "I don't know about these Cumberland Creek Police."

When the phone rang at 2:30, the boys were playing outside. It was unusually warm for November.

"We found her," Bryant said. "She's not right, but she's alive."

"What do you mean, she's not right?" Annie asked.

A hush came over Annie's kitchen. All the women were looking at her, as if they could hear the entire conversation if they stared hard enough.

"She's either on drugs or has had some kind of mental collapse. Maybe both." His voice was strained.

"Who did this to her?"

"Zeb McClain."

"Jesus," Annie said.

"Look, I promised you an exclusive. I should be back at the station in about twenty minutes. Can you be there? This is going to be one hell of a story."

"Yes, I'll be there," she said.

"They found her. She's still alive," Annie announced after hanging up the phone.

"Thank God," someone said among the sighs of relief.

Annie's husband wrapped his arms around her. "Oh, Annie," he said. "My Annie."

She wanted to stay there in his arms forever at that moment.

Beatrice came up behind them and circled her arms around them. Soon Vera, Sheila, DeeAnn, and Paige were surrounding them.

GURU OF JENKINS MOUNTAIN
By Annie Chamovitz

Zeb McClain had a vision. In his vision, a ghostly specter came to him and told him he had been "chosen" to lead his people. He could rebuild the economy of his mountains with the money he'd earn by selling methamphetamines. Only the weak took drugs, and for the "race" to strengthen, drugs were necessary to help "weed" them out.

"The voices came to him only during certain times. Other times he received messages in runic patterns," said Detective Bryant of the Cumberland Creek police force.

"We often see delusions of grandeur, hear about voices in these cases where a person sets him or herself up as a spiritual leader," said Dr. Jane Ivan, consulting psychiatrist. "This man also suffers from a kind of post-traumatic stress syndrome. He still relives his parents' brutal murder."

Whether as a victim, a misguided spiritual teacher, or simply a drug trafficker, McClain was not stupid. He set up a complicated system of trafficking drugs in and out of Jenkins Mountain and Jenkins Hollow, using cutting-edge technology, such as calcite. Only a few people are actually skilled enough to configure calcite in such a way that it would render their stash and lab invisible. Because of his money, he was able to attract and pay brilliant young scientists—like Luther Vandergrift—to experiment with the calcite, which Jenkins Mountain is filled with.

Invisibility? Isn't that the stuff of fairy tales and Harry Potter?

Not according to researchers at the University of Birmingham, England. Using a paperweight-size lump of calcite, researchers were able to hide a paper clip or pin from view. The lead researcher, Shuang Zhang, noted that hiding a large dog would be possible with a crystal twenty feet long and around six feet thick.

The basic premise is that calcite is naturally birefringent, which means it sends light waves along different paths depending on their polarizations. Once polarized light is shone on the prism of calcite, the object within becomes invisible to those looking at it from outside.

Take a brilliant but misguided young scientist, like Luther Vandergrift, and now Jenkins Mountain has the largest "invisible" calcite compound in the world.

"Vandergrift's DNA was all over the crime scenes," Bryant confirmed. "But so was McClain's. Vandergrift, of course, confessed to save McClain because he thought he was doing important work as a messenger of God. This is also why he carved messages into the body parts of the women who were killed, and tried to kill a baby, who was a product of one of these women and therefore could not be allowed to live."

But the child, left to die of exposure, did survive and is now happily with its mother's parents. Despite the shunning of their daughter, they accepted her baby into their home.

The New Mountain Order (NMO) group had 113 members living in an area just outside what is known as the "Nest" in Jenkins Hollow. They live in a dorm near the compound that housed the calcite and the drug lab. Many of its members claim no knowledge of the methamphetamine lab, the trafficking, or the murders. They claim they have come from far and wide just to learn the spiritual secrets Zeb McClain offered. Of course, the "secrets" McClain offered were in actuality old concepts, dusted off and placed in his own book—a mishmash of Eastern philosophy, Norse paganism, and Mennonite beliefs.

A search on the background of his followers reveals a group of drifters and outcasts. Whether they call themselves artists, healers, or scientists, they believed they found a home on Jenkins Mountain and a leader in Zeb McClain.

Hannah Bowman was a good friend of both of McClain's earlier victims. Sarah, the mother of his child, had been shunned by her own community because of her association with him. She was adrift, staying with him for a while, then staying at Rebecca's home. The two of them sometimes chatted with Hannah about NMO and Zeb's visions and, chillingly enough, about the need for sacrifices.

"The term *sacrifice* was used like a metaphor—or so I thought. People gave their money to the organization. Women gave themselves to Zeb. All of this was done in the name of sacrifice. His spirit needed to be fed in order to maintain clear contact with God," Hannah said.

But soon, she explained, the terminology became violent, and the next thing she knew, they were sacrificing animals.

The last time Hannah saw Sarah alive, Sarah was so frightened that she could barely speak. Though Hannah was able to calm her down, she still made no sense, muttering words about seeing Zeb with another woman and something about meth.

"I'm finished," Sarah said to her. "I'm taking the baby and going to Pennsylvania to stay with my cousin. I want nothing to do with drugs."

When Hannah read about the body of a red-haired young woman washing ashore in Cumberland Creek, she knew it was Sarah. When Rebecca's body was found, Hannah grew even more frightened. Who to turn to? Who would believe her?

She knew she was in trouble the day Zeb McClain walked into the bakery with Luther Vandergrift.

"It was just the way they looked at me. I can't explain it."

Little did they know, she was expecting them and had already left a note asking for help.

Annie's editor was pleased with the first article. Their paper was the first to break this story—of national significance because of the cult slant and the millions of dollars in illegal drugs that were found, in a cave in Jenkins Mountain, in a huge crevice that was covered with the "invisible" calcite crystal, which was discovered by complete accident. An officer tripped over it. She promised her editor more interviews and write-ups on this case. But after she was finished, she told him, she wanted to take an extended vacation. What she didn't tell him was the rest of the story.

Chapter 69

Annie sometimes found herself back at Cookie's yellow house. Nobody had rented it yet, and it was still wide open. She loved to walk through those empty rooms. It was a place of peace and quiet. Even though it hurt that Cookie left them, Annie still found the place that her friend had called home to be comforting. *Strange.*

She looked out the huge window at the mountain range—a place of splendid beauty, especially with the first snowfall lying in clumps on the grass and on the trees.

"Pretty, huh?" Someone came up behind her.

She turned around quickly, startled. It was Detective Adam Bryant.

"Didn't mean to scare you," he said, smiling. "I thought I might find you. Mike said he thought you might be here."

Mike and Bryant had struck up a friendship. Annie wasn't sure how she felt about that.

"What's up?" she said and smiled back.

"I wanted to thank you, once again, for not reporting on the FBI involvement and all that," he said.

"Sometimes, even when you know the truth, it's best not to write about it. Thanks for telling me everything," she said.

"You had me cornered." He laughed, and then his deep-dimpled smile faded quickly. "I'm still pissed about it."

"C'mon," she said. "You had no idea."

"I should've known they were setting me up, using me. I should've smelled that a mile away. Sometimes I wonder if I've outlived my job as a cop. Maybe I'm getting too slow-witted," he said, his head tilting, brow knitting.

"Funny, I just said the same thing to my husband about reporting," she said. "But there was no way you could have done anything about it—even if you had known the FBI was setting you up or setting up Cookie. You would have still kept her. You would have still done your job. Even though it came down to this, justice was served."

"Let's hope it will be served, that Zeb will get convicted," he said.

Bryant walked over to the other side of the window, looked out to the mountains. "I didn't know why they wanted me to keep Cookie. I just knew that I had to. That's all they told me. Just wanted her out of the way. Me too, evidently. I wanted you to know that. I had orders from them. They were supposed to be working with us. But you know how that goes. FBI comes in and trumps all of us."

"I hope that she's okay," Annie said, suddenly feeling warm and taking off her parka. She sat down on the floor. "I've been going over the scenarios."

He sat down next to her. "You know, me too."

"I think of that scrapbook she had, full of tarot cards, bits and pieces of hair, crystals, maps."

He frowned.

"I'm just saying that it felt like she was here for a reason. She researched Cumberland Creek, yeah. But there was more to it than that."

He shrugged. "What are you thinking?"

"Undercover agent?" she said.

"Witness protection program?"

Their eyes locked as they sat together on the floor, the winter sun streaming in, the sunlight reflecting off the bright snow. Annie felt a sudden rush of heat or embarrassment and felt her face reddening. Was this the flush of attraction? She shrugged it off and thought of her husband immediately. She stood up.

"I'm sorry. I've got to go," she said.

Could she be friends with or even attracted to this cop? He was infuriating, maddening, and yet . . . Mike was right. He was basically a good guy. She could not write up the story in a way that would make him look like an ass. Yeah, ten years ago, she'd have done it and not flinched. But she was a different person today.

"Oh yeah. Yeah, sure," he said. "Oh wait, I have something for you. Come out to the car with me."

She trailed behind him and watched him open the car door.

"Close your eyes," he told her.

"What? C'mon," Annie said. "Are you serious?"

This was a side to him she'd never seen. Playful. Who'd have thought?

"Close them," he said.

"Okay," she sighed. "Whatever. Get on with it, Bryant!"

"Hold out your hands," he told her.

She did so.

"We found this when we were traipsing around up on

the mountain. It's a bit torn up in some places. Missing pages. Kind of ragged. But I thought you might want it."

A heavy item was placed in her hands. Cool. Metallic. She felt a warm wind come over them as she opened her eyes and read what was written in beautiful hand-printed letters: "Cookie Crandall's Scrapbook of Shadows."

Chapter 70

Vera had been playing detective, and it resulted in a new scrapbook for Beatrice. She'd been racking her brain for weeks as to why her mom never shared many photos from Paris. Then it came to her one morning while she was feeding Elizabeth scrambled eggs. Her daughter asked for Jon, who made a kick-ass scrambled egg.

It was then that she figured out that Beatrice must have more photos and that Jon was in them or had taken them. So, one evening while Beatrice and Jon were out together, Vera sneaked into her house and her computer, downloaded all the photos. Jon was in many of them. There they were at the Eiffel Tower. Jon's arm was placed naturally across Beatrice's shoulders. Beatrice was beaming. She looked twenty years younger. Vera could not deny that her mother had been extremely happy since Jon came to town.

"I'm almost finished with this one," Annie said. "Wow. I can't believe Bea was at the Louvre and didn't mention it."

"Uncharacteristic," Vera said, taking the last drink of eggnog. "I think she was trying to come to terms with the whole Jon thing. I mean, he was there. And at some point Paris became all about Jon."

"I think it's fantastic for her," Sheila said, took another sip of eggnog, and burped a little. "Excuse me."

"She's going to be shocked when she sees this," DeeAnn said, reaching for a gingerbread cookie. "What fun."

"It's going to be a great Christmas," Vera said. "Elizabeth, Jon, all of us together. It's so much fun playing Santa."

"What about Tony?" Annie asked, dropping her scissors.

"Oh, that's over," Vera said in a tone that she hoped let her friends know she really didn't want to talk about—because she did not. She didn't know what happened between them, but did know that Tony was not the man for her. Neither was Bill. The surprising truth was that for now she liked being alone with her daughter. She liked her life.

"Too bad," DeeAnn said, getting up from the table with her empty glass for a refill of the eggnog.

"Careful," Sheila said, smiling. "Don't have too much. You know that's spiked."

"No kidding," DeeAnn said and laughed.

"Speaking of things being over," Paige said, gathering up all the stickers and ribbons from the table. "Are they going to be able to make the charges stick on Zeb?"

"I don't know why not," Annie said, handing Vera the last page of the Paris scrapbook.

"You never know. You get lawyers involved, and God knows what they will come up with," Paige said.

Nods of agreement around the table. Holiday music filled the room.

"I woke up the other night from another strange dream. Not like the one I had before. Just strange.

There were several redheads in it," Vera said after a few minutes. "I'm not sure I'm ever going to get over this."

"It's funny. We all thought the red hair had something to do with the murders, and it turns out it didn't," Sheila said as she held up a page for Vera to slide a page protector over. "It turns out it was a simple reason. They knew too much. The fact that they both had red hair was happenstance."

The women gathered in a half circle around Vera and Sheila, checking the completed scrapbook—all in black and white. Stunning. Sheila turned the page to the Eiffel Tower pop-out that she'd worked into the book.

"That's delightful," DeeAnn said.

"I'd never even have tried it if it wasn't for Cookie's book. I thought if she could do it, so could I," Sheila said.

An empty hush came over the Cumberland Creek Scrapbook Club. They searched one another's faces for answers. Where was Cookie? What did it all mean? The book, the dreams, her involvement?

"I've been thinking about her scrapbook," Annie said. "At first, I thought it was just a spiritual journaling exercise. But sometimes when I think about it, that book was full of clues. The mountain. The crystal. The map. We just didn't know it."

"Hindsight," DeeAnn said.

"I also think it was clear that she studied this place. She was here for a reason. So . . . I guess she's gone for a reason, too," Annie said, blinking back a tear.

"Have some more eggnog," DeeAnn said, taking her glass. "I'll get you more."

Vera placed a big red velvet bow on the black album. It was edged in silver. The black, the red, the silver, all came together in a classic visual feast. "I'm not going anywhere. I was born here, and I guess I'll die here." She pressed down on the bow and looked up at all her friends looking at her. "Oh, don't worry. I'm not planning on dying anytime soon." She laughed.

"Oh, well," Sheila said, "that's good to know."

Vera looked around the table as the Cumberland Creek Scrapbook Club members finished up their holiday treats before strolling down the street with the scrapbook for Beatrice. Vera thought of the past few months and everything. . . . Hell, they had even been in jail. Oh, but it wasn't all bad. There were some moments that Vera loved: DeeAnn knocking over the man on the mountain, which still made Vera smile; Paige sitting cross-legged on the jail cell floor and refusing to give her name at first to the police; Sheila wagging her finger in Detective Bryant's face; and hearing about Annie smacking Zeb across his face in DeeAnn's Bakery. As Vera looked around the table, she had to wonder what they would get into next.

"Are we ready to go?" Sheila asked. They gathered their coats and bags.

They walked together down the street, laughing and chatting, as the snow fell. Beatrice's pink Victorian house looked something straight out of a Christmas greeting card—beautiful white bows in each of the windows and a huge wreath on the front door. Vera gave it a knock.

"What do you want?" Beatrice said when she opened the door. "What do the scrapbook queens want with me?"

"We have something for you, Mama."

Vera watched her mother's face as Beatrice gradually realized what they had done—in the midst of all the turmoil and the hectic holiday season, these women had artfully placed photos in an album for her.

"What?" she said, as if still trying to make sense of it all. Then it gradually washed over her face. The joy. And for the first time in years, Beatrice was rendered speechless.

Glossary of Basic Scrapbooking Terms

Acid-Free: Acid is a chemical found in paper that will disintegrate the paper over time. It will ruin photos. It's very important that all papers, pens, etc., say acid-free, or eventually it can ruin cherished photos and layouts.

Adhesive: Any kind of glue or tape can be considered adhesive. In scrapbooking, there are several kinds of adhesives: tape runners, glue sticks, and glue dots.

Brad: This is similar to a typical split pin, but it is found in many different sizes, shapes, and colors. It is very commonly used for an embellishment.

Challenge: Within the scrapbooking community, "challenges" are issued in groups as a way of motivation.

Crop: Technically, "to crop" means the cutting down of a photo. However, a "crop" is also when a circle of scrapbookers gets together and scrapbooks. A crop can be anything from a group of friends getting together, or a more official gathering, where there are scrapbook materials for sale and there are games and challenges and so on. Online crops are a good alternative for people who don't have a local scrapbook community.

Die-Cut: This is a shape or letter cut from paper or cardstock—usually by machine or by using a template.

Embellishment: Embellishment is the enhancing of a scrapbook page with trinkets other than words and photos. Typical embellishments are ribbons, fabric, and stickers.

Eyelet: These small metal circles, similar to the metal rings found on shoes for threading laces, are used in the scrapbook context as a decoration and can hold elements on a page.

Journaling: This is the term for writing on scrapbook pages. It includes everything from titles to full pages on thoughts, feelings, and memories about the photos displayed.

Matting: Photos in scrapbooks are framed with a mat. Scrapbookers mat with coordinating papers on layouts, often using colors found in the photos.

Page Protector: These are clear, acid-free covers that are used to protect finished pages.

Permanent: Adhesives that will stay are deemed permanent.

Photo Corners: A photo is held to a page by slipping the corners of the photo into photo corners. They usually stick on one side.

Post-Bound Album: This term refers to an album that uses metal posts to hold the binding together. These albums can be extended with more posts to make them thicker. Usually page protectors are already included on the album pages.

Punch: This is a tool used to "punch" decorative shapes in paper or cardstock.

Punchies: The paper shapes that result from using a paper punch tool are known as punchies. These can be used on a page for a decorative effect.

Repositionable Adhesive: Magically, these adhesives do not create a permanent bond until dry, so you can move an element dabbed with the adhesive around on the page until you find just the perfect spot.

Scraplift: When a scrapbooker copies someone's page layout or design, she has scraplifted.

Scrapper's Block: This is a creativity block.

Strap-Hinge Album: An album can utilize straps to allow pages to lie completely flat when the album opens. To add pages to this album, the straps are unhinged.

Template: A template is a guide for cutting shapes, drawing, or writing on a page. They are usually made of plastic or cardboard.

Trimmer: A trimmer is a tool used for straight-cutting photos.

Vellum: Vellum is a thicker, semitransparent paper with a smooth finish.

Making Your Own Scrapbook of Shadows

A "book of shadows" is actually a book that modern witches or pagans often keep; it is a journal of sorts about their beliefs. It often includes rituals, spells, prayers, and personal reflections. When scrapbooking techniques are used to make the book, the result is a "scrapbook of shadows," which is less like a journal. No matter what your religious or spiritual beliefs, a scrapbook of shadows can be a worthwhile and creative endeavor, as well as a tool for personal growth. Choose a special scrapbook, binder, or journal for your scrapbook of shadows, something that inspires you.

Here are some things you might include in a scrapbook of shadows:

- ☞ Prayers
- ☞ Poems
- ☞ Photos of meaningful items or people
- ☞ Pressed flowers and/or herbs
- ☞ Astrological information
- ☞ "Found items" from a special day, such as feathers, leaves, wrappers, and so on
- ☞ Notes about your dreams
- ☞ Notes about spiritual or religious events/ holidays
- ☞ Special symbols

Other Ideas For
More Reflective Scrapbooking

A yoga scrap-journal. In *Scrapped,* Annie is journaling her yoga classes.

An inspiration scrap-journal. Gather photos, magazine clippings, bits and pieces of art, and poetry centered around a theme that inspires you.

A gratitude scrap-journal. Gather photos, magazine clippings, bits and pieces of art, and poetry that express what you are grateful for.

Scrapbook Essentials
for the Beginner

When you first start to scrapbook, the amount of products and choices can be overwhelming. It's best to keep it simple until you develop your own style and see exactly what you need. Basically, this hobby can be as complicated or as simple as you want. Here is all you really need:

1. Photos
2. Archival scrapbooks and acid-free paper
3. Adhesive
4. Scissors
5. Sheet protectors

Advice on Cropping

Basically, two kinds of crops exist. An "official" crop is when a scrapbook seller is involved. The participants sample and purchase products, along with participating in contests and giveaways. The second kind of crop is an informal gathering of friends on at least a semi-regular basis to share, scrapbook, eat, and gossip, just like the Cumberland Creek croppers.

1. In both cases, food and drinks are usually served. Finger food is most appropriate. The usual drinks are nonalcoholic, but sometimes wine is served. But there should be plenty of space for snacking around the scrapbooking area. If something spills, you don't want your cherished photos to get ruined.

2. If you have an official crop, it's imperative that your scrapbook seller doesn't come on too strong. Scrapbook materials sell themselves. Scrapbookers know what they want and need.

3. Be prepared to share. If you have a die-cut machine, for example, bring it along, show others how to use it, and so on. Crops are about generosity of the spirit. It can be about something as small as paper that you purchased and decided not to use. Someone will find a use for it.

4. Make sure there's a lot of surface space, such as long tables where scrapbookers can spread out. (Some even use the floor.)

5. Be open to both giving scrapbooking advice and receiving it. You can always ignore advice if it's bad.

6. Get organized before you crop. You don't need fancy boxes and organizing systems. Place the photos you want to crop with in an envelope, and you are ready to go.
7. Go with realistic expectations. You probably won't get a whole scrapbook done during the crop. Focus on several pages.
8. Always ask about what you can bring, such as food, drinks, cups, plates, and so on.
9. If you're the host, have plenty of garbage bags around. Ideally, have one small bag for each person. That way scrapbookers can throw away unusable scraps as they go along, which makes cleanup much easier.
10. If you're the host, make certain there is plenty of good lighting, as well as an adequate number of electricity outlets.

Frugal Scrapbooking Tips

✂ Spend your money where it counts. The scrapbook itself is the carrier of all your memories and creativity. Splurge here.

✂ You can find perfectly fine scrapbooking paper in discount stores, along with stickers, pens, and sometimes glue. If it's labeled "archival," it's safe.

✂ You can cut your own paper and make matting, borders, journal boxes, and so on. You don't need fancy templates, though they make it easier.

✂ Check on some online auction sites, like eBay, for scrapbooking materials and tools.

- ✄ Reuse and recycle as much as you can. Keep a box of paper scraps, for example, that you might be able to use for a border, mat, or journal box. Commit to not buying anything else until what you've already purchased has been used.
- ✄ Wait for special coupons. Some national crafts stores run excellent coupons—sometimes 40 percent off. Wait for these coupons, and then go and buy something on your wish list that you could not otherwise afford.
- ✄ If you have Internet access, you have a wealth of information available to you for free. You can find free clip art, ideas for titles for your pages or even poems, fonts, and so on.

Turn the page for a special preview of the next book in
Mollie Cox Bryan's
Cumberland Creek Mystery series

A Kensington mass-market paperback coming soon!

Chapter 1

A green velvet dress, the skirt of which was flung over top of the right hip of the victim, revealed that she was naked from the waist down. Her white thigh and buttocks were so muscled, taut, and perfect that she almost looked like a statue, lying twisted, face down on the floor. Her long brown ponytail of curls was askew, but the green ribbon was still intact. A pair of hose was crumpled in the corner of the dance studio. Her underwear, if indeed, she wore any, was missing. One of her shoes was lying next to the hose—and it was without laces, of course, because its laces were still wrapped around Emily McGlashen's neck.

"How long has she been here?" Annie asked Detective Adam Bryant, after settling her stomach with a deep breath and calming thoughts.

Poor woman. So young. So talented.

He shrugged. "As far as I can tell, maybe all day. We think it happened sometime early this morning. She was supposed to be at a meeting this afternoon. Her friend came looking for her and this is what she found. You here officially?"

Annie grimaced. She'd been working on her book about the New Mountain Order and had taken a leave of absence from her freelancing, and he knew it. But her editor called her to see if she'd cover this. Big news— well, to a certain segment of the population, namely those that followed Irish dance.

"Maybe," she said.

"Not much of a story here," he went on. "Just a murder of a person who maybe was just in the wrong place at the wrong time. "

"She was sort of in the public eye. And a strangling is a personal act, isn't it?" Annie twisted a curl around her finger. She was wearing her hair down—all of a part of the newer, more relaxed version of her former self. She didn't need to pull it back. She didn't need to control it. It was a relief. Chalk that bit of advice up to her mysterious friend and yoga teacher Cookie Crandall, still missing.

"Most of the time, yes," he said, his blue eyes sparkling. "But there was a robbery. Looks like the safe was ransacked. Maybe she surprised the perp. Maybe he didn't have another weapon."

"So he used her shoe laces?" Annie said. "C'mon."

The detective's mouth went crooked.

Still, it probably had nothing to do with the NMO. There were none of the symbols they had used in the past. Maybe it was true. Maybe they had really cleaned up their act.

"But she was a famous Irish dancer," Annie said, almost to herself.

"And?" he said with a crooked smirk. "One of her fancy-dancing competitors offed her?"

Annie crossed her arms and glared at him.

The police photographer entered the studio and his camera flashed in the dim room—a large dance studio with beautiful floors, a mirror along one wall, and bars that ran along the side of it. Posters of Irish dancers, medals, and trophies decorated the facility. You could say what you wanted about Emily—and many towns-folk did—but she knew her Irish dancing. An international champion who came to Cumberland Creek and opened a new studio, Emily made a splash in town—right away.

A couple of uniformed officers pulled Bryant away to show him something they found. Annie stepped out of the way of another officer, now bending over the body. A glint of a flash from the camera reflected in the mirror.

"Damn, it's going to be hard to get good pictures. These mirrors are a problem," the photographer said as he looked around for another angle. "Can you run and get some sheets from the van?" he said to a younger person who was assisting him.

"Well, that's an interesting piece of evidence," Bryant said.

Annie turned around to see the detective reach for a red handbag that looked vaguely familiar to her. She was not a handbag kinda woman—she was more a designer-shoe-turned-into-a-sneaker aficionado. She didn't pay much attention to purses, given that she avoided carrying one as often as possible.

But she was certain she'd seen that bag somewhere.

The detective reached in and pulled out the wallet—still there and full of money, credit cards, and the driver's license, which caused a huge grin to spread across his face.

"Vera Matthews," he said and looked at Annie. "And I think we all know what Vera thought about Emily McGlashen."

"Don't be ridiculous," Annie said, but her heart sank. Vera had made no attempt at hiding her feelings about Emily—and Vera hadn't been herself. But still she was far from being a cold-blooded killer. Vera? Not likely. "Vera Matthews may not have liked Emily, but she didn't kill her."

"But, Ms. Chamovitz, her purse is here. How do you explain that?" Bryant smirked, as he placed the handbag in a plastic evidence bag.

"I don't have to explain it. You do," she said.

"You're wrong about that, Annie. She does," he said, slipping off his gloves.

She knew he was right. But she walked away from him nonchalantly. It took every ounce of restraint she could muster to not run out of the studio and call Vera to warn her that Bryant, or one of his underlings, would be stopping by to question her. As if it mattered, really, she was certain Vera would not kill anybody, especially after seeing the compassionate way she'd behaved over the past few years. Still, a little warning would be nice.

But Vera's life had changed drastically over the past year. Her ex-husband Bill had moved in with a woman in Charlottesville and was rarely around to help with their daughter Elizabeth. Her mother, Beatrice, was also living with a new man in her life. Vera was alone and claimed she preferred it. But her business income had plummeted after Emily McGlashen came to town, stealing many of Vera's students by offering cheaper classes and preaching against the "archaic" dance form of ballet. Vera was in such financial trouble that she was renting her house out, hoping to sell it, while she and Elizabeth lived in the apartment above her dance studio.

"Didn't she write a letter to the editor recently about Ms. McGlashen?" the detective asked, still holding the purse. Annie refrained from smiling at the decidedly manly-man holding the bag with the purse in it.

"Yes. Wow, you read," she taunted him. "Did you also see the letter she was responding to? The one that Emily wrote?"

"Oh gee, I must have missed that," he said. "I'm sure I'll be reading it in about an hour, right, Johnson?"

"Yes sir, right on it."

He started to walk by her and brushed up against her. "Sir," he said in a low voice. "I like that. If only I could get a little of that respect from you. "

His breath skimmed across her neck as he walked by. Telling him that she was a married woman, again, would do no good. He had been blatantly flirting with her for months—sometimes right under Mike's nose. If they hadn't shared that one kiss during a moment of drunken weakness, she'd have more solid ground. But he knew.

He knew what he was doing to her. And he was enjoying every minute of it.

Chapter 2

When Vera opened her apartment door to Detective Bryant, who held her purse in a plastic bag, her first thought was one of relief.

"You found my purse," she said. "Oh thank heaven. I was looking everywhere for it." When she went to reach for it, she was interrupted by a crashing sound. "Oh shoot," she said, taking off toward where the crash was coming from. "Come in, Detective," she managed to say, waving him in.

"Oh Lizzie!" she said to her grinning daughter who was sitting in the middle of a huge stack of CDs that had been piled nicely in several stacks around the floor. They were just too tempting for an inquisitive two-year-old. At least the silver disks were all still inside the covers. Lizzie hadn't gotten around to that yet.

Vera reached for Lizzie and pulled her up to her hip. She looked at the Detective, who stood by awkwardly with her purse. Annie had just walked in behind him.

"Hey," she said.

Lizzie squealed and squirmed down from her mother. "Annie!" She ran to her.

"You want to come and play at my house?" Annie said. "Yes!"

"Annie, why do you want my daughter? Don't you think you should check with me first?" Vera asked, smiling. She was so glad that Annie and Lizzie got along so well. After all, Lizzie's father was mostly nowhere around.

"Detective Bryant wants to talk to you. I just thought I'd help out by taking Lizzie home with me for a little while. Do you mind?"

Vera sighed. "Look at this place. No. I don't mind. I'm still trying to unpack."

Lizzie grabbed Annie's hand. "Her diaper bag is in the hall closet there, just in case," Vera said. Lizzie was mostly potty trained. Mostly. Sometimes Lizzie was indignant at the thought of diaper bags, because she took great pride in using the potty.

After she kissed her daughter goodbye and watched as she and Annie left the room, she turned back around to face the handsome but annoying detective Adam Bryant.

"Well," she said, starting to straightening out the stacks of CDs on the floor. "What can I help you with?"

"How long has your purse been missing?" He asked.

"You know, it's the craziest thing," she replied, stacking up the last group of CDs. "I woke up this morning and thought I should charge my cell. I meant to do that last night when I got in, but was exhausted. I just fell into bed. So I looked for my purse this morning and couldn't find it. I thought maybe I left it downstairs. "

"Your cell is usually in your purse?"

"Usually," she replied. "So where did you find it?"

"Before I tell you that, can you tell me where you were last night?"

"After the Saint Patrick's Day Parade and show,

Lizzie and I went to my mother's house. We had dinner with Jon and mom. Why?"

"Any reason your purse would be in Emily McGlashen's studio?"

"What? Why? No. That bitch. Did she take my purse? I knew the woman had some screws loose. But to take my bag? As if ruining my business wasn't enough, she had to steal my purse?"

"Sit down, Vera."

"Why? What's going on?" she said, but sat down on her second-hand couch. Oh how she longed for the comfortable light blue, deep-cushioned couch sitting in her house. This couch was uncomfortable and stiff. Not very pretty, either, with it green plaid cushions. In fact, her apartment was full of mismatched, uncomfortable furniture. She had rented her house, fully furnished, which is what her Realtor advised. And it went quickly. A visiting University of Virginia professor snapped it up.

He looked deflated, momentarily. His eyes scanned the room. "You really do have your hands full, don't you? Big changes, heh?"

"Yes," she replied. "At last we have a roof over our head and food for the table."

He sighed. "Emily McGlashen is dead, Vera."

She gasped, her hand went to her mouth. "What—what happened to her? So young . . ."

"Twenty-eight, to be exact," he said. "She was strangled. Murdered at her studio late last night or early this morning. Time of death is inconclusive."

Vera felt the room spin as her mind sifted through the recent murders in her small town. Cumberland Creek had always been so safe. Except for the past few years.

"Vera, your purse was found at the scene of the crime. I'm going to have to take you to the station for questioning," he said.

"I don't know anything about this, detective. Why would you need to question me?"

"Vera, you're the only suspect I have right now. "

"Suspect? Me? I've just told you that I was with Mom and Jon last night."

"What time did you leave?"

"Around eight," she said. "I had to put Lizzie down."

"What did you do after?"

"Nothing. I mean, I took a bath and went to bed, if you must know."

"And what was your purse doing in the studio?"

"I don't know."

This is the same detective who took her good friend Cookie to jail because they'd found one of her earrings at a crime site. Could he take her to jail? Who would stay with Lizzie? Who would run the few classes that she had left at her studio?

"It's a matter of public record that you two didn't get along," he said.

"I won't deny that. I didn't like the woman," she replied, meeting his eyes. "Maybe she took my purse. Maybe that's why you found it there."

"Maybe," he said. "I think you better call your lawyer. I'm taking you in for questioning, Vera. Just procedure."

"Well now, my lawyer happens to be in a love-nest in Charlottesville. God knows when he'll get back to me. At least our daughter is in good hands. Annie will take care of her."

The detective looked off into the distance—a stiff, pained expression came over his face. Was it the mention of Annie? Was he still brooding at her rejection of him? What made him think that a happily married woman would give it all up for him?